# Summer in the City

# Summer in the City

Lori Wilde
Priscilla Oliveras
Sarah Skilton

KENSINGTON
PUBLISHING CORP.

www.kensingtonbooks.com

KENSINGTON BOOKS are published by

Kensington Publishing Corp.
119 West 40th Street
New York, NY 10018

All Kensington titles, imprints, and distributed lines are available at special quantity discounts for bulk purchases for sales promotion, premiums, fund-raising, educational, or institutional use.

Special book excerpts or customized printings can also be created to fit specific needs. For details, write or phone the office of the Kensington Sales Manager: Kensington Publishing Corp., 119 West 40th Street, New York, NY 10018. Attn. Sales Department. Phone: 1-800-221-2647.

ISBN-13: 978-1-4967-3268-2 (ebook)
ISBN-10: 1-4967-3268-5 (ebook)

ISBN-13: 978-1-4967-3267-5
ISBN-10: 1-4967-3267-7

First Kensington Trade Paperback Printing: June 2021

10 9 8 7 6 5 4 3 2 1

Printed in the United States of America

# Contents

# Night at the Museum

## LORI WILDE

*To Alicia Condon, whose hard work and phenomenal editorial guidance made this book possible. You're truly a standout in publishing. Thank you for inviting me along on the ride.*

# Chapter 1

*When the lights go out, there's a million stories in the dark. For us, serendipity was the start of it all.*
—Ria Preston

Holy Picasso, it was *him*!

Fine-art restorer and lover of beauty, Ria Preston ogled the sexy guy as her heart skipped a beat.

Okay, full disclosure, it skipped *a lot* of beats.

The mysterious man she'd been crushing on for the past four months was right here, right now, gliding smooth as cream through the lobby of her Chelsea apartment building.

She pushed her glasses up on her nose for a better look and wished she had her contact lenses in.

Today, he wore what she'd come to think of as his Wall Street persona—black suit, crisp white shirt, and snazzy silk tie. This time the tie was an azure paisley print. Last time it had been maroon plaid. The time before that, a dove-gray chevron pattern.

Yes, she'd noticed and remembered.

But while he rocked a tailored suit like a hurricane, she preferred him on the High Line in exercise attire. Tan muscular legs on full display in nylon shorts, Boston Marathon T-shirt, feet shod in trendy running sneakers, and wearing an iPhone strapped to his biceps with a Velcro armband. In his height and handsomeness, he stood out in the sea of joggers, owning the park like a boss.

Her stomach fluttered.

Whether he was in a business suit or athletic attire, whenever she spotted him in the city, she found it hard to catch her breath.

He was, in a word, *magnificent.*

It was her second sighting this week. She'd seen him on Wednesday at the Chelsea Market. She'd been at the bookstore. He'd been in the coffee shop across the way. She glanced up from browsing the latest bestselling romances and *bam!*

He was watching her back.

Just like now.

Their eyes met, and a slow, sexy grin lit up his gorgeous face. She felt the impact hit her throat first and then slide down her body to lodge in a hot tingle right between her thighs, and she thought illogically, *Serendipity.*

Although maybe not so illogically after all. He did resemble the handsome male half of the romantic couple in the painting she'd spent four months restoring.

*Serendipity* was one of four works in the artist's *Soul Mate Seasons in the City.* The series focused on a pair of lovers in New York City during the shifting seasons of their lives in the late 1800s. *Serendipity* featured spring when the couple were young and first falling in love. And tonight, Ria was giving a presentation about her labor of love during a fundraising event at the Metropolitan Museum of Art.

Right after the party, she was leaving the city for her parents' summerhouse in Sag Harbor to get ready before her best friends, Vanessa and Alison, arrived for their all-girls weekend. It had been too long since they'd spent time together. They were so busy with their careers that every time they set up a get-together, something managed to derail it at the last minute.

But not this time!

Ria had the keys to the summerhouse, and she was bubbling over with excitement. She'd planned everything in minute detail. *Nothing* would go wrong this time. She was sure of it.

An active evening lay ahead of her, and the last thing she should be doing was standing spellbound in her lobby grinning at Mr. Gorgeous.

He sauntered straight toward her, and she thought, *At last, he's going to speak to me,* and her heart was off again on that hop-skip-gallop pattern.

To her right, she heard the elevator ding as it settled to the ground floor, but her entire attention was locked and loaded on *him.*

This masculine walking work of art.

Her breath was shallow, and she felt her eyes growing wider with each step he took in her direction and . . . and . . .

She moistened her lips, this time determined to say something to him if he didn't initiate a conversation with her, but before she could get out a breathless "Hi," an elderly couple burst from the elevator and barreled into the lobby.

"Ria!" called Mrs. Markowitz. "Yoo-hoo, honey, over here."

Reluctantly, Ria let go of his gaze and turned to her neighbor, opening her arms for a hug. "Second Grama! There you are."

Maxine Markowitz hustled over, her husband, Harry, following her like an imprinted duckling.

Purple-haired Maxine was a pixie-size, four-foot-eleven powerhouse with a personality that more than made up for her lack of height. Harry was her polar opposite, towering well over six feet with a solid beer belly and an easygoing nature. He was mostly bald, save for a few tufts of flyaway white hair that ringed the back of his head, and Ria thought he looked a bit like former NYC mayor Ed Koch.

"We dropped by your apartment." Maxine enveloped Ria in a hug. "But you weren't there. We came to tell you to break a leg tonight, didn't we, Harry?"

"Break a leg," Harry echoed. "But *don't* break a kneecap."

Ria laughed. "Harry, you're priceless."

"That's what she said." He cocked a lazy grin at Maxine.

Ria gazed over Maxine's head in search of *him*, but in the hubbub, Mr. Gorgeous had disappeared.

*Well, fiddlesticks. Another missed opportunity.*

She'd almost spoken to him two weeks ago when she'd seen him in the park, stretching before his run. She'd worked up a whole conversation in her head and had even strolled close enough to notice that he wasn't wearing a wedding band. She'd primed her mouth to speak, and just as she'd been about to say hello . . .

A drop-dead beautiful woman pushing a baby stroller walked up to him.

The child leaped from the stroller and into his arms. Laughing, he'd swung the boy up on his shoulders for a piggyback ride.

Giggling, the toddler clung to his hair, and shouted, "Giddy-up, horsey," while the woman had slipped her arm through his, leaned in, and whispered something intimate to him.

Feeling like a fool for thinking the silent flirtation they'd had for the past four months had meant something, Ria kicked herself for believing in things like soul mates in the city—working on that darn painting had scrambled her brain—and she'd slunk off.

He had a girlfriend / wife / significant other *and* a child, and here she'd been dreaming impossible fantasies. She blamed her heart-surgeon parents. Their romantic, thirty-five-year marriage that engendered false hope in their impressionable daughter.

Then she'd heard Mr. Gorgeous exclaim, "That's wonderful, Cuz! Best news I've had this year. Congratulations! Another baby!"

The woman was his cousin. Whew! And *whoosh*, Ria's faith was at it again, believing there *was* such a thing as serendipity.

But alas! Today was not destined to be the day they finally spoke their first words to each other. He was long gone.

"Snap out of it, Ria," she mumbled under her breath.

"You'll have to speak up, dear." Maxine cupped a hand around her ear. "My hearing is the worst."

"Because she's too vain to wear hearing aids," Harry supplied.

A bit absentmindedly, Ria drifted over to where Mr. Gorgeous had been standing and caught the faint hint of manly cologne: sandalwood, basil, oak, and a sophisticated something she couldn't quite identify.

*Mmm.* He even left a delicious aroma in his wake.

Talking nonstop, Maxine trailed after her. Ria had been so busy inhaling she hadn't heard what the woman said.

"Have you seen that man before?" Ria asked her.

"Pardon?" Maxine blinked, and feathers from the purple boa she wore floated up around her chin.

"The guy who was standing here when you and Harry got out of the elevator?"

Maxine was plugged into everything that went on inside their building. "Aww, the *looker*. He was here checking out the vacant third-floor apartment."

Really? Mr. Gorgeous was apartment shopping? Now that was fated.

"Quite the cutie patootie, no?" Maxine winked and nudged Ria with her elbow. "Maybe he'll move in. It's been far too long since you've had a boyfriend."

"Maxine," she protested. "I'm too busy for a love life."

"Your pink cheeks tell me you're lying." The elderly woman reached up to pat Ria's cheeks. "No shame in having your eye on someone."

"No shame at all," Harry said, slipping his arm around Maxine's waist and drawing her gently to his side. "Come along and let's leave Miss Ria alone. She's got a big night to prepare for."

Maxine wriggled her fingers goodbye, said, "Break a leg," again, and let Harry lead her out the door.

Smiling at the elderly couple, Ria said goodbye. Would she ever have a solid, lasting relationship like Maxine and Harry's? Like her own parents' and grandparents'.

*He might be moving into your building*, hope whispered in her ear. *How about that?*

If he did, that was a sign, right?

It seemed as if time and time again, the universe kept pushing heaven and earth to put them in the same place at the same time.

The scientific side of her that loved research and logic said that was utter nonsense. The universe was not interested in what was happening in her measly human life.

But the romantic part of her that loved art and beauty and the breathless idea of one day finding the kind of deep and lasting love her parents had found told her seeing him today, in her building, was nothing short of serendipitous.

Sweet bull market! It was *her.*

Money manager and lover of the bottom line, financial adviser Victor Albright couldn't stop smiling. He'd been within seconds of finally striking up a conversation with the ravishing redhead who looked so studious and brainy with her dark-framed rectangular glasses and serious blue eyes.

Vic liked intelligent women. He found them challenging in the best kind of way. You had to stay on your toes with the smart ones, and he enjoyed keeping his reflexes sharp.

Although a part of him was reluctant to ruin the exciting eye-flirting they'd been doing all around the High Line for the last four months, he did ache to talk to her. From the first time he'd seen her sitting in a café sipping hot tea and drawing in a sketchbook, he'd been smitten.

He'd felt an instant pull of longing, and it surprised him. Vic was not the type who spent much mental real estate on feelings. Feelings came and went. They weren't something to invest in.

Yet, every time he saw *her*, he felt bowled over by her beauty, refinement, and self-containment. She looked like an oasis.

He feared that once they actually spoke to each other, the fantasy would crumble, ruining this fun diversion. He liked the allure of mystery and the thrill of the chase. In his experience, actual relationships didn't hold up to the promise.

Cards on the table?

Her calmness, empathy, and intelligence weren't the only things he admired. She also had a rocking hot bod, although too often she kept it camouflaged in loose-fitting clothes. She wasn't one to flaunt her gifts, but what he wouldn't give to see her in a formfitting dress that showed off all her assets.

Red was not his usual type. She seemed studious, serene, and circumspect.

While Vic was serious about his career, he was casual about everything else. And that's the type of woman he normally went for—busy with her career, but up for fun whenever the workday was done.

Red had a soft-focused, rose-tinted glow about her. The romantic who'd spin happily-ever-after fantasies about love. Then again, maybe he'd pegged her all wrong. He shouldn't be judging books by their covers.

She'd made eye contact, oh, yeah, in the lobby of that apartment building, and this time, she hadn't shyly glanced away.

Everything inside Vic pushed him toward her.

But then the elderly couple getting off the elevator captured her attention. He'd been wildly relieved while at the same time deeply disappointed.

Unnerved by so many conflicting emotions, he'd sprinted out of there, avoiding the revolving door to get outside more quickly through the side exit, bursting into the hustling crowd, eager to end the workweek.

Red had been so close, almost within touching distance, and he'd run away.

Retreat wasn't like him.

Not at all.

What was it about her that caused him to flee?

Maybe that was the wrong question. Maybe he should be asking why *was* he taking off, especially when staying would have been more satisfying?

He didn't have the time to dwell on those questions. He'd stopped by what he now presumed was her apartment building to check out one of the units in which a client was considering investing.

But now, he needed to get home, change into his tuxedo, and grab a car to the black-tie event at the Metropolitan Museum of Art. His boss, Mort Lewis, was dangling a promotion in front of Vic.

Tonight, Mort planned to introduce him to Jake and Lilah Stevenson, the billionaire couple Mort had been courting. He hoped to convince them to let his company manage their wealth.

The Stevensons had been at their villa in the French country-side for the spring so Vic hadn't met them in person yet, but they'd already put him through his paces, with tasks and assignments to prove his worthiness, and he'd aced them all.

Finally, they'd issued one last chore before committing to Vic's company.

They'd decided they wanted to add some fine art to their portfolio. His assignment? Find the perfect painting for them to invest in at the Met party, so they could buy it at the subsequent art auction on Monday. With the budget his potential clients had given him, placing the winning bid should be a no-brainer.

The problem was, Vic knew little about art and had no idea which investments were likely to appreciate in value. That's what the Stevensons' challenge was all about. His task? Find a fairly obscure artist on the cusp of discovery.

Yeah, piece of cake.

Mort had told him to learn fast. Vic had watched some videos, taken an online art-appreciation class, and read a few books, but what he knew about the topic he could fit into a tablespoon. He wasn't the best person for the job, but Vic didn't back away from a challenge.

Winning the Stevensons' business would be a feather in his cap and could earn him the promotion he'd been striving for his entire life.

While Vic wasn't wild about attending the museum fundraiser, he *did* want that executive position. A few of his regular clients would be there and so would Mort. Besides, who knew? With the museum's impressive VIP guest list, Vic might be able to pick up a few extra clients along the way as well.

Yes, it was Friday afternoon. Yes, he was officially off the clock, but working in finance in New York City took hustle and grit, and sometimes it felt as if half the people in Manhattan were money managers.

By staying sharp and on his toes and always going the extra mile for his clients, Vic had carved out a nice living, but he couldn't ever afford to let up. He'd grown up dirt-poor from a farming community outside Philadelphia. He'd clawed and fought his way out of poverty, and he wasn't ever going back.

With that mission and motivation in mind, he put thoughts of the stunning redhead aside. Tempting as she might be, he needed his head in the game 100 percent.

Tonight's fundraiser had the all earmarks of a pivotal career turning point, and he wasn't about to blow it.

Not for Red.

Not for any woman.

# Chapter 2

Stepping out of her Uber in front of the Metropolitan Museum of Art, Ria marveled at her surroundings. Instead of heading into the museum through the employee entrance as she did every workday, she got to arrive like a guest.

She paused on the street, watching the flow of well-heeled guests scale the steps of the museum, talking and laughing. Excitement crackled in the air.

In the crowd, Ria spotted celebrities, dignitaries, and VIPs who'd paid a pretty penny to attend. Normally, she wasn't overly impressed by star power. Rich people put on their pants like everyone else. But tonight was the unveiling of the painting she'd spent months restoring, and she was thrilled to show it off to such a large crowd.

Mentally, she'd rehearsed her presentation on the ride over. She knew it by heart. Double- and triple-checking quelled her anxiety. She didn't much like public speaking, but she loved talking about art. As long as she was well prepared, it would all work out.

To keep the details of art restoration from being too dry for the general public, as part of her presentation she'd give a guided tour on nineteenth-century artist Laurice Renault.

Her phone dinged a text. She slipped it from her purse, took a peek at the screen. It was from Vanessa: *Good luck 2 nite.*

Her friend Vanessa had an impressive night ahead of her as well, and Ria couldn't wait to hear all about it when she and Alison arrived at the beach house tomorrow morning.

*U 2,* she texted back.

Vanessa sent a heart emoji.

Smiling, Ria was about to slide the phone back into her clutch when it dinged again.

Alison this time: *Take the Met by storm!!*

Ria texted, *TY. Rock your evening 2.*

Alison: *Can't wait to see U.*

Ria: *Ditto.*

Alison sent her favorite emoji: the zany face.

Aww, Ria had the best friends in the world. She was so lucky.

More cars arrived, doors slammed, people pooled on the sidewalk beside her. Time to get a move on. She needed a few minutes of solitude to collect herself before the festivities.

Taking a deep breath, Ria tucked her clutch under her arm and moved to join the stream of people headed into the museum. The hot, humid air sent a trickle of perspiration rolling down Ria's cleavage. She needed to get inside the air-conditioning while her deodorant was still effective.

"Ria! Hold up a minute." It was her boss, Latoya Taylor, the head conservator of her department.

Ria halted.

Latoya caught up with her. "You look amazing."

Ria flushed. She'd dressed carefully tonight, in a simple little black cocktail dress with red high heels, hoping to project a polished professional image, but nothing flashy to overshadow *Serendipity,* the star of the night.

"Thank you, so do you."

Latoya twirled for effect and laughed. She did look impressive in an emerald ball gown and designer shoes. She was a beautiful tall Black woman who carried herself with grace and dignity. As a boss, she was exacting but fair, and if she trusted you, she gave a lot of latitude in how you did your job. The director trusted Ria, for which she was eternally grateful. Ria worked best in situations with few interpersonal demands.

She'd gotten the job based on the strength of her NYU art professor's personal recommendation, but she'd kept it based on her talent and attention to detail. She was good at what she did, and she knew it, but Ria took nothing for granted. Her paternal grandmother, from whom she'd inherited her Chelsea apartment, had taught her to appreciate everything that came her way in life, both good and bad. In Grammy's book, everything that happened was a valuable life lesson.

"Listen," Latoya said, taking Ria by the arm and pulling her aside. "I wanted to be the first one to break the news."

*Uh-oh. That sounds worrisome.* Ria's smile drooped, but she thought of Grammy and lifted it back up again. "Oh?"

"You did such a fabulous job restoring *Serendipity*. I can't praise you highly enough. You should be so proud of yourself."

"Thank you," Ria said, waiting for the *but* . . .

"But . . ." Her boss met her gaze, and Latoya's eyes softened the way they did when she was breaking unpleasant news.

Ria blinked, holding on to her smile for dear life now. Whatever Latoya was about to tell her, she would handle it. *Appreciate everything that comes your way, Ri-ri, for what it can teach you,* her grandmother's voice reminded her. *It's all a gift.*

"You did such an exemplary job with the restoration, and your research on Laurice Renault for our blog has generated a huge spark of interest in Renault's work. We're getting hundreds of inquires a day about Laurice and *Soul Mate Seasons in the City* on our social media accounts."

"That's good news, right?" Relief loosened her spine.

All was well.

The painting was a stunning portrait of a young couple holding hands and darting lovesick glances at each other as they sat on a park bench beneath the vibrant blooms of Central Park cherry blossoms.

Laurice Renault had perfectly captured the spirit of a young couple in the throes of new love, and to Ria, the painting depicted serendipitous good luck in finding one's own true love.

Her viewpoint might be fanciful, but she believed in fated love. Her grandparents had had it, and so did her parents. She was spoiled, she supposed, having two examples of such radiantly successful marriages.

Alison said Ria's beliefs about love were old-fashioned. Vanessa said maybe Ria's views clouded her vision of reality and that no guy could ever live up to a fairy tale. Maybe her friends were right. Maybe she was too hopeful about romance.

All Ria knew was that the past four months she'd spent restoring that sweet, optimistic painting, her mood had been upbeat and hopeful. Starting work on the painting had coincided with the first time she'd seen Mr. Gorgeous. In her mind, the two things had become intertwined.

Grammy would have said it was a sign. Ria didn't know about that, but the timing was what it was.

"Yes, yes," Latoya said. "It's very good news for the museum, but . . ."

Here they were back to *that* word.

"But?" Ria echoed.

"The museum believes that at this time, rather than keep the painting, they'd like to include it in Monday night's auction."

Ria kept right on smiling. She was a trouper, but she couldn't deny her disappointment. She'd thought she'd get to see the painting in the museum for a little while at least.

"I know how invested you are in this painting and how

much you wanted it to hang in the Met, but I also know you're a professional who can roll with the punches."

"They added it to the auction catalog last minute?"

Latoya shrugged and looked a little guilty. "Not really. They decided last month. I just didn't want to upset you while you were still working on the restoration."

"I'm not upset."

Just disappointed. She adored that painting and wanted the whole world to have a chance to fall in love with it the way she had.

"Fabulous. I knew you'd handle this like the professional you are. The sale of *Serendipity* will help fund the expansion of other collections."

Ria could read between the lines. They were selling Renault's work to raise money for more "important" collections.

"Cheer up," Latoya said. "This expansion will bring in additional work for you restoring new acquisitions. You've got a bright future with the Met, Ria. We're all seriously impressed with your skills."

That's when Ria realized she'd dropped her smile and was letting her heartbreak show. She should cheer up. She'd just received a grade A compliment on her work from one of the world's premier museums. The world, as Grammy would have said, was her oyster.

"Thank you," she said, and dipped her head. She'd never been quite comfortable accepting compliments.

"Let's get out of this heat, Ria, I'm about to melt." Latoya lifted the hem of her long gown and started up the steps. "The evening begins."

Shaking off her disappointment, Ria rallied and followed her boss.

When he was a kid, Vic slept in a cramped room with his three older brothers and dreamed of making millions and living in New York City.

At thirty-one, he'd made a good start on his career. He loved NYC and being at the hub of everything, hobnobbing with the rich and famous, and helping people achieve their financial goals.

His lifestyle sustained and fulfilled him. He was happy.

For the most part.

Once in a while, on the rare occasion that he had some downtime, he'd feel a stab of emptiness, a longing for something more, for a deeper experience of life. But rather than trying to figure out what that feeling was about, he'd go for a run or stay late at the office or take in a Yankees game with his friends.

Right here, right now, he was totally in his element—on the lookout for new clients and taking care of existing ones.

Lately though, mostly after first spotting Red, Vic had wondered if his friends were right. That at some point everyone settled down in one way or the other.

That thought scared him.

The finality of picking just one person to spend the rest of his life with seemed, well . . . untenable.

Stepping out of the town car depositing him at the entrance to the Met, Vic straightened the sleeves of his tuxedo jacket, turned and saw . . .

*Her.*

His breath came out like a wild pitch over first plate, too high, and too short.

She was standing on the sidewalk just a few feet away, speaking to a striking older woman. Red's formfitting cocktail dress showed off every inch of her shapely figure.

He gulped and thought a bit triumphantly, *I was right.*

A hard thrill ran through him. He should go talk to her. Damn, but she was a stunner. He was suddenly tongue-tied. She wore a strapless little black dress and sexy red stilettos, and her long wavy hair was out of the bun she'd been wearing when he'd seen her earlier in Chelsea.

Imagine, twice in one day.

What were the odds?

Horns honked. Car doors slammed. Brakes squealed.

"Vic! Hold up."

In the middle of the crowd, Vic stopped at the sound of his boss's voice and turned to see Mortimer Lewis waving him curbside. He bounded over to join his boss, who'd just stepped from a limo.

Mort was old-school. He'd made a name for himself in the financial district back when Reagan was president, but even nearing his seventies, Mort was still a force to be reckoned with, and Vic considered himself beyond lucky to have landed a position at Mort's prestigious firm five years ago when Vic had come to the city fresh out of Wharton's MBA program.

Don't get him wrong. The job hadn't been easy, and Mort had surely put him through his paces, but he'd taught Vic so much. He was forever grateful to the man and was determined to snag the promotion Mort had promised if Vic made his next quotas.

A couple in their fifties got out of the back of the limo after Mort. The guy was lean and fit, the sort who ran marathons, and his wife was decked out in a glittering diamond necklace big enough to choke a giraffe.

Vic darted a gaze over his shoulder, looking for Red. Yep, she was still there talking to her friend.

He willed her to turn and look at him.

She did not. She seemed intently focused on her conversation.

Oh, well, he had a conversation of his own going right now. He could find her later inside the museum. He made up his mind right then and there, he was speaking to her tonight no matter what.

And when Vic made something his mission, it *happened.*

"At last. You get to meet Jake and Lilah in person." Mort

made the introductions and shot Vic a look that said, *Land these whales tonight.*

Message received.

"Jake, did you know that Vic is a runner, too? He qualified for the Boston this year," Mort said.

"Really?" Jake's eyes lit up. "What was your time?"

"Two forty."

Jake's mouth dropped. "No kidding? You gotta give me some tips. I'm as slow as a turtle and lucky to finish a 10K in under an hour."

"Sure, be happy to." Vic gave an easy smile. He could talk about running all day long. "We could run together if you'd like."

"Plan on that." Jake pointed a finger at him.

"And, Lilah . . ." Mort motioned Mrs. Stevenson closer. "In his spare time, Vic volunteers at the animal shelter in his neighborhood."

That was stretching the truth. Vic had volunteered for the animal shelter one time as part of a charity challenge at work. Mort made it sound as if it were an ongoing thing.

Lilah immediately started talking about pet rescue, and Vic opened his mouth to set the record straight on his involvement with the cause. "I'm not—"

Mort purposely stepped on Vic's toe and shot him the side-eye. *Ouch. Got it. Stretch the truth if it gives you an advantage.* No harm really, but it didn't sit right with Vic. Blame it on his Catholic upbringing, but a lie of omission was still a lie.

"May I escort you up the steps?" Vic offered Lilah his arm.

She flushed and smiled and latched on to him. The sweep of people arriving pushed them over closer to where Red and the other woman were standing. Close enough to overhear their conversation as he and Lilah passed.

Red's companion said, "Let's get out of this heat, Ria."

*Ria.*

Her names was Ria. Such a beautiful name for such a beautiful lady. He got a soft mushy feeling inside and found himself wishing he could snap a picture of her as she stood looking so stunning.

Tonight, she'd left her glasses at home and done her makeup perfectly. She was a living sculpture. A masterpiece come to life. Hmm, maybe he *should* take more of an interest in art.

He stared at her, willing her to look in his direction.

She smoothed the skirt of her dress, adjusted the sheer black shawl around her shoulders, and lifted her head just as he went by with Lilah Stevenson on his arm.

Their eyes met.

He smiled at her.

Ria smiled back at him, wide and warm and welcoming.

And Vic couldn't help thinking the evening ahead looked promising. Business on one arm, and pleasure on the other.

# Chapter 3

*F*ocus.

Ria had to stop looking over her shoulder for *him*.

She had a job to do. A job she loved with all her heart and soul. Even though she wasn't keen on the museum's putting *Serendipity* up for auction, her job was to spin such a compelling story about the painting and Laurice Renault that people would rush to bid on it at Monday's auction.

Crossing the threshold into the room where the guests who'd signed up for her tour waited, she flashed a bright smile and welcomed them to her presentation. The signage read SERENDIPITOUS SPRING: LAURICE RENAULT'S SEASONAL CELEBRATION OF LOVE IN THE BIG APPLE.

Quickly, she did a head count, surprised that almost fifty people had signed up to hear about art restoration. She didn't really need to count them since the various tours were part of the gala entry fee and people could wander in and out during her presentation, but doing math calmed her nerves.

Public speaking was not her strong suit, but Ria was passionate about her topic, so that was what she homed in on. She started off with an introduction to the artist. Who Laurice Renault was and how, eighty years after her death, she'd suddenly become a newfound darling in the art world.

"The four paintings were found in the attic of a row house in Harlem by the new owners last year. They donated the artwork to the Met, and though the four paintings were in sad condition, our restoration team was immediately struck by Laurice's artistic skill and the powerful positive emotions that her work evokes."

"Cool find," someone said.

"Indeed. I did a little digging and learned that Laurice had a fascinating history. She was born in France in 1860, and when she was growing up, her mother worked as a servant to Édouard Manet."

"*The* Édouard Manet?" murmured a Rubenesque woman in a butter-yellow dress.

"Yes, the Édouard Manet. When Laurice was fifteen, her family emigrated to America. They came through Castle Garden, now known as Castle Clinton, and ended up in Harlem, living in the same house where the paintings were found."

"What an exciting backstory," the woman murmured.

Ria crooked a finger. "Please follow me into the Manet exhibit area. As you study the paintings, be sure to note the use of broad brushstrokes in his work, and you'll be able to see his influence in Laurice's emerging style."

People milled around. She took a deep breath, surveyed the crowd to see if she was keeping them engaged, and . . . saw *him* hovering at the fringe.

Watching her.

Intently.

With those mesmerizing dark blue eyes.

He was alone. No longer with the affluent-looking couple she'd seen him talking to earlier. Had he expressly come looking for her?

Ria's heart took an elevator straight to her throat. Flustered, she turned and motioned for the group to follow her into the next room.

Once she'd assembled everyone, Ria clasped her hands behind her back, expressly *not* looking for *him* so she could keep her mind on her work as she addressed the black-tie-clad attendees.

"When we first received Laurice's four paintings, we weren't sure we could salvage them, but due to new techniques, which I'll discuss when we view *Serendipity*, we were able to fully restore the painting."

That got a round of applause.

"What about the rest of the paintings?" someone asked.

"It looks like we'll be able to restore the other three as well using the same method. I'll be starting *Fortune* next week."

"What are the names of the four paintings?"

"*Serendipity* is set in the spring, *Fortune* is summer, *Nourished* is the fall season, and *Everlasting* is winter."

"So beautiful," a teenaged girl sighed.

Encouraged by the audience's enthusiastic response, Ria went back to her presentation. "All four paintings are set in the same location. We project that we'll have the entire series finished within two years. Please, enjoy the Manet paintings for a few minutes and then we'll proceed to the next room."

Hands still clasped behind her back, she moved over to stand by the security guard, watching the crowd as individuals stepped closer to study Manet's brushstrokes.

Despite her intention of staying fully present for the tour, she found her gaze trailing over the attendees.

*Stop looking for him.*

Aah, but it was too late. He was so tall and broad shouldered, he definitely stood out in the crowd.

He was at the opposite side of the room, but he was staring straight at her.

Their gazes collided.

High impact.

She felt his stare hit her stomach with a one-two punch.

He grinned.

Smiling, she ducked her head, felt her cheeks heat and perspiration trickle between her breasts. *Head in the game, Ria. You've got a job to do.*

*Right, right.*

Gently, she clapped her hands to gain the group's attention again and raised her voice slightly to be heard over the chamber music being played by a string quartet in the hallway. It was Vivaldi's "Spring."

"In the next room, we have an exhibit of Laurice Renault's contemporaries. Another influence on Laurice's style was impressionist Mary Cassatt. From Cassatt she picked up her use of a lighter color palette than what was common at the time."

The violins sounded bright and joyful. Just like spring. Just like *Serendipity*.

She tossed a glance over her shoulder as she ushered the guests into the other room, but he'd disappeared.

Her heart jumped back into the elevator and took it all the way down to her shoes. He was gone.

Good. Now she could concentrate.

Except she couldn't.

She went through her spiel by rote, wondering where he'd disappeared to.

*Settle down.*

This was Laurice's night.

*Keep the spotlight on her.*

Leading the group to another area featuring various forms of art from the same time period, she talked about the political, cultural, and artistic framework that defined Laurice's work. This room was dominated by a sculpture of embracing nudes deep in the throes of an impassioned kiss. It had been sculpted during the years Laurice had been creating her paintings.

Ria gave the attendees time to examine the artwork, again stepping out of the flow of traffic and into the corner, affording more space for the guests. Smiling, she kept an eye on everyone, not wanting to rush them, but not wanting them to get bored or lag behind either.

And then *he* strolled into the room.

Her heart jumped.

Mr. Gorgeous was back.

He made eye contact with her, then directed a lopsided grin at the naked sculpture, wriggled his eyebrows, and met her gaze again.

He looked so comical, she almost burst out laughing, but even as his antics tickled her funny bone, a hard, hot rush of sexual desire flooded her system.

Holy Picasso, she *wanted* him.

And not just a little bit.

Maybe tonight they could finally have a conversation? That thought stoked both fear and desire. She'd been living inside her work, restoring the painting, for so long, she'd forgotten about sex, but she longed to get reacquainted.

*What the hell, Ria? Tone it down, girl.*

Mr. Gorgeous had gotten her so hot and bothered that she could hardly think.

The final room contained *Serendipity*.

The second she walked into the hall, her eyes and her heart were drawn to the painting on the central wall in its place of honor. How she loved this painting! One look at the couple depicted and you knew without having to be told that they'd just met on the park bench under the cherry blossoms and it was love at first sight.

The guests oohed and aahed. Folding chairs had been set up, and her PowerPoint presentation was projected on the wall beside *Serendipity*. Ria launched into the meat of her presentation, highlighting the challenges and rewards of restoring the painting.

What she didn't admit was that during her work, she'd fantasized that it was she on that park bench with *him*, Mr. Gorgeous, who'd surely captured her interest over the past four months, but whose name she didn't even know.

It was fanciful. Whimsical. Romantic.

Just like Laurice's artwork.

For four months the painting had held Ria spellbound, but so had Mr. Gorgeous. The two events were forever linked in her mind. A glorious painting and a four-month flirtation in which not a single word had been spoken between them.

Perhaps she should have been born in the 1800s. That era seemed a much better fit for her quiet personality than the high-intensity twenty-first century.

Every so often, she'd sneak another peek around the room, but he hadn't yet entered. Where had he gotten off to?

Probably another engagement. Several simultaneous events were going on throughout the museum. Numerous topics for numerous interests.

After this, she was free to head out to Sag Harbor and get her weekend started. No reason to be disappointed that Mr. Gorgeous hadn't come over to talk to her. No regrets that she hadn't approached him.

It was what it was.

A lovely moment. A lovely evening. Whether she ever spoke to him or not.

Ria finished her presentation in the allotted twenty minutes and then took questions for ten minutes afterward. There were so many questions, it gratified her to discover the attendees seemed as entranced with *Serendipity* as she was.

"We have time for one final question," she said.

A hand shot up.

And there, looking resplendent in his tuxedo, one shoulder leading against the wall, was Mr. Gorgeous.

Instant heat flooded her body. Ria blew out her breath and posted a winning smile. "You, sir, at the back of the room. What's your question?"

His gaze hit her like a laser. "Where do we go from here?"

Vic watched Ria's startled reaction to his question.

Good. It was his intention to rattle her.

Except she was as cool as cucumber sandwiches. "Why, thank you for asking. There's a cocktail party on the Roof Garden Bar and you're all welcome to attend."

"Will you be at the party?" he asked, enjoying the hell out of himself. "You know, in case any of us want to learn more about *Serendipity*?"

"I wasn't planning—"

"Oh, please stay for the cocktail party," a middle-aged woman in a lemon-colored dress said. "I have *so* many follow-up questions."

"Me, too," someone else added.

Vic held Ria's gaze. He had a feeling she'd been about to leave now that her presentation was over, and he worried he wouldn't get the chance to speak to her privately. He liked this game they were playing and wanted to know if she was on board for taking it to the next level.

That is, have an actual conversation and see if there was more to their flirtation than instant chemistry.

"I can stay for a bit." She gifted the audience with a beautiful, earnest smile.

That smile got him right in the heart. He put a palm over his chest. *Ria, I can't wait.* He moved toward her, but the woman in yellow hogged her attention.

Vic got a text.

Mort: *Where R U? We're at the cocktail party and the Stevensons are asking 4 U.*

Vic: *Be right there.*

When he glanced up, the crowd had dispersed, and Ria was gone.

*Darn it.*

He hoped she'd keep her word and appear at the cocktail party. On his way out, he strolled by the painting for a closer look, remembering how she'd described the restoration in her presentation, the laborious work involved.

Bigger question: Was *Serendipity* the kind of painting that could double the Stevensons' investment? He knew they were in it for the appreciable value of the painting, not for the art itself. If they'd been that kind of art buyer, they wouldn't have needed him.

But it was a beautiful painting, and from what he could tell after listening to Ria's presentation, it would be a good investment.

There was something compelling about it that he couldn't put his finger on. As if the painting's very existence was serendipitous, and he found the art even more compelling because Ria had been the one to bring the painting back to life.

Leaving *Serendipity* behind, he made his way to the rooftop. The outdoor space was filling up as the sun set. The weather was sticky as hell, especially in these clothes, and so hot that he'd gotten a text alert warning of possible brownouts for the metropolitan area. The smell of deep summer was in the air, but Vic's heart was still in the cherry-blossom spring of Laurice Renault's painting.

"Vic!" Mort called to him, and waved a hand.

His boss and the Stevensons had staked out a great spot at the boundary hedges that overlooked Central Park. Down there somewhere was the park bench where the *Serendipity* lovers had met under the cherry trees.

He wondered if the lovers in the painting had been real or if they were just figments of the artist's imagination. If he got a chance to talk to Ria, he'd make sure to ask.

The painting sure had gotten under his skin, which was weird since he didn't pay much attention to art. The pieces that hung in his own apartment had been put there by the interior decorator he'd hired. He felt the urge now to buy art that actually meant something to him.

He took a glass of champagne from a passing waiter and wandered over to where Mort and the Stevensons stood. They talked about marathon running and pet rescue and the new yacht that Jake Stevenson had his eye on and not much about art at all.

Vic was a master at small talk. It was where he excelled. He was good at keeping things light, superficial, and buzzing right along.

Then they discussed art and he told them about *Serendipity*, and they acted intrigued but didn't seemed overly anxious to go view it.

"I could arrange for the art restorer to talk to you about it," he said.

"Write up the specs and send it to us," Jake said.

"And we'll see it at the auction on Monday," Lilah said. "For now, I need more champagne." She trailed off to refresh her drink.

The string quartet had moved from the lobby hallway to an area just off the open-air lounge, and the soft sound of their music spilled out into the deepening twilight. A few people were waltzing. Mort was talking to Jake about the Yankees and their chances for a winning season. Vic was only half listening as he scanned the crowd for Ria.

He spotted the woman in the yellow dress, but Ria was no longer with her.

Had he missed her already? He got the feeling she wasn't one for crowds. He wasn't sure how he'd arrived at that conclusion. Perhaps the solitary nature of her job. The way she blushed and ducked her head whenever their eyes met. The fact that nine times out of ten, whenever he'd seen her, she'd been reading or drawing in a sketchbook.

An introvert.

Then he spotted her.

In that sexy black dress and red high heels. She caught his gaze and an instant smile spread across her face.

He raised his champagne glass, telegraphed her a message: *A toast . . . to you.*

For once she didn't duck her head or look away. Instead she lifted her chin and squared her shoulders and hoisted her champagne flute, too.

This was it. A clear signal: *I'm waiting for you.*

He was going in.

"Jake, Mort," he said. "I see someone I must go speak to. It was a great pleasure meeting you in person, Jake, and I'll be in touch about the painting." To his boss, Vic said, "See you on Monday."

Mort gave him a look that told him to stay and keep playing nice with the Stevensons, but Vic was off the clock and had only attended the event as a favor to Mort. Vic had a right to cut out a tiny slice of personal time.

Lilah came back with her drink. "You're leaving?"

"No, I just spotted someone I want to dance with."

"Oh, go get her." Lilah laughed and waved a hand. "Maybe I can convince Jake to dance with me."

All Vic's attention was centered on Ria. He sauntered toward her, striking a casual stance—he hoped—keeping his gaze locked on hers the entire stroll across the rooftop.

She didn't flee.

The crowd seemed to part, giving him a straight path to her. His smile widened.

So did hers.

His pulse hit a pace reserved for the fastest footraces. Four months of eye contact and smiles, and this was about to turn into something bigger—he could feel it. He was close enough to smell her. His chest expanded as he sucked in a big breath of sweltering twilight and her unique scent—books and oil paints and knowledge.

Oh, he was awestruck.

He stopped in front of her. "Hey."

"Hello."

*She's way too cool for school, folks.*

"You didn't wear your glasses," he said. "I like your glasses."

"Contacts. I usually don't bother with them since I'm not in the public eye, but tonight—" She gave a little shrug. "Concession to looking good for the event."

"Well, you succeeded. You look"—he let his gaze travel over her body, and he touched his top teeth to his bottom lip—"stunning."

"Thank you. You're not half-bad yourself. You're made for tuxedos."

"Well," he said, not feeling nearly as smooth as he wanted to be, "I found out tonight that your name is Ria." He pointed to her name badge.

"I still have that on?" Laughing, she peeled off the badge and slipped it into her clutch.

He held out his hand. "Nice to meet you, Ria Preston, I'm Vic Albright."

She took his hand. Her palm was much firmer than he imagined it would be, but he wasn't disappointed. The firmness of her hand made her seem even more competent.

"*Vic,*" she said as if testing it out on her tongue. "Short for *Victor?*"

"It is."

"Nice to finally speak to you, Vic."

"Ria." He canted his head. "I have something very important to ask you."

Her cheeks colored a sweet shade of pink. "What's that?"

"Would you like to get something to eat from the buffet?" He pointed his thumb toward the buffet set up under the twinkle lights, where chefs were carving up roasted meats. "And sit down for a private conversation?"

Her laugh was rich and light, and her eyes, those enticing blue eyes, drilled straight into him. "Vic, I thought you'd *never* ask."

# Chapter 4

Being with Vic was so easy.

He was witty and smart, just as she'd imagined he would be. Up close, he was even more gorgeous, which oddly enough didn't fuel her insecurity. Ria marveled at how effortlessly the conversation just rolled out of her. Normally she had trouble talking to super-good-looking guys.

They took their food to a spot with tables and chairs, and Vic scouted out a place for them to sit. He pulled out her chair for her. She was flattered. He dropped food on his tux and told a self-deprecating joke. She was disarmed. He spoke Cantonese to an older gentleman who'd asked for directions to the restrooms. She was impressed.

He seemed, in a phrase, too good to be true.

"Cantonese? Seriously?"

He gave a half smile and a shrug.

"Where did you learn Cantonese?"

"Hong Kong. Work-study program in school."

"That sounds adventuresome."

"It was a game changer. I came back with a whole different perspective on another culture and my own."

"I bet living in a foreign country would open up the way one looks at things," she mused, meeting his gaze.

"How long have you lived in the city?"

After swallowing the mini-quiche that she'd stuffed in her mouth, Ria dabbed her lips with a napkin. "Since college."

"So a year?" His eyes twinkled.

"I'm twenty-eight. I've been in New York City for six years. But I visited a lot before then. My grandparents were from Chelsea."

"Really?" He seemed surprised. "I thought you were younger."

"Disappointed?"

"No way." His grin lit up her heart. "I'm thirty-one myself."

"How long have *you* been in the city?"

"Five years. Since getting my MBA from Wharton."

"You're in finance!" Ria hooted.

"Why do you say it like that?" He looked bemused.

"I suspected you were. In fact, whenever I'd see you out and about in a suit and tie, I called you Mr. Wall Street." When she wasn't calling him Mr. Gorgeous.

"Oh, yeah?" He gave her a lopsided grin.

"You're Mr. Adidas on running days."

"Am I?'

"You are. You're easy to read."

"How so?"

"You're all about the bottom line. In life and in exercise. You want results and you get them."

"You think you have me pegged, huh?" His grin widened.

"Not at all. First impressions aren't everything." Her gaze hung on his mouth. He had one crooked tooth, and that slight tilt gave jagged balance to his otherwise perfectly symmetrical face. She was glad he'd never gotten the tooth straightened.

"And you . . . you're all about beauty." His gaze latched on to hers and held on tight.

An electric thrill ran through her body. It had been too long since she'd been kissed, and now she was yearning for *his* kisses.

"You mean art?" she murmured.

"That, too." His eyes smiled as engagingly as his mouth.

She felt her cheeks burn and knew they'd turned flaming pink. The curse of the natural redhead. Easy blush.

"It's the red hair," she said because she was uncomfortable with compliments about her looks. She didn't like that much attention.

"It's way more than that." He paused and kept right on holding her gaze.

Her pulse shot up and she couldn't look away. He smelled so good. A provocative earthy hint of sandalwood and musk that belied his sharp tuxedo and expensive haircut.

*He works at it,* she thought unexpectedly. The upwardly mobile urbanite. He cultivated the image he needed to do his job successfully, but buried underneath it she got a sense of wide-open pastures and burbling creeks.

Why?

Was he ashamed of where he'd come from?

She tried to identify his origins in his accent, the place where his bare feet had first hit the dirt, but he'd scrubbed his vocal identity from his voice, shaped and shined it into an *I'm from nowhere, but I'm going somewhere* narrative.

A wave of sadness fluttered through her and she had no idea why.

"And the work you did on that painting?" He let out his breath in a low whistle. "I don't know a thing about art, but I gotta say, the painting blows me away."

"Really?" She was shamelessly grateful for his praise. She'd worked so hard to honor Laurice.

"The restoration is unbelievable."

"It was my joy to work on *Serendipity* for four months. I can't wait to get started on the second one in the series."

"*Fortune.*"

"You *were* listening." She felt inordinately pleased.

He chuckled. "You gave a fascinating presentation."

"You kept trying to throw me off my game." She laughed and shook a finger at him. "Playing cat and mouse all through the museum and then grinning at that sexy sculpture."

"What sculpture?" he asked, feigning innocence. "There was a sexy sculpture and I missed it?"

He had a fantastic voice, lacking as it was in cultural identity, rich and even. Maybe it was because his voice had no cultural identity that it sounded so soothing. She could listen to him talk all night.

"May I ask you a question?"

"Surely," she said.

"How much value did your restoration add to the painting?"

She processed his question, felt a twinge of disappointment. The bottom line. Money. But why did that bother her? He was a money guy. That's what financial people did. Asking him not to think about the bottom line was like asking a bird not to fly.

Art versus commerce. The age-old debate.

Luckily, they lived in a city that could support both. Shaking off her expectations, she told him how much she suspected the painting would fetch at the auction and how much it would have earned without restoration.

"Really? Wow. If it sells for that amount, I'd say the Met owes you a big raise or at least a significant bonus."

She was fortunate to do what she loved for a living and grateful she had the talent to continue doing it. "For me, the bonus is that the sale of the painting will give us the opportunity to restore more art."

He studied her for a long moment. "You don't want it to go to auction, do you?"

She widened her eyes. "How do you know?"

"Your face lights up whenever you talk about it."

"It's an amazing painting and I wish it could hang in the gallery instead of in a private collection. Is that selfish of me?"

"Quite the opposite."

"I want people to know and understand Laurice Renault in the way I've come to know and understand her." She crinkled her nose and then, in an impulsive move that surprised her, told him her biggest dream. "She was an exemplary woman who never got her due. She died penniless. I'd like to write a book about her life and the struggles she went through to create art in a time when art by women, especially minority women, wasn't particularly encouraged or valued."

"Do it." He nodded.

"That's it? Just do it."

"It's my motto."

"And Nike's."

"They let me use it." He winked.

She laughed.

"So why not just write the book? Jump right in."

"I'm not really a writer."

"Then hire someone."

"What?"

"Hire a ghostwriter."

"I don't have the money for that."

"You're a big reader. I've seen you." His grin was the sun, shining directly on her. "You can write a book."

"You really think so?"

"Absolutely."

"It wouldn't be to make money. It would be to honor Laurice and her amazing series."

"What's wrong with making money?" he asked, lowering his voice and his eyelids.

And now they'd come to *his* passion.

He leaned forward. "You know, I wish I could see the creative environment where you work. The tools of your trade. You can learn a lot about someone from the things they love."

Was he angling for a tour of the restoration offices?

"Do you want to see the second painting?" She held her breath. Was she being too forward?

"Inviting me to the inner sanctum?"

Did she really want to make this invitation? It would be just the two of them, alone, in the vault-like work space.

A fresh thrill shot through her. Her friends had been telling her it was way past time she got interested in a guy again. While throwing herself into the painting for the past four months, she'd severely neglected her sex life.

"We've got the canvas of *Fortune* stretched out in the workroom. I'm starting the restoration process on Monday when I get back from a weekend in the Hamptons with my two best friends." She rubbed her palms together in anticipation of diving in. "I can't wait to get started on it."

"Do you know that you have an absolutely electric smile?" His eyes were soft, appreciative.

This evening was turning out far better than she'd hoped.

"I have a feeling *Fortune* will be even more spectacular than *Serendipity*. It depicts the summer season on the same park bench, featuring ripe cherries and the deepening connection between the lovers."

"Ria, you are simply captivating."

Lifting her shoulders to her ears, she gave a coy grin. In her memory, she was seven years old again, when her Grammy took her to the Met for the first time and she fell totally in love with the museum. "C'mon then."

"Really? You mean it?"

Grinning giddily, she crooked a finger at him. "Follow me."

Ria took him to the basement. The corridors were narrower here and the lights dimmer. It was also cooler than upstairs.

In her sleeveless dress and thin shawl, Ria shivered.

"Cold?" he asked as their shoes echoed against the tile.

"A little." She rubbed her bare forearms.

"Here." Feeling gallant, he whipped off his tuxedo jacket and draped it around her shoulders. "How's that?"

She dipped her head and slanted him a sidelong glance. "That's very nice. Thank you."

Her smile left him tongue-tied. Gone was his normal self-assurance, and in that moment he was the small farm boy who'd grown up lean and hungry, yearning for something more than the scant living he could eke out from rural Pennsylvania soil.

His quest for a better life had brought him here, to one of the most vibrant cosmopolitan cities in the world. To one of the premier museums in the world.

To a woman who fascinated him beyond measure.

And right now, more than anything else, he wanted to know her better. He'd almost forgotten the reason he was actually here. To scout out a painting for the Stevensons.

From what he could tell, especially if Ria wrote a successful book about the artist and her restoration process, *Serendipity* was bound to increase in value. It was one of those rare, gold-mine finds.

The very thing that got Vic's blood flowing.

*Profit.*

But standing beside Ria as she tugged his jacket more tightly around her shoulders, inhaling her lovely scent and knowing that soft fragrance would haunt his clothes after he got home, Vic thought illogically, *I may never take it to the dry cleaner's again.*

"It feels secretive down here," he said. "Mysterious."

"To me, it feels sacred. The restoration workroom is where the art comes back to life." She looked so adorable when her eyes were lit with that inner fire.

He knew the feeling. He felt the same way when they rang the opening bell on Wall Street.

"Here we go." She accessed the room through a series of security measures. She turned and waved to the camera. "Hi, Helen."

Vic glanced over his shoulder. "Who's Helen?"

"She watches the security cameras, and she used to be a Rockette. You should see her legs."

*I'd rather look at yours.* "No kidding?"

"The stories Helen can tell!" Ria chuckled. "You should hear."

*I'd rather listen to you.* "Next, you'll be telling me she bakes great cakes and I should taste."

Laughing, she waggled a finger at him. "It just so happens . . ."

*Yours is the only cake I want to be tasting.* That thought hit Vic like an avalanche, and then he thought, *Sweet bull market, I really like this woman.*

And that's when things got dicey.

# Chapter 5

Ria led Vic into her inner sanctum.

The intoxicating aromas of linseed oil and turpentine greeted them. How she loved that smell.

The large room was highly organized and almost sterile in its stark cleanliness. Artwork was laid out on tables fitted with microscopes for the detail work. Overhead, there were numerous lighting choices. Easels, rag bins, and boxes of gloves sat at each workstation, along with art tools organized in caddies—brushes, sponges, putty knives, angles, rulers—painting restoration was as much a science as an art.

"Don't you need natural light for painting?" Vic looked around the windowless room.

"We have several conservation areas and while there *is* a stage where I will take the painting into natural light, sun can damage the paintings. That's why much of the conservation is done down here."

This area had three open-concept rooms, one with a small kitchenette and a landline phone.

"Why the landline?" he asked as she led him through the kitchen area.

"No cell reception down here."

"Throwback." Looking bemused and a little bewildered, he shook his head.

"Honestly? It's nice not being in constant contact with the outside world. Here, we can withdraw and fully immerse ourselves in our work."

"It takes a lot of concentration."

"Probably no more concentration than your job. Just different. Your job rewards big-picture thinking, while mine rewards the detail oriented."

"I like that way of looking at things." He grinned. "I never really considered whether I was big-picture or detail oriented, but now that you mention it, I do see the big picture first."

"A visionary." She nodded.

That was easy enough to read him. She'd gathered that information the second time she'd seen him in the park in his running clothes, on the phone, animated, talking a mile a minute, using his body gestures as punctuation. But he'd been so engaged in his conversation, he'd walked off and forgotten his pricey stainless-steel water bottle. She almost called to him as he jogged away, but suddenly he jumped and ran back to snatch up the bottle, looking sheepish for being so distracted.

"Nah." He waved a hand. "I just have trouble staying still. My grandfather used to tell me I had ants in my pants and if I got too restless, he'd send me to weed the garden."

*Ooh, personal information.* Ria leaned in, wanting to hear more about his childhood.

But Vic dropped eye contact as if he'd revealed too much, too soon. "Huh. So, the restoration room is a communal area. For some reason, I imagined you toiling all alone in some lofty tower."

"I do have my own office, but that's mainly for administrative work and building a digital blueprint for the project. Would you like to see the space?"

"Sure."

"I have to warn you, it's small."

"No worries. Maybe one day, I can show you my office."

Did that mean he wanted to see her again?

*Yes, please.*

A little shiver ran through her that had nothing to do with the cool temperature needed to preserve the artwork and everything to do with this interesting man looking at her as if she were a delicious Thanksgiving meal.

Gulping, Ria touched the tip of her tongue to her upper lip and snuggled deeper into Vic's jacket.

The garment smelled of his cologne, a sophisticated urban scent. She was visual by nature and not overly prone to identifying smells, but his fragrance made her sit up and take notice. The fresh scent was a bold mixture that could see him through any boardroom agenda—zesty grapefruit, woody bay-leaf undertones, fertile oakmoss. He smelled, in a word, like *victory.*

Like Victor.

Vic.

Oh, but his name was just too damn perfect. *He* was too perfect. No one was that perfect.

*No, but there is perfect* for you. Her friend Alison's voice was in her head.

*Alison, thank you for your opinion, but I'm busy right now.* Ria eyed Vic, who was standing a few feet away with his hands in his pockets, checking out the artwork, trying—it dawned on her—to look nonchalant.

Was he nervous?

Yay! She wasn't the only one.

She took a step back, did a flirty little dip with her hip that she'd had no intention of doing, and motioned with her head for him to follow.

When he fell in behind her, Ria's heart slammed into her chest with each footstep.

Where she'd been acutely aware of his scent before, now, her ears, highly tuned and hypersensitive, flooded with sounds— the snap of his dress shoes on the tile, the gentle rasp of his measured breathing, the ding of an electronic timer.

*Ding.*

The sound was coming from the cell phone in his front jacket pocket that she wore. Not a text since there was no reception, but some kind of alarm, as if telling him it was time to take a medication or something.

She reached into the front pocket of his jacket, felt around for the phone, and discovered the outline of a foil-wrapped condom.

*Holy ever-loving Picasso!*

He'd come prepared.

*For her?*

But that was ridiculous. He hadn't known she was going to be here. . . .

Or had he?

Fear and doubt played havoc with her. Had he followed her? Had he rented a tuxedo, bought an expensive ticket last minute, and come stalking her after seeing her that afternoon in her apartment-building lobby?

Yes, that fear was a little over-the-top, but really, what did she know about him?

Sure, they'd been flirting for four months, but in all that time, they'd never spoken. She'd assumed things about him. Good things. Sexy things that attracted her. But what if all her assumptions were wrong? What if he was a stalker who'd just been stringing her along from the beginning?

*Whoa. Slow your roll. That's a substantial leap.* She'd found a condom in his pocket. Something any reasonable sexually active single person should carry. Why was she building a crazy story around it?

You're *alone* with him.

No, not totally alone. There was Helen on the security cameras.

But there were no cameras in her office, where they were now standing. Only a desk, a chair, a computer, and a vegan-leather love seat.

Her mind spun, spewing out rapid-fire thoughts in seconds.

The phone timer kept dinging. Oddly, the overhead light seemed to flicker, and Ria thought about the news reports warning of a brownout. *Hmm.*

"Here you go." Her voice came out too breathless, but he didn't seem to notice.

Without even looking at the phone, he stuffed it into the back pocket of his pants.

"What is it time for?"

"Huh?" He seemed a little dazed.

"The phone?"

"Oh." He smiled. "It's my meditation timer."

*Aah.* "You meditate?"

"I'm trying."

"To tame those ants in your pants?"

His gaze drilled into hers. "Exactly."

"Well . . ." She held her arms wide and felt so vulnerable it was all she could do to keep from hugging herself. "This is it. My home away from home."

"You have a couch in your office."

"Love seat."

"Aah, okay."

"I sleep here sometimes when I'm so deeply embedded in a project that I lose track of time and suddenly realize it's two in the morning."

"Another workaholic." The gleam in his eyes brightened.

"I just love what I do so much that sometimes I don't know when to stop."

The lights flickered a second time.

He raised a hand. "Guilty."

She thought of the condom again and let her gaze slide down his body. Even through his dress shirt, she could make out the hard planes of his muscles. The room, which had seemed cold earlier, was now overwhelmingly warm.

He was close enough to touch. All she had to do was reach out her hand and—

"I'm having a really fun time with you," he murmured.

She met his gaze again. "Me, too."

"You're even more amazing in person than I imagined you'd be." He stepped closer.

Ria's heart quickened and she licked her lips. "Ditto."

"I regret that I didn't say hi to you weeks ago."

"Why didn't you?"

"I"—he gave a self-deprecating snort—"was afraid to ruin things."

"My thoughts, too."

"I don't know why I was afraid to take a risk. That's what I do for a living. Why should I be afraid of a risk?"

"Because," Ria said, feeling philosophical, "those are monetary risks. They're much easier to calculate. Math is indisputable. Relationships, on the other hand . . ."

"Are a whole new level of risk."

They both took a step toward each other. Ria's breath came in short, shallow pants as if she'd just finished a strenuous run in high humidity.

"Ria," he said on an admiring sigh.

"Vic."

He dipped his head.

"Would it be okay if I kis—"

But that was as far as Vic got.

Because in that moment, the lights went out in her tiny office at the Met. Leaving them in darkness so deep, Ria wondered if she'd gone blind.

* * *

"Wh-what was that?" Ria whispered.

"Not to sound like a genius or anything, but I think the electricity went out."

That made her laugh and he felt good for having coaxed it from her.

"Hang on." He fumbled for his phone, got the flashlight feature turned on. The thin beam cast shadowy light between them.

"What now?" she asked.

"We wait for it to come back on."

"Oh."

"It should be fixed soon."

"You sound certain."

"I lean toward optimism."

"I lean toward worry."

"Worry doesn't solve anything."

"I know."

"Self-aware," he said. "I like that about you."

"Neurosis cast in a favorable light. Thank you."

"You're not neurotic. Or at least not any more neurotic than the next person."

"How do you know?"

"Even if you have inner turmoil, you don't show it much."

"No? Good feedback. Thanks." She paused.

They were standing close. Kissing close. He'd positioned himself for a kiss when the lights had gone out.

"How long?"

"Huh?" He blinked, jolted from thoughts of her lips and what they might taste like.

"Since the lights went out."

He glanced at his cell phone screen. No bars. She was right about there not being any cell service down here. "Two minutes."

"How long do we wait?"

"I dunno."

"I'll call Helen," Ria said. "She'll know what's going on."

"Good idea."

He held the light for her, and they made their way from her office back to the kitchenette so Ria could use the landline. She picked up the cordless receiver—punched in three numbers. Helen's extension? Put it on the speaker feature.

From where he was standing, he could hear it ringing.

After the fifth ring, the breathless former Rockette said, "Ria?"

"What's happening up there?"

"Can't talk. It's nuts. Total mess. We're trying to get everyone out of the museum safely. Looks like a citywide blackout. Stay down in the restoration room with that handsome hunk of man I saw you with. Lock the door. Kick back and relax. It's gonna be a while."

"Thank you, I—"

"Gotta go!"

"Bye," Ria said, but there was already a dial tone. Ria hung up and found his eyes in the wan single beam of light. "Wow!"

Wow indeed.

"It sounds crazy out there," she said. "I'm going to check on my friends. We were supposed to have a girls weekend in the Hamptons."

"Sure."

She called one friend on the landline. Got no answer. Left a message. Same thing with the second friend. "They both had big evenings ahead of them. I bet they're caught up in their own situations."

"There's gotta be a million stories out there in the dark."

"Um . . ." She licked those sweet full lips of hers.

"Yes?"

"Maybe I should have mentioned this before, but I'm a tiny bit afraid of the dark."

"What happens to you?"

"Nothing, I just feel insecure."

"That's totally normal."

"Is it?"

"Yes." He hope he sounded self-assured and reassuring. Truthfully, the sudden darkness was unsettling no matter how you sliced it. They were just starting to get to know each other. This could be a make-or-break situation.

*Sure, put extra pressure on this moment. That'll ease the tension.*

"My fear of the dark stems from a hurricane that hit when I was a teen."

"You were in a hurricane?"

"Hurricane Rita, right on the heels of Katrina, and Houston took it seriously that time. All the roads out of town got blocked with traffic as everyone in the city tried to evacuate at the same time. My parents and I got snarled in a traffic jam for twelve hours. People abandoned their cars. There was looting when it got dark. It was so scary."

"Sounds like you could have some PTSD related to that."

"Do you think so?"

"PTSD is far more common than people think. It's not just visually flashing back to a disturbing incident. There's often an emotional component as well, and you can have flashbacks to feelings, no visual imagery involved."

"You speak as if you know something about PTSD."

"All three of my older brothers served in Afghanistan."

"No kidding?"

"In the little town where we're from, there's not much of a way to make a living. Farming is the main industry, and small farmers live hand to mouth. Thirty percent of my high school class joined the military."

"But not you."

"Not me."

"Why not?"

"I had a plan from an early age."

"A plan for what?"

"The kind of life I wanted to live. I had it all mapped out by the time I was thirteen. Dreams, goals, wishes. I still have the mind map."

"That's awesome. What a cool kid you were."

"I've achieved most everything on that list," he mused. "Way sooner than I thought I would."

"Time to make new goals."

"You've got a point."

They fell silent.

"You said you were in Houston during a hurricane? What was that about? Why were you there?"

"I grew up in Houston. And there, we pronounce it *Hyoo-stuhn* not *How-stun*."

"You don't have a Texas drawl."

"My dad's family are New Yorkers. He met my mom when he went to medical school in Houston."

"Are you an only child?"

"Yes. And you have three older brothers. Four boys? That must have been a lively household."

"That's one word for it." He smiled into the darkness. "Mom called it 'bedlam.' "

"Good word. This night is taking on a bedlammy feel."

He chuckled. "It's a memorable first date. We'll never forget it."

"One for the record books."

In the shadowed light, he stared deeply into her eyes. "Our relationship isn't on a routine trajectory, is it?"

"No, it's not."

*Our* relationship? Had he actually said that? Vic stifled a groan. He was moving too fast. The darkness had escalated their intimacy, and he didn't know how to slow things down. Honestly, he didn't know if he wanted to slow things down.

"Our courtship has been rather unique." Her tone shifted, lowered, and from what he could see of her eyes in the feeble phone light, they said, *We're fated.*

The hairs on his nape lifted.

Were her eyes really saying that? Or was it his fear of commitment trying to head off anything meaningful? It wouldn't be the first time he'd sabotaged a romantic relationship just when things started to get deep.

"You're trembling," he said, surprised.

"I'll be okay. It's the fear-of-the-dark thing."

"I'm here with you." He slid an arm around her. "You're not alone."

She leaned her head against his shoulder, and it felt so good there that he didn't want to move. His job? To distract her.

"Before the lights went out, you were about to say something," she said. "What was it?"

"Was I?" He was half teasing, half a little scared. He was trapped in a blackout at the Met with the object of his neighborhood crush and worried he was going to blow it with her.

"Oh, yeah." She turned in his arms until they were face-to-face again. "You were."

He stopped breathing.

"Do you want to ask the question now?" she asked, and darn if she didn't lean in and purse her lips.

"You know, I think I'd rather just do it."

"Live your motto?"

"Exactly."

Then, before he got cold feet, Vic set his cell phone on the counter, pulled Ria close again, and kissed her.

# Chapter 6

The kiss was off the charts.

Ha!

Vic's lips obliterated the entire concept of charts. When it came to his kiss, charts as a unit of measurement had zero meaning.

Although, strictly speaking, it was more a series of kisses than a single event. A red-hot coming together of eager lips, exploring tongues. It was a full-on personal investigation of each other. His mouth was spectacular.

It was her downfall.

His kisses were just like the man himself—goal oriented, eager, responsible, and persistent.

And she couldn't quite figure out if he'd ruined her or saved her.

Maybe both.

At the same time.

Whatever the consequences, she floated in his arms, absorbing the flavor of him. He tasted of tart cherries, and that made her think of cherry blossoms, and that made her think of *Ser-*

*endipity*, and that made her think of soul mates finding each other in the teeming city, and it all seemed fated.

Which was a dangerous idea.

Yet, she couldn't help believing that something magical was unfurling in her life, and it had started with her work on *Serendipity*. The day she'd begun the project was the same day she'd seen Vic for the first time.

Here was the deal—whether they ended up as a couple or not wasn't important in the long run. Through a series of fortunate events, they'd found their way to each other, and the fortuitous encounters meant something to her.

As if they were cosmically destined somehow. At least for tonight. It was as if an invisible hand had been guiding them to this moment.

She was grateful for everything and determined to live in the moment because moments like this did not come around that often for her. This was the moment she'd been dreaming of for four long months.

The kisses were getting hotter, and if they didn't do something now, there'd be no stopping.

Thing was, she didn't want to stop.

After one last soul-stirring kiss, Vic pulled his mouth from hers and stepped back. "Ria." He panted. "I gotta, I need—"

She didn't give him time to retreat. She wrapped her arms around his neck, tugged his head down, and this time, *she* kissed *him*.

Weakly, he sagged against her.

"Love seat?" she asked.

"Are you sure?"

"Absolutely."

"Love seat is fine by me."

Uh-oh, they were doing this!

She'd never before slept with a guy on the first date. *It's not really a first date. You've seen each other four or five times a week for four months.* That had to account for more than first-date-level intimacy. *Yes? Maybe?*

*It's not even a real date. You picked him up at the party.*

Technically, he was a one-night stand.

Scandalous for her. Her friends? Maybe not so much. But Ria didn't form close attachments easily, which was why her friends were so important to her. When she did commit to someone, it was for the long haul.

Big question: Was she capable of casual sex? Could she do this thing, walk away with a smile on her face and zero expectations?

His tongue tickled the outside of her ear, and she shivered so hard she lost her balance and sagged into him.

*Oh, yes, I can!*

"I've gotcha." His arm went around her waist and he held her tight.

"Let's go back to my office." She breathed audibly. It was a startling sound in the dark, cavernous room.

He grabbed his phone—their only source of light—off the counter and directed the narrow beam at the floor.

Carefully, they picked their way through the thick blackness. It panicked her a bit. This oppressive night. The air felt heavy, and if she'd been all alone, she might have given in to her fear of the dark and panicked.

But she wasn't alone.

Vic was here with her, smelling and tasting so good and doing and saying all the right things. He was supportive and encouraging and he kissed like the dickens!

She didn't know much about him, but what did she need to know except that he treated her with kindness and respect?

While also giving her sizzling-hot kisses, mind you.

A dazzling mix.

She couldn't help feeling cosmic forces were at play. It was as if they'd stepped into alignment with the stars and entwined the threads of their story into the tapestry of life.

Cheesy?

Maybe, but, hey, she'd worked on a romantic painting called *Serendipity* for four months. She was susceptible.

The trip from the kitchenette, through the main workroom, to her office seemed to take an eternity, and they had to go slowly. They couldn't risk bumping into a painting in the dark and damaging it.

Just as they made it into her office and closed the door, Vic's phone winked off.

Ria gasped. His cell must have lost its charge.

"Are you okay?" He reached for her in the pitch black and connected with her elbow. From there, he moved his hand down her arm to interlace his fingers with hers.

Holding hands.

He was holding her hand and squeezing gently, reassuring her.

Ria tried not to swoon. "I'm good."

"You sure?"

She nodded and then smiled because he couldn't see her. "We've got my phone, but it's in my purse and I'm not sure where I dropped it when we came in."

"Do you need me to find it?"

"I'm okay without a light...." She hauled in as deep a breath as she could take. "As long as I'm not alone."

"Should we find that love seat and sit down?"

"Yes, please."

Stumbling against things in the dark, they fumbled their way to the love seat and sank down on it together, still holding hands.

He was so freaking sweet.

She leaned against him.

Vic slid his arm around her, and they were kissing again. Kissing and kissing and kissing until they were feverish and frantic.

"Ria, do you want to—"

"Yes! Yes, Vic."

She was still wearing his jacket. The condom was right there in his front pocket. They were prepared.

He groaned happily and leaned back on the love seat, pulling her on top of him. She straddled him, slightly disoriented because she couldn't see his face. But in some way, being essentially blind intensified her other senses. She was so aware of him, his novel sounds, scents, feel, and taste.

His fingers found the zipper of her dress, and slowly, in between kisses, he started easing it down.

She tensed.

"Do you trust me?"

After four months of fantastic silent flirtation, she had to say that she did trust him. "Yes."

"If at any time you change your mind—"

"I'm on board, but there's something I've been meaning to ask you."

"What's that?"

"Why did it take you four months to talk to me?"

"I could ask you the same question."

*Touché.*

He drew in an audible breath. "Honestly, I wasn't in a place where I was ready to speak to you. I figured I'd only get one shot at it, and I wanted to make sure the time was right."

"What changed? Why tonight?"

"Why not tonight?"

Hmm. Interesting question. She turned it over in her mind. "Personally, I kept quiet because I was afraid of ruining the fantasy."

"Is that what you're worried about?" His tone lightened, laughter running through it. And his fingers—oh, those skillful, naughty fingers—had completely unzipped her dress.

He slipped the dress off her shoulders, and the air, still chilled from the air-conditioning that had been running before the power went out, hit her bare skin. But she wasn't cold. Not with her body pressed against his.

She heard him rub his palms together, warming his hands, and his thoughtfulness touched her.

Gently, his heated palms cupped her breasts. He sucked in his breath on a hard hiss. "Do you have *any* idea just how incredibly sexy you are, Ria Preston?"

"I am?"

"You are to me."

"Even in the dark?"

"Even in the dark. In the dark, I get to discover all the ways in which you're beautiful."

She grinned. Okay, that was smug, but he made her feel so good about herself, she was allowed a little smugness.

They kissed some more, and their hands got busy, then she was naked, and he was naked, and she was on her back and things just went wonderfully wild from there.

Vic's mouth planted a trail of hot, wet kisses from her lips to her chin, to her jaw to the hollow of her throat. He surprised her by how he took his time. He was a bottom-line guy, he'd told her as much himself, but he wasn't rushing this in any way.

It meant something to him.

She meant something.

*Don't read too much into it. Maybe it's got nothing to do with you. Maybe he's just sex starved like you.*

As he kissed his way down her belly, she slipped her fingers through his silky hair and clutched his head close. Everywhere his mouth touched, her nerve endings were aflame as if he'd set a hundred little forest fires with his tongue.

By the time he got to her most responsive spot, her muscles were so tense she could scarcely breathe and her fingers tightened in his hair. Her body went stiff as a stretched canvas.

"Just let it all go," he urged, his buzzing lips sending sweet vibrations rippling through her. "Relax."

Not happening. She was too charged up for that. Especially when he kept doing what he was doing. She couldn't even think. How in the world was she supposed to relax and let go?

Excitement churned through her and she felt the way she did whenever she restored a painting—eager, anticipatory, submersed in her work. And there was the attention to detail that she brought to the table . . . er . . . love seat as it were.

She wouldn't allow an inch of his body to go unexplored either.

Having sex with him was as sacred as art, and she vowed to savor every second in his arms. Even though she felt some higher force had been shepherding them toward each other, she wasn't going to tell herself a happily-ever-after fairy tale. They were making each other feel good, *right now.* It was enough.

In the meantime, if she wanted this experience to last as long as possible, she needed to cool his jets. Hers, too.

"Wait." She wriggled underneath him so he'd let her up.

"What is it?"

"Just need a breather."

"Did I hurt you? Did I do something wrong? Please, teach me what it is that you like. I aim to please." He sounded genuinely worried that he'd misstepped.

How she wished she could see his face and smile at him, reassure him that he was better than fine. "No, no. You are awesome sauce, Mr. Gorgeous."

"Mr. Gorgeous?" He laughed.

"My nickname for you when I talk to my friends about you."

His voice deepened. "You talk to your friends about me?"

"Whenever there's a Mr. Gorgeous sighting, they get a text from me. It's a whole thing."

"Wow. I had no idea I was so entertaining."

"Oh, yeah. Very. Now, where were we?"

"You asked me to wait. . . ."

"I just wanted to slow things down. I want to savor every part of this. We were going so fast I was afraid—"

"Gotcha."

They went back to kissing and foreplay until they were both worked to a fever pitch again. They flipped and flopped and slipped and slid on the short sofa.

She was on top again, teasing him with her hand.

"Woman!" He grunted and sank his fingertips into her fanny. "You're driving me insane."

Giggling, she rocked into him, stimulating both of them.

"What a goddess!" he cried, rising up to meet her, burying his face in her breasts to kiss each one before fisting her hair in his hand, and holding her in place while he captured her lips and kissed her as they moved.

They gave her love seat a vigorous workout. She'd never be able to look at it again without remembering this night.

Reeling with the newness and joy of their joining, she let go.

"That's right, Red," he said, giving her a nickname. "I've got this. I've got you. You're safe."

His voice was soft as a wool sweater, fluffy and warm. He nuzzled her neck, nibbled her earlobe, and licked the hollow of her throat.

Goose bumps scattered on her skin, engulfed her entire body.

Without warning, he tucked his arm around her waist and flipped them over in one smooth unit. He was on top, cradling her head in his hands, and once more she wished she could look into his mesmerizing eyes.

"Next time," he said, seemingly reading her mind. "We're going to do this with all the lights on."

*Next time?*

Hope unfurled wings in her heart. *Next time? Yeah, baby!*

"I want to be able to see every inch of your gorgeous body," he murmured. "I've imagined you naked in my bed from the moment I first saw you."

"Really?" She smiled, feeling a bit self-conscious. While seeing his face would be pretty great, she was grateful for the darkness, too. It made her feel less vulnerable.

"You're a dream."

In his voice, she heard awe and realized he truly meant it when he said he found her beautiful. That touched and humbled her.

"But . . ." Vic stroked her cheeks with his fingers and pressed kisses everywhere he'd touched—her forehead, her chin, the tip of her nose. "It's more than just your beauty that gets me charged up."

"Oh?" She could barely manage to whisper.

"You have this powerful, self-contained grace that I admire so much."

"I do?"

"You have a wise, peaceful quality about you." He paused to kiss her lips again and position her above him. They were in the middle of the love seat. He was inside her and they both had their legs at the level of each other's waist.

In the modern *Kama Sutra*, position #406 was called the Oasis. Ria knew because: one, she loved to research, and, two, Vanessa had given her the book as a gag gift to encourage her to get out of her head and into her body and have fun while doing it.

For a second, her mind drifted to her friends and she wondered how Vanessa and Alison were doing during the blackout.

"Come back to me," Vic murmured, and drew one of her nipples into his mouth.

Bam! Ria was right back in her body. She felt him grow harder inside her and let out a little moan.

"That's it. That's right."

He tugged her closer, penetrating deeper, and started moving again. Slowly at first, an easy pace. He tilted his pelvis against hers, rubbing the spot that sent electric-indigo sensations flooding through her.

Being in her body was so much fun. She made a mental note to thank Vanessa for the book. Then Ria surrendered.

To Vic, to the heat, and the blazing hungry need inside them both. Caught in the swirl of lips, tongues, arms, and legs, they were entangled in the best possible way.

In the darkness, they were one.

She was hyperaware of everything—the brush of his hand, the spiciness of his scent, the ragged sound of his breathing, the saltiness of his skin.

Her nerve endings tingled and glowed. The mysterious dance of two people getting to know each other.

He picked up the tempo and it ended in a whirlwind.

And then, oh, she was falling, falling, falling into the sweet release. Headed for a majestic, splintering plummet into uncharted terrain.

Vic was pushing her up and over, his body thrusting into hers. She writhed above him, pleasure claiming her and pulling her down.

"I'm with you," he gasped. "All the way."

Trapping her between his knees, he arched his back, bucking upward, and his skill blew her mind.

For the finish, he quickened the pace, accelerated the pressure, rocked himself into her. The world staggered. The universe spun off course. The galaxy split wide open. Sending their sweaty bodies climbing, clinging, crashing together.

She saw golden stars that lit a path in her head and heart, until it seemed that every inch of her was vibrating and glowing.

"Vic!" she cried.

"Ria," he answered in a hoarse groan.

A final plunge. That last thrust and she split into two pieces as a rich shuddering release chopped her down the middle, stealing her breath, draining her strength, sapping all the energy from her body.

Leaving her shaking and laughing uproariously with delight. She'd never in her life laughed so hard during sex.

She felt freer than she'd ever before felt.

Vic made sounds of his own, which were masculine, raspy, and raw.

She grinned into the darkness, and in that moment she felt like that goddess he claimed she was—sensual, earthy, and oh so powerful. She'd reduced him to a quavering mass. Aha!

But he'd done the same to her.

Vic cradled her, kissed her cheek, and tightened his grip as if reluctant ever to let her go. She felt cherished and cared for. What an amazing fantasy. What beautiful serendipity. Soaking it all up, she floated.

Only afterward, as she lazed in the circle of Vic's arms, did Ria realize he'd never answered her question about why he had finally struck up a conversation with her.

Ria had fallen asleep with her head on his chest. Vic's arms were wrapped around her. Honestly, his right arm was starting to go numb, but he hated to move and ruin their connection.

*Say what?*

It was his older brothers' collective voices in his head. He could hear them as clearly as if they were back at Thanksgiving dinner the year that he'd turned eighteen and announced he wasn't following in his brothers' footsteps and joining the military, that he had bigger goals in life. His announcement hadn't endeared him to the family, who'd already painted him with a scapegoat brush for acting "uppity."

*Let me get this straight. You're scared of ruining your connection with a woman you've slept with once?*

The goose bumps that spread up his arms answered that question.

How could that be? They'd just met. He felt . . .

Vic paused. What *did* he feel?

Contentment, but that was just the orgasm. Underneath that feeling, he sensed something else. Anxiety. Yes. Definitely anxiety.

What was he anxious about?

*Hmm, let's see. Citywide blackout, that's a start.* His cat, Charlie Whiskers, who'd take a poop in Vic's shoe if not fed on time. And, oh, yes, he'd just had sex with his gorgeous red-haired fantasy girl, and he was stark raving terrified because she'd stirred complicated feelings in him.

He had to ask himself one question: Was Ria spinning what-ifs about their future just like he was?

And that's when Vic moved.

# Chapter 7

Sudden light, and the rebooting noises of computers and equipment coming back to life yanked Ria and Vic instantly awake.

They jumped apart, blinking wide-eyed at each other.

*Holy Picasso, so you were the one who was doing such wonderful things to me last night.* Followed by *Oh, crap, I have morning breath and no toothbrush.* She slapped a hand over her mouth.

"Me, too." Smiling, Vic grabbed for his pants on the floor and pulled out a tin of Altoids. He took a mint and passed one to her, and now they were sitting side by side on the love seat totally naked.

Their gazes met, then sparked off each other like striking marbles.

"Um . . ." He jumped up to wriggle into his trousers.

She kept her eyes averted and hoped he was doing the same. She spied her underwear in the corner and, feeling far too vulnerable, went for her lingerie.

"Here's your dress."

She turned to find him holding her black cocktail dress. He was shirtless and his feet were bare. Standing there in nothing but his tuxedo pants, his hair raked back off his forehead, he looked absolutely breathtaking.

"I—"

"We—" She accidently interrupted him as they spoke at almost the same time.

"You go first," he said with a flourish.

"No, you. Please."

"Last night was . . ."

"Beyond, beyond."

"*Beyond,*" he echoed, looking a little dazed.

She had so many things she wanted to say, but it was all jumbled up inside her head. She was scared to tell him what was really on her mind. That last night had been special to her.

"But . . ."

"But." He nodded.

She pulled her dress down over her head, twirled to put her back to him. "Could I get a zip?"

"Sure." Only when he came closer did she realize they'd been standing as far apart as the small room would allow.

He reached her, his fingers putting light pressure on her back as he tugged up the zipper. She flipped her hair to one side so it wouldn't get caught in the track and felt his warm breath on her nape.

*Don't shiver, don't shiver.*

Too late.

"There. All zipped up."

"Thank you." She stepped away from him as fast as she could.

"Do you have a phone charger I could borrow?"

"Sure, sure. Let me just find my purse." After a short search, she found her purse in the kitchenette.

Vic had followed her.

She opened her purse, got out her charger, and handed it to him.

He smiled, but the warmth didn't reach his eyes, and plugged the charger into the wall switch. "I'll just charge it for a couple of minutes. Enough to get me home."

While he was doing that, she'd taken out her own phone to check the time. Six a.m. With no cell service, she had no texts or messages. As soon as she was out of the basement, she'd call Alison and Vanessa to see how they'd fared during the night.

She left Vic to his phone charging and went to use the restroom. Ria took extra time reapplying her makeup. Partially because she wanted to look good for him and partially because she didn't want to stand around making awkward conversation while he waited for his phone to charge.

When she emerged from the bathroom, Vic unplugged his phone, gave back her charger. He looked as if he might say something profound.

She paused. Waited.

He said nothing.

Their fairy-tale night together was over. Time to get back to her regular life.

Before he had a chance to give her a see-you-around-the-neighborhood goodbye, she said, "I'm headed home."

"I'll walk out with you."

Silence rode up the elevator with them to the main floor. People were everywhere in the clothes they'd worn the night before, looking groggy and confused. Apparently, many of the party attendees had stayed at the museum until the lights came back on.

That made sense. A dark city in the chaos of a major power outage was hardly a place to wander at night.

Ria checked her phone once they were out of the basement. No texts from Alison or Vanessa.

"May I have your phone number?" Vic asked.

"You don't have to call me."

He looked disappointed. "You don't want me to call you?"

"No, no, I do, I just didn't want you to think I had any expectations."

"So, you don't want to exchange phone numbers?"

*Yes!* Of course, she did. They swapped numbers.

They stared into each other's eyes.

Vic cleared his throat. "Do you want to share—"

"Vic! There you are," a man's voice boomed out across the lobby.

Ria looked over to see the middle-aged couple that Vic had been talking to last night at the party.

They came over.

Vic introduced them as Jake and Lilah Stevenson. He introduced Ria as the conservator who'd restored *Serendipity.*

"What a delight to meet you!" Lilah Stevenson exclaimed. "We adore that painting and feel so grateful that Vic found it for us. We plan to bid on it when it goes up for auction next week."

*Wait. What?*

"And"—Jake Stevenson pantomimed a drumroll—"we've decided to let you manage our money."

"Really? Jake, Lilah, you won't regret this." Vic's face lit up. "We're going to make a lot of money together."

Ria felt sick to her stomach. Vic had been scouting out art for these people to buy in order to convince them to let him manage their money. Had he been using her all along?

Stunned, her mouth dropped open.

Vic turned back to her, his face flushed with excitement, but the minute he met her gaze, his posture changed from loose and lighthearted to concerned. "Ria? Are you okay?"

Well, she wasn't okay, but honestly it was silly to be upset with him. They barely knew each other, but somehow, weirdly, this new knowledge felt like a betrayal.

"I hope you enjoy the painting," Ria told the Stevensons. "It was a labor of love for both me and the artist. Although, I was hoping it would stay in the gallery. I believe art should be shared so it can be enjoyed by others and not hidden away from the world."

From the looks on their faces, she could tell Lilah and Jake Stevenson didn't agree. Ria was a little touchy on the subject of private collectors hoarding great paintings, but she admitted it was her personal bias and she couldn't expect others to feel the same way.

"Glad we all survived the night. Please get home safely. If you'll excuse me . . ." She waved and headed for the door.

"Ria, wait!" Vic called out, jogging to catch up with her in the crowd of well-dressed but wilted guests who'd spent the night at the museum, all trying to exit the building at the same time.

Even though she didn't want to hear his song and dance, she stopped. It was silly to feel so much for a man she'd just met, but she couldn't help the way she felt. After last night, she was connected to him in a way she'd never before experienced, but was that because of some silly idea she'd had about fate and serendipity and soul mates in the city? Had working on the painting for so many months turned her into a silly romantic fool?

"What is it?" She tried her best not to snap at him.

"It's not what you think."

"What's not?"

"I didn't introduce myself to you because I was scouting art for the Stevensons."

She canted her head, folded her arms over her chest, and shot him a chiding glance.

"Okay, okay, I did come here last night to meet the person who'd restored the painting because the Stevensons wanted to get into art, and I wanted to demonstrate that I could handle all their investment needs even though I know squat about art. But the minute I saw that the restorer was you, any motivation I had beyond—"

"Getting me in bed?"

"No!" Vic cringed as his *no* echoed off the marble and lowered his voice. "I'm sorry. I didn't mean to say that so loudly."

"Look, Vic, it doesn't really matter what your motives were. We barely know each other. So what if I'm disappointed in you? You owe me absolutely nothing."

"B-but—"

"I've got things to do." She waved a hand and rushed away, her heart pounding in her ears as she threw over her shoulder, "Have a nice life."

She was *disappointed* in him?

Shaken, Vic stared after her. He'd only been doing his job. Did she honestly believe he'd led her on? Deceived her? Taken advantage of the situation?

Apparently.

*Well, you didn't tell her why you were at the Met. You could have done that. You should have done that before you slept with her.*

In his defense, he hadn't intended on having sex with her. The electricity had gone out and it had just happened. He hadn't meant to hurt her. He needed her to know that.

But she was already out the door.

He took off after her. "Ria!"

Outside, car horns honked as scads of weary-looking party-goers climbed into taxis and ride-share vehicles. Ria was standing at the bottom of the steps with her phone in hand, and he presumed she was calling for a car.

He jogged over. "Ria, could I speak to you?"

"What is it, Vic?" She looked at her screen, then peered at the heavy traffic blocking the street, but she didn't look at him.

He had a sick feeling way down in the pit of his stomach, as if he'd blown an important meeting. "I should have told you I was scouting artwork for the Stevensons. That was wrong of me."

Finally, she looked at him, her eyes forgiving.

His hopes hopped.

"You really don't owe me anything, Vic. It doesn't matter if your clients are the ones who buy *Serendipity*. I'm just the restorer. I shouldn't have gotten so attached to the painting. That's on me."

She said it didn't matter, but when he reached out to touch her shoulder, she shied away and said rather breathlessly, "It was really great spending time with you."

*Ahh, the brush-off.*

What did he expect? Some kind of fairy-tale ending? That was just nuts. But he found himself saying, "Look, I'm not an art expert. I got roped into this by my boss. The Stevensons are billionaires, and Mort really wants me to land their account. So, I said I'd broker the art deal, but I have no idea what I'm doing and the last thing I wanted was to hurt you. It's not my choice, but I'm going to talk to Mort and the Stevensons about *Serendipity* and—"

"Honestly, Vic, that's sweet of you to offer to intervene, but someone's going to buy the painting. Let the Stevensons have it. You get the brownie points with your boss and all is well. Oh, here's my car. Bye."

She wriggled her fingers at him, jumped in the car that pulled curbside, and was gone.

Vic was bothered by Ria's distress more than he wanted to let on. Normally, he shook off drama like this, but he couldn't stop seeing how hurt she'd looked when she'd learned he was acting on behalf of the Stevensons.

"Albright," Mort called out to him in the diminishing crowd.

"Hey, you spent the night here, too?"

"Yes, a night at the museum is not as appealing as it sounds." Mort grinned.

*Speak for yourself,* Vic thought.

"But you didn't waste your time." Mort clamped a hand on Vic's shoulder. "Good work."

"About . . . ?"

"Landing the Stevensons. We ran into each other and they

told me, because of your ability to adapt and dive into something you don't know anything about and your dedication to them even when they weren't yet clients, they've decided to let us manage their money. You, Albright, are a shining asset to our group."

Mort's words were golden. The sort of praise Vic lived for, and yet they felt hollow. So what if he scored points with the Stevensons if, in the process, he'd hurt Ria.

"And," Mort was saying, "if you keep the Stevensons happy, the promotion is yours."

Vic stared at his boss as reality hit him. He'd been determined to find the Stevensons before they left the museum and ask them not to buy the painting, but if he did that, he'd lose the promotion he'd spent his entire adult life working toward. If he blew this with the Stevensons, he could even lose his job.

That was a sobering realization.

On the other hand, how could he ignore Ria's feelings? She felt betrayed. She thought he'd gotten to know her simply because he was interested in buying the painting for his clients. He didn't know how to convince her that wasn't true.

Because on the surface it sure *looked* true.

Then Vic saw the Stevensons coming down the steps of the Met arm in arm in their black-tie finery, grinning at each other as if they were still just as madly in love today as when they were newlyweds, and he had an epiphany about how to solve his dilemma.

Now, all he had to do was convince the Stevensons that he had a perfect plan.

# Chapter 8

Back at her apartment, Ria collapsed on her couch, and her kitty, Schrödinger, hopped into her lap. She'd left him a bowl of food last night, so he wasn't hungry. He just wanted her affection.

"At least someone does," she muttered, and scratched the orange tabby under his chin until he started purring.

While scratching him with one hand, she slipped her phone from her purse with the other to text Alison and Vanessa. She was still hoping they might salvage their weekend. After fifteen minutes, her phone pinged. It was Vanessa: *You are not going to believe the AH-mazing night I had. Are we still on for Sag Harbor? Must share details . . . ALL GOOD!*

It sounded like Vanessa's night, at least, had ended well. Ria supposed she could head on out to Sag Harbor and get things ready as she'd planned, but honestly, she just didn't have the energy.

Not at the moment.

She was still reeling from learning that Vic had been with her just because he'd wanted to purchase *Serendipity* for his potential clients. She shouldn't be feeling so sensitive. Normally, she wouldn't be, but last night had meant something to her, and she'd believed it had meant something to Vic as well.

That's what she got for believing in soul mates and love at first sight and all that silly malarkey.

Why was she so emotionally invested in Laurice Renault's paintings?

Yes, she'd spent four months restoring *Serendipity* and had many more months of restoration work on the series ahead of her, but it was more than that. Somehow the artist had captured on canvas what true love looked like, and smitten with possibilities for her own happily ever after, Ria had fallen in love with the idea of fated love.

And that silliness had led her to spin fantasies about Vic.

Fantasies that had no basis in reality.

She was disappointed in herself for believing their night together meant more than it had—at least to him.

That's where the problem lay.

Not with Vic, but with her.

Just because *Serendipity* spoke to her, that was no reason to get upset because it was being sold off. It was like a cattle rancher being upset because she had to take her cattle to market. Ria needed to fully accept reality. Yes, she'd been the one to draw attention to Laurice Renault, but she didn't own the artist's work.

None of this was Vic's fault, and if the Stevensons didn't buy the painting, someone else would. He might as well be one who got some benefit from the sale.

Ria smacked her forehead with her palm, startling Schrödinger, who stopped purring to stare at her. "I'm an idiot," she told the cat. "I handled this so poorly."

Schrödinger meowed.

"You think I should call him?"

Schrödinger thumped his tail against her arm.

"I see." Time to eat crow.

Ria was just about to look up his phone number in her contacts when her cell phone rang. Startled, she dropped the phone. It was most likely Alison calling in response to her text.

The phone buzzed her ringtone again and she scooped it off the floor and glanced at the screen.

It wasn't Alison.

"It's him!" she told Schrödinger. "It's Vic."

The cat gave her a lazy look as if to say, *Answer the phone, woman.*

"Hello." She tried to keep the excitement from her voice. Playing it cool.

"We need to talk."

"Okay. Where are you?"

"I'm at your building, but I don't know your apartment number."

She told him, and then had just enough time to brush her teeth and run a comb through her hair before her doorbell buzzed.

Ria opened the door and looked into his handsome, smiling face. Her heart did that weird little thing it always did whenever she saw him. "Hey."

"May I come in?"

"Please." She stepped aside.

"You have a cat!" he said enthusiastically, crouching down to pet Schrödinger, who'd strolled over to greet the new arrival. "What's his name?"

"Schrödinger."

Vic laughed. "I love your sense of humor. I have a cat, too."

"Really?" That revelation made her like him even more.

"His name is Charlie Whiskers and he's a tuxedo."

"I wouldn't expect anything less from you." She chuckled, noting he was still wearing his own tuxedo. "You haven't been home."

"Not yet. I had to come see you first."

"Before you tell me what you want to say, I'd like to speak."

"By all means." He straightened and brushed cat hair from his palms.

"I was wrong to react the way I did when I learned who the Stevensons were and that you were working on their behalf. They have every right to buy the painting. I got too attached."

His eyes held hers and he said in the gentlest of voices, "It's easy to get attached to something you admire."

"Thank you for understanding. I'm not usually so emotional."

"I know," he murmured. "I've watched you in action for the past four months. Each time I see you, I admire you just a little bit more. The fact that you're willing to examine your reactions and question your motives says a lot about you as a person."

"I'm actually happy that the painting is going to people who are so excited about it."

"You might be able to have it both ways." He grinned big.

"What did you do?" she asked, curious as to what that grin was all about.

"I had a talk with the Stevensons after you left." He paused, his grin widening.

"And?" Excitement tightened her chest.

"I convinced them to put in the winning bid for the painting and then donate it back to the museum. They get a welcome tax write-off along with all the fanfare and accolades of making such a donation, and museum visitors will get to enjoy *Serendipity*."

"Oh, Vic, I can't begin to thank you." She placed a palm to her heart, overcome by strong emotion. He'd done this for her. He'd taken a risk, put his reputation on the line.

For her.

"You know," he went on, "I've been thinking about what you said."

"Which was . . . ?" She tilted her head in the opposite direction from his as they studied each other with great, heartfelt smiles.

"Your theory about fate, destiny . . . soul mates."

"Oh." She felt her pulse quicken at her throat. "That theory. Gotta say, I was caught up in the moment, and you were right . . . soul mates. Ridiculous. That idea does not hold water. At all."

"I wouldn't say 'at all.' "

"What people call 'love at first sight' is just chemistry, and while that's fun, it's nothing *magical*." Although last night had been pretty darn magical. "A real relationship, a lasting relationship, takes time."

"Like taking four months before introducing yourself to the person you're interested in?"

"Well, that *was* slow." She laughed and sliced her arm away from herself in an arcing gesture, showing him just how goofy her romantic babblings had been the night before. "You convinced me. Love at first sight makes absolutely no logical sense."

"Aaah, that's too bad." Vic made a tsk-tsk noise.

"It is?" She ticked her head the other way, mirroring him.

"Because I gave your theory some thought." He stroked his chin with his thumb and index finger and his eyes got even brighter.

"You did?"

"While I agree with you that it takes time to learn about another person and build a healthy relationship, I also feel . . ." He paused.

She waited.

He bobbed his head and loosened his grin. "I'm not good at talking about my feelings."

She waited.

His shoulders went up and he scratched his forehead while he looked down at her bare feet.

"Yes?"

He raised his head and met her gaze head-on. "When I first saw you, I wanted you. You were this hot, brainy redhead who wouldn't give me the time of day and I was intrigued."

"What do you mean I wouldn't give you the time of day? You never asked."

"Whenever I'd come close, you'd stick your nose in a book or start drawing in your sketch pad."

"I didn't." She crinkled her nose.

"You did."

"Did I?"

"Face it, we both hesitated because we could feel that this"— he toggled an index finger from her to him and back again— "has the potential to be something big."

"Do you think that too?" All the air leaked from her lungs in a long exhale. Her heart was beating crazy fast and she was glad she'd taken the time to brush her teeth because he had an *I'm about to kiss you* look in his eyes.

"I've had some casual flings in my life," he went on. "I know from the get-go whether it's something that can last or not."

"Are you saying what I think you're saying?" Inside she was shaking like a leaf, but somehow outwardly at least, she managed to play it cool.

"I'd like to see where this thing could go."

*Bam, bam, bam*, went her heart. "Really?"

He leaned in. "Really."

She couldn't believe what he was saying. She'd felt inextricably drawn to this man from the beginning, but she'd been working on a romantic painting and feared she was just being fanciful. But if he said he'd felt something from the beginning, too . . .

His mouth claimed hers and she let go of her inner musing

and just savored his heat. She melted into his arms, and as he lifted her up and carried her to the bedroom, one last thought rolled through her head.

This weekend was supposed to have been about fun with friends, but what she hadn't counted on was that serendipity had other plans.

Sometimes, fate really did know best.

# Lights Out

PRISCILLA OLIVERAS

*Para mi querida Gueli (abuela), la que inculcó en mi el amor por el juego de béisbol y un tremendo orgullo por Roberto Clemente. Le encantaría estar en el opening night de Mateo.*
*¡Me haces mucha falta y te quiero, Gueli!*

*For my beloved Gueli (grandmother), who instilled in me a love for the game of baseball and tremendous pride in Roberto Clemente. She would have loved to be at Mateo's opening night.*
*I miss and love you so much, Gueli!*

# Chapter 1

"He's just a man. And you're *just* doing your job. Cálmate, chica," Vanessa Ríos chided herself under her breath, willing her racing heart to calm.

"Excuse me?" The elderly theatre usher's confused frown deepened the wrinkles lining her round face. Her cap of short gray curls bounced softly as she angled her head in question.

"Oh, nothing. Just . . . just mumbling to myself." Embarrassed heat climbing her cheeks, Vanessa smiled politely and took the usher's proffered *Playbill*. "Thank you, I can find my seat."

Dios mío, the man had her so wound up, she was talking to herself out loud. In public.

She sucked in a deep breath. Alison's pep talk, delivered via text earlier today before the two of them and Ria had headed their separate ways for the night, drifted through Vanessa's mind again.

*You are the queen of your universe, girl. Own it.*

Damn straight, she was.

Tonight had nothing to do with the past. And everything to

do with reminding herself of what her present and future held. Claiming her title as one of the "30 under 30 Voices to Heed" thanks to her stellar writing skills and reputation for speaking the hard truth.

Shoulders back, head high, Vanessa followed a young couple down the crowded aisle between the center and right orchestra seating areas in the standing-room-only packed Booth Theatre. She was a woman on a mission. One that did not involve butterflies in her stomach or tingles in places that should not be tingling over a guy who could, at best, only be a professional contact.

The couple in front of her slowed their progress toward the front, drawing Vanessa's attention away from her private antagonist. She tuned back in to the excited buzz of conversations and palpable excitement in the historic theatre.

Around her, people of all ages settled into their seats, perused their *Playbills*, snapped selfies, or sipped their expensive cocktails. Anticipation hummed in the air like cicadas awakening from their slumber.

"I can't believe you surprised me like this!" the young woman ahead of Vanessa gushed to her partner.

Based on the woman's beaded black halter dress and the guy's crisp, white button-down and fitted suit ensemble, along with his hand splayed protectively on the small of her back and the adoring look they shared, the couple were obviously on a date. An expensive one, at that.

Ticket prices for this opening-night performance of *Clemente: Legend & Hero*, written by and starring Broadway's rising heartthrob, were steep. As in, hand-over-your-firstborn steep. Every die-hard theatre fan and some with serious FOMO had for months been salivating over a chance to be in the room where it happened.

Fear of missing out wasn't something Vanessa usually had to worry about.

Thanks to her gig with *The Fix*, New York's number one, in-the-know online magazine, she had an all-access pass to a majority of the hottest spots, events, and goings-on in Manhattan and the rest of the five boroughs. Amazingly, *The Fix* paid her to keep her finger on her adopted city's pulse. The powers that be actually wanted her to attend—and review—the plays and musicals she'd once dreamed about performing in as a teen. Her editor even expected her to hit up the after-parties or visit backstage to interview actors, tech crew, producers, and those involved in the NYC arts scene. Like the one later tonight celebrating *Clemente.*

It was a dream job. One she did damn well, too.

Forget the few who whispered behind her back at the office. The petty ones complaining that she'd risen too fast, grumbling about how she had managed it, implying there had to be some hidden connection aiding her. Vanessa never listened to their negativity. She'd gone through the ranks from college intern to assistant to full-time staff writer covering the arts, entertainment, and culture section by busting her own culo. Not by kissing someone else's.

Hell-bent on proving to herself that she had made the right decision when she'd changed course in college. Distancing herself from the career her papi had boasted was proof that they were made of the same cloth.

An old antsiness she rarely felt anymore skittered across her shoulders. It tiptoed down her chest, into her belly. Resolutely, she shook it off and slid her gaze past the bottleneck of theatregoers to trail over the musical's set, a welcome distraction from her mind's unwanted memory-lane detour.

Tropical trees and foliage adorned the area on either side of and behind a one-story, weatherworn home's façade at center stage. Two classic aluminum lawn chairs with frayed orange webbed fabric sat open in front of the brown wooden door. Stage right resembled the inside of a bodega. A checkout counter sat on the far edge, and two low shelves stocked with cans of criollo products like gandules and various types of beans, bottles of Malta India and other sodas, and bags of plantain chips mixed with Doritos, Fritos, and more ran parallel to the stage wings. In the far background, wispy white clouds dusted a clear blue sky that melded into the Caribbean Sea's horizon. A baseball glove and bat sat haphazardly on an empty park bench angled at stage left.

The Puerto Rico of Clemente's time—and that of her abuelos as seen in the old pictures lovingly displayed around her grandparents' homes—came back to vivid life through the much-anticipated musical.

At the moment, the stage sat still. Quietly, expectantly waiting. But she knew that in the halls and dressing rooms throughout the historic building, actors ran through their lines, marked choreography in their heads, performed last-minute makeup checks, or engaged in whatever pre-curtain routine helped them step into character.

That might have been her life, had she stuck with her original plan. Instead of letting her father's "You're a chip off the old block, ha, nena?" tip the hand she had already been considering folding.

"Stop it."

Her muttered command had the young blonde in front of her shifting a wary glance over her shoulder.

Vanessa widened her eyes in mock excitement, spreading her lips and adopting the same "Oh my gosh, I can't believe I'm here for this" expression worn by countless others around them.

The girl returned it with a tentative smile of her own as the crowd snaking down the aisle started moving again.

Hiking her small tote purse higher on her shoulder with one hand, Vanessa slapped her *Playbill* against her leg with the other. The glossy paper stuck to her skin where the hem of her short minidress hit her midthigh. *Ay, Dios mío, nena, get your shit together.*

Maybe writing for *The Fix* hadn't been the career she'd imagined as a young . . . bueno, more like naïve . . . college coed. Instead, as an FU to her philandering, narcissistic father, she'd surprised everyone by closing her backstage dressing-room door for good only one year into her musical theatre BFA at the University of Central Florida. After switching her concentration to writing and theatre studies, she never looked back.

Most of the time.

Tonight being one of those damn anomalies.

As she'd walked into the Booth, her past had risen like an uninvited specter, its aura shimmering with what-ifs armed with a current that threatened to zap her if she let them get too close. All because of the charismatic leading man, writer, and brains behind the show she was here to review.

Or, more pointedly, *confirm* her already-written review. Something she never did. She always trusted her gut instincts. Confident in her abilities.

Except when it came to this musical. Or, more precisely, the man whose vision and talent and determined drive had brought this show to life.

No wonder her editor had given her a *What the hell!* scowl when Vanessa had asked for a chance to edit her already-submitted piece, if need be, before it went live later tonight.

She had reviewed countless plays and musicals when they'd still been in preview. Never had she second-guessed herself or her work. Her shoot-from-the-hip, don't-hold-back straight talk resonated with readers. They wanted it; she gave it to them.

Until her previous review of Mateo Garza's performance in another show three years ago.

A familiar stinging prick of guilt made her wince.

Doggedly, she ignored it, as she usually did. Bueno, except

that one time she had slipped and accidentally mentioned her private dilemma during a girls' night in with Ria and Allison and way too much wine.

Alison had immediately pounced, demanding details.

Ria had remained silent, her intense pale blue eyes assessing Vanessa like one of her prized art pieces undergoing restoration.

Thankfully, Vanessa's alcohol-loosened lips hadn't tattled the whole shameful secret. Leaving out the part about the potentially misguided correlation her head, and then her metaphorical pen, had made between Mateo and her father.

Emphasis on *potentially*.

Because, frankly, Mateo's previous interviews had fueled the rumors confirmed by Vanessa's "anonymous" tipster. Plus, when it came to recognizing the signs of an ego-driven man with little regard for those he hurt along the way, experience with her sinvergüenza of a father had turned her into a pro.

Her mami's "Por favor, don't call him that" rang in Vanessa's head. Hell, she had called her father much worse than *shameless*. Deservedly so.

Annoyed that her past—the painful memories and discord, the lingering misgivings born of her choices—had snuck in to color her mood black, Vanessa tucked her chin and tried picturing the relaxing beach scene her therapist recommended as a calming visualization exercise. The *Playbill*'s edge wrinkled in her tightened grasp, drawing her attention.

She gazed down at the image of Roberto Clemente in his old-timey 1960s-era white, black, and yellow Pittsburgh Pirates baseball uniform. A man who had fought both on and off the field for equality. A strong voice for the often-overlooked and unappreciated.

Exactly what she intended to do with her new human-interest column. If *The Fix* agreed to make it a regular addition to the magazine.

How best to ensure that happened was what she should be concentrating on. Not the Broadway star who dogged her mental steps far too often.

Progress down the crowded aisle stalled again and the house lights flickered.

Almost curtain time.

Her thumb riffled through the edges of the *Playbill*'s pages, stopping when she spotted the musical's cast list. Unable to resist, she opened the booklet, spreading the pages wide.

Mateo Garza stared back at her. The high school boy she'd crushed over from a distance now a grown man. All smoldering dark eyes, square jaw, and straight white teeth flashing against his warm bronze skin. That single dimple in his left cheek winked at her. Teasing. Enticing.

Vanessa slapped the pages closed between her hands. There was absolutely nothing enticing about him. There couldn't be. She knew better.

Rising on her toes in her sandaled heels, she peered at her seat through the crowd blocking her path.

"Vanessa!"

A familiar voice whisper-shouted over the din. She glanced to her left, scanning the mid-orchestra-level section to find Greg Vickers, a veteran reviewer with *The Times*, waving from a few rows ahead.

She grinned back at the tall, wiry man with thinning gray hair and sharp gray eyes who'd become her mentor of sorts over the past few years of rubbing elbows at many of the same events. Despite his occasional grumble, in his thick Jersey accent, about "youse millennials," and the rise of digital media undermining the demand for print, he'd been a fountain of insider info and advice. Along with a fair amount of good-natured teasing.

Lips pursed, Greg narrowed his gaze in a mock glare, fisting his hands and holding them up to feign a boxer's fighting stance. A move the old geezer made when he teased her about what he called her "pugnacious nature." The way she rarely held back in her articles and reviews. Giving readers the bald truth—good, bad, and indifferent—just as she'd done when sharing her thoughts about Mateo Garza after his previous role as a self-absorbed lothario.

That same scrappy fighter mentality had gotten her where she was right now . . . and she did *not* mean acting like a wet-behind-the-ears newbie, talking out loud to herself, second-guessing her already-submitted review, secretly fangirling over a guy who was undoubtedly just like countless other guys: destined to break a girl's heart.

The reminder straightened her spine. She shot Greg a smirk. Gave him a blasé shoulder hitch and head tilt that the dastardly butterflies in her stomach belied.

Greg mimed giving his own jaw a punch as if she had thrown it, then laughed and sat down when she rolled her eyes at him.

Chuckling, thankful for the stress relief his teasing offered, Vanessa tipped her *Playbill* at him, before fiiiinally moving down the aisle again.

Moments later she settled in her fourth-row seat. Smoothing her hands down her short floral skirt . . . okay, wiping her slightly clammy palms on the material . . . she took a slow measured breath and finger-combed her blowout.

The lights dimmed. The audience hushed. Excitement pulsed in the air.

The band nestled in the back left corner of the stage struck up the beginning strains of "En Mi Viejo San Juan." The trumpet player's strong, vibrant notes melded with the melodic, sensual guitar as the violinist plucked an engaging beat that invited the audience to tap their feet. The woman in front of Vanessa swayed to the sultry music, and she found herself doing the same.

Love, pride, and anticipation pulsed through her. The memory of her abuela singing the lyrics, an ode to their beloved Old San Juan, brought a nostalgic smile to her lips.

Then the ballad's music shifted, the familiar lyrics faded away, and an upbeat, salsa rhythm infused the notes.

Onstage, the home's front door opened, and Mateo Garza stepped out onto the makeshift front porch. Vanessa's heart tripped. Her breath lodged in her chest as he strolled downstage, coming to a stop a step away from the front edge.

Casually dressed in slim-fitting dark jeans and a pale blue button-down, the sleeves rolled up to reveal the muscles in his tanned forearms, he exuded confidence and magnetism. A warm smile tugged up the corners of his mouth, sparkling in his dark eyes. Arms outstretched at his sides as if preparing to wrap the entire audience in a welcoming bear hug, Mateo greeted them.

"Un campeón. A champion. An All-Star. That's how many describe Roberto Clemente. Rightfully so. Pero, para nuestra isla, to *our* island . . ." Mateo angled his body, motioning with his left arm to encompass the stage and the world it evoked, before slowly bringing his hand to his broad chest. "To those who knew him, those whose lives he touched, then and now, he was and still remains larger-than-life. A reminder of how one person can make a difference. How we can *all* make a difference."

Sí.

The word whispered from her soul, the musical's message resonating with her on an intimate, personal level.

That it had been created by Mateo Garza, a man who both drew and repelled her, had been wreaking havoc on her psyche for weeks—more like months—now.

Mateo took in the crowd filling every seat in the house, those standing in the back fringes. Chin raised high, his expression earnest, he stared up at the mezzanine, moving his gaze toward the stage right side of the orchestra-level seating, opposite her.

"Tonight we celebrate the life of a legend. Una inspiración."

Vanessa's pulse pounded to the bongo beat as Mateo's gaze slid closer toward her section. Arms spread wide again, his dimple making a charming appearance beside his pleased grin, he continued the opening monologue. "And now . . ."

His gaze reached her and stopped. For a split second she could have sworn he flinched. But then he gave a cheeky wink and dipped his head in greeting.

Her eyes widened in surprise. Heat crawled up her cheeks.

"Bienvenidos, my friends." Mateo's voice deepened, warm and husky. Far too sexy. "Welcome to our celebration!"

The music swelled, trumpets blasting, bongo drums beating with a fast salsa rhythm. Mateo swiveled his hips to the song, his feet smoothly moving into the steps. His grin widened when a woman in the audience called out a "¡Wepa!" of encouragement.

Dancers dressed in street clothes, baseball uniforms, or beach attire swarmed out from the wings to fill the stage around him in a mix of vibrant colors and motion. When she'd seen the show in preview, the high-energy opening number had blown Vanessa away with its intricate choreography. But while she found herself caught up in the pageantry of it all once again, for some reason tonight . . .

Tonight she only had eyes for Mateo Garza.

# Chapter 2

Mateo's chest heaved as he sucked in a deep breath after the vigorous number near the end of act one. He palmed the base-ball bat and lapped up the audience's cheers.

Cortez had absolutely outdone himself with the show's choreography. Sharp, energetic combinations, lifts, and foot-work highlighting the music's rhythm and soul. Even using the bats and devising intricate exchanges among the dancers. Brilliant.

Although Mateo still sported a bruise on his left biceps after one of the understudies had accidentally smacked him with a bat during rehearsals last week. The pain and injury were worth it given the crowd's reception.

Given one particular person's reception.

Unbidden, he sought out Vanessa Ríos. Stage left, fourth row, on the aisle. Light brown hair blown straight, no wild curls tonight. The waves teased her left shoulder, bared by her one-sleeved floral dress. Her expressive eyes alight with won-der. A rapturous smile curving her full lips, until she realized he was looking her way. Again.

Her grin slipped. She scowled at him and a tiny groove wedged between her brows.

Great, his inexplicable need to gauge her reaction to the show seemed to piss her off. Practically begging her to bash him in her next write-up for breaking the fourth wall.

Needing every positive review possible, Mateo blinked and made himself look away. Smiling down at his dance partner, he forced his attention back to where it should have been—the show.

The applause began to quiet, and Juan, the talented Afro-Latinx actor who portrayed their Clemente, moved into his next line. Most of the ballplayers and fans hustled offstage, leaving behind Mateo and the actor playing Willie Mays, another baseball great and Clemente's teammate during winter ball in Puerto Rico.

"At tomorrow's youth baseball clinic," Clemente began, "I want to—"

The stage lights flickered unexpectedly and Clemente broke off.

A heartbeat later, the entire theatre went dark. A collective gasp sounded from the audience.

Onstage, at the back of the theatre, up in the box seats, even . . . Mateo shot a glance toward the stage-left wings. Darkened.

¿Qué carajo?

There were several seconds of stunned silence as Mateo—his *What the hell?* reverberating in his brain—and everyone else waited for the lights to come back up. Instead, soft yellow emergency lights strategically placed around the historic theatre switched on.

Murmurs swept through the house, increasing with volume and shocked intensity when it became clear this wasn't a momentary glitch.

Heads swiveled as people looked about the place, searching for answers. In the muted lighting, Mateo exchanged confused glances with his fellow actors.

The stage manager's voice over the speakers interrupted the escalating din. "Everyone please remain calm. It appears that we have experienced some sort of power outage in the building. We're seeking further information and appreciate your patience."

Groans of disappointment and complaint arose, rippling through the crowd. Discord threatened, despite the manager's request for patience.

Hands raised in a conciliatory gesture, Mateo strode to the stage edge. "Por favor, do not worry. I am sure we'll have answers shortly."

He sure as hell hoped so. When the news sites and social media reported about tonight's performance, he needed it to be about how the actors, music, story line, choreography . . . every freaking aspect of the show . . . had wowed and taken the reviewers' and audience's breath away. Too much was riding on *Clemente*'s success.

The past eight years of his life had been spent thinking about . . . brainstorming, researching, writing, pitching, rewriting, *living* . . . this show. His familia and friends believed in him. They had *invested* in him, literally pooling their hard-earned money to help fund his vision and dream. He couldn't let them down.

The show was good. No, it was fucking incredible.

And that wasn't just his ego talking because he'd written most of it. Or because he starred in the cast.

*Clemente* was his passion project. It had been since sophomore year of his BFA, when he'd first started working on the idea. Since then, he'd eaten, slept, breathed, *Clemente*, even when he was performing other shows. Especially the occasional roles he had accepted mainly as a means of maintaining his union health-care benefits.

Bringing his vision for *Clemente* to the stage had consumed him. Some would say to a degree that proved detrimental. He obviously disagreed.

Frustration growing, Mateo shoved a hand through his hair. He stared blindly out at the house. The darkened area glowed with the light of cell phone screens as people frantically searched for information or a connection with someone outside.

For some harebrained reason, he sought out Vanessa Ríos.

Head bent, her shapely legs crossed so that her short skirt rode up her tanned thighs a little higher, she tapped her thumbs quickly across her phone screen.

What the hell was she doing here again? She'd already attended a preview show. He knew because he'd specifically asked to be alerted when she was in the house.

That meant her poisoned pen should already have done its work.

Unease slithered through him as he recalled her last, less than glowing review of his work. Bad critiques were part of his profession. Any fool knew that. Her unvarnished critique of him in *Sin with Me* had created a few waves with one *Clemente* investor, but Mateo had weathered the defection. He'd been more disappointed in her clear disdain, realizing she'd bought into the offstage playboy role he had assumed as part of publicity for the play. *Sin with Me*'s producers had loved it.

But her review of *Clemente* . . . that had serious ramifications.

This wasn't only about him.

If *Clemente* flopped, people who counted on him, who had put up money he felt certain they couldn't easily have parted with, would lose. Everyone who'd sweated blood and tears and spent round-the-clock hours with him would be let down.

It was on him to make sure that didn't happen.

Intellectually, he understood that Vanessa Ríos represented only one *Clemente* review. But hers . . . for him, hers hit a personal chord.

Mainly because of their past connection, as hard to describe as it might be. How exactly did a guy classify the teen crush he'd secretly had on the star performer from his rival high school's theatre troupe? The closest they'd come to being a couple was the one time they'd been paired up as duet partners during a Theatre Fest vocal workshop senior year.

At the time, their respective competition shows had featured songs from *In the Heights*, with her singing the role of her namesake and him, Usnavi. In his infinite wisdom, the workshop instructor had asked them to sing one of the show's ballads together. The song "Champagne" had never again been the same for Mateo. Not to mention, his and Vanessa's chaste kiss had fueled far too many of his youthful fantasies.

Vanessa wasn't exactly the girl who got away. More like the girl he couldn't have. The one he had dreamed about as a teen, then a college kid. So, he couldn't help but take her reviews personally. Knucklehead that he was.

Whatever Vanessa read on her phone screen must not have met with her approval because she shook her head and dropped the cell in her lap. Her chin came up, her brow still furrowed as she gazed around the darkened area. She caught her plump lower lip between her teeth, and Mateo's gut clenched. Lust shot through him.

"Oye, what do you think?" César asked. He and Juan huddled up with Mateo near the long wooden bench replicating the home team's dugout in the 1960s Santurce Cangrejeros' ballpark.

"This can't be good, 'mano," Juan muttered. Hands on his trim dancer hips, their Willie Mays shook his head with a worried grimace.

"I'm praying it's only a minor brownout, and we're back on soon." Mateo's gut clenched with unease, a reaction that was never a comfortable feeling onstage in the middle of a performance.

"You and everyone else in this place, bruh," Juan said.

Arms crossed, the three of them heaved deep, shoulder-lifting, disappointed sighs like a choreographed move.

Forty-five minutes later, the opening night Mateo had dreamed of for close to a decade had devolved into a pandemonium-fueled debacle courtesy of an NYC in the midst of a complete, all-boroughs-wide blackout.

The theatre had been safely cleared, but chaos ensued on the streets and outside the stage door in Shubert Alley. Fans normally flocked here for preshow miniconcerts in the style of the #Ham4Ham shows made popular by the Tony-winning musical *Hamilton*. The actors never performed after a show, stopping only to greet the fans clamoring for autographs and selfies.

Tonight was different.

Tonight people crammed the alley and streets, cell phones held aloft as a light source. On either side of the alley, taxis crawled by on Forty-Fourth and Forty-Fifth Streets, filled with strangers opting to ride together if headed in the same direction. With the subway system shut down, taxis and other ride-share options were at a premium.

Pedestrians swarmed the streets, and drivers leaned on their horns in frustration. The sound reverberated off the alley walls, heightening the tension palpable in the hot and humid July air.

In an attempt to quiet the unrest while patrons tried to figure out how they might make their way home, Mateo and a few fellow cast members had agreed to a second miniperformance after changing into their street clothes. Now they stood behind the rail barricade in front of the stage door after having sung three numbers.

"Thanks so much for hanging out with us," Mateo told the crowd, who responded with cries of "One more!" and "Sing 'My MVP!' "—the request a soundtrack favorite of many. Also one of his solos.

" 'MVP'!"

" 'MVP'!"

The cries heightened, and Juan nudged Mateo with his elbow. "Dales lo que quieren, 'mano."

"Yeah," César agreed, mopping his sweaty brow with a hand towel. "You gotta give the people what they want."

Gloria, who played Clemente's wife in the show, nodded her encouragement.

"Okay, okay!" Mateo caved, and the crowd let out a cheer.

Off to his right, a group of fans shifted to gather closer. He caught sight of Vanessa standing behind two blond teens leaning against the railing.

Once again her presence surprised him. Her no-nonsense, sharp-witted personality didn't peg her as the type to hang around stage doors for a glimpse at a star. With her press credentials and contacts, she didn't have to. Yet there she was, eyeing him with guarded interest.

Unnerving him like an uncomfortable itch under his skin.

Heat arced through him, arousal darting low in his body.

Ignoring his reaction to the woman who'd made no secret that she wasn't signing up for his fan club—not that he had one anyway—Mateo turned away. He brought the mic close to his mouth, then signaled the understudy sitting on a stool by the stage door to start the accompaniment music.

Soft cheers and a few swooning sighs greeted the song's first notes. Encouraged by the response, Mateo closed his eyes and let the music pull him into the character of a young ballplayer awed and inspired by his mentor, Clemente. He sucked in a diaphragm-expanding breath, ready for his first line of lyrics.

A loud bang ripped through the night.

A quick smattering of what sounded alarmingly like return gunfire followed out on the street. Shrieks of fear and shouts of dismay pierced the air. Pedestrians swarmed off Forty-Fifth and into Shubert Alley. The crowd gathered around the safety railing surged forward in a rising tide of hysteria.

"What the fu—?"

A woman cried out in pain, and Mateo broke off when he caught sight of Vanessa, now sandwiched between the metal railing and the mob behind her. The top rung cut into her waist as she was forced against it, one foot shoved at an awkward angle between two of the thin vertical bars.

A theatre security guard in black pants and tee threw his arms over Gloria for protection, at the same time yelling at Juan and César to head inside. The guard reached for Mateo's elbow to pull him along, too, but Vanessa cried out again and Mateo shook the burly guy off.

Mateo raced toward her at the same time two other guards and a few stage-crew members hurried out. Hands outstretched, they tried to bring order to the panicked masses. One of them yelled into a bullhorn, calling for calm to no avail.

"Stop! Back off!" Mateo shouted when he reached Vanessa. He shoved the shoulder of a heavyset guy who loomed over her. The dude didn't budge, and Mateo shoved harder, desperate to lift the pressure off her. "Mike, help!"

The guard, who was built like a New York Giants lineman, sidestepped closer to Mateo.

Bent at a nearly ninety-degree angle over the top bar, Vanessa craned her neck to look up at him. Through the light brown tresses spilling over her face, he spotted the stark fear clouding her hazel-green eyes. Pain pinched her beautiful features. Her lips parted with a guttural gasp as the crowd surged again.

Bracing his legs, Mike pushed the heavyset guy's torso, grunting with exertion. The crowd shifted, and Mike lunged forward to force the big guy off Vanessa. Mateo grabbed her by the underarms to haul her up and over the railing. She whimpered when her left foot jammed, still caught between the vertical railings. He jerked to a stop and she wiggled her foot free, grimacing with the effort, then threw her arms around his neck as he scooped up her knees and lifted her in his arms.

"Back the hell up!" Mike yelled, his deep voice bouncing off the alley walls.

Mateo didn't stick around to see if the crowd listened.

Instead, he hurried inside, leaving the clashing sounds of a city in turmoil behind him. The floral scent and soft feel of a woman who'd been an unwanted, far-too-desirable distraction in his life tucked safely against his racing heart.

# Chapter 3

Eyes squeezed shut, Vanessa sought to slow her panicked breathing. In for a count of three. Out for a count of three. Again. Again. Desperately trying to quiet the simmering hysteria.

Her heart pounded, the whoosh of blood coursing in her veins loud in her ears. A light sheen of perspiration dotted her upper lip and brow, left a clammy sensation across her upper back and between her shoulder blades. Her stomach ached, both from the crush of the guardrail against her hips and belly and the anxiety roiling her insides in shock waves.

"I can walk," she mumbled, as Mateo carried her through the tiny hall leading backstage at the Booth Theatre.

It would be on shaky legs, more than likely, but she hated being at a disadvantage and showing any sign of weakness.

"Not until I take a look at your ankle. And make sure you're all right," Mateo insisted, his voice a low grumble. His strong arms tightened around her as if punctuating his words.

She peeked up at him, taking in his angular jaw and cheekbones, intense dark brown eyes, and wavy black hair in the 1960s style that had sent girls swooning over charmers like Cary Grant. Mateo Garza wore the look well.

Too well.

His gaze cut down to her and she glanced away. No need to be caught admiring his Casanova good looks. Unlike the charming boy he'd been in high school, Mateo as an adult had an ego that seemed to have ballooned. Based on his innuendo-riddled interviews anyway.

What she couldn't ignore, though, was the warmth from his firm chest seeping through the thin material of her minidress, heating the entire right side of her body where it pressed against him. Her short skirt crept up her thighs, coming dangerously close to being inappropriate for anything other than a beach cover-up. And she definitely wasn't wearing the blue bathing-suit bottoms she had planned to pack for her girls' weekend with Ria and Alison. More like a black lacy thong that would give an onlooker a nice view of her butt cheeks if Mateo didn't put her down soon and her dress rode up any higher.

Thankfully, it looked like the majority of the cast and crew had already bugged out, braving the masses outside in a bid to get home.

"I'm fine," she assured Mateo. "Really. A little spooked for a second. But I'm good now."

A lot spooked, actually. But no need to reveal that to him.

She didn't need a man to save her.

Bueno, not if she could help it.

She refused to think like her mami.

Mateo grunted in response.

They reached the backstage area, and he slowed his pace. The normally dimly lit space sat even darker now thanks to the blackout. Emergency lights emitted a garish, yellow-tinted glow, casting bleary shadows over the long hanging rack filled with costumes waiting to be cleaned before tomorrow's matinee show. If, as Vanessa was sure all of NYC prayed, whatever had caused the power failure was resolved by then.

"Here we go." Mateo stopped beside one of the prop tables,

this one littered with the baseball gloves used throughout the musical and a collection of oversized Spanish fans Vanessa remembered from a number in the second act. A part in the show tonight's audience had missed.

"It's around here somewhere," Mateo mumbled.

"What is?'

He bent forward slightly, and Vanessa yelped in surprise. She tightened her arms around his neck, instinctively tucking her head against him. Her nose accidentally brushed his skin above the rounded collar of his soft gray T-shirt. A musky oak and leathery scent, slightly sweat tinged after his performance under the hot stage lights and the humidity out in the alley, filled her lungs. Desire, unwanted and raw, curled through her.

"I got you," he assured her.

Face still pressed to his neck, she felt his words rumbling against her cheek.

"Just looking for . . ." His body dipped again, and one of his legs swiped underneath the prop table. "For this."

Something scraped across the floor, and Vanessa twisted to glance over her shoulder. In the muted light she watched him drag a wooden stool out with his foot, his white Vans sneaker vivid in the darkness.

"Can you stand?" He ducked his head to look at her.

And, coño, this close she caught the reflection of the emergency lights in his nearly black eyes. Worry floated among the tiny circles shining in their depths.

She nodded dumbly, surprised . . . okay, touched, but she didn't want to be . . . by his concern. "Uh, yeah, I'm good."

Her bumbling reassurance didn't erase the frown wrinkling his forehead.

Still, the arm he had crooked beneath her knees slackened, and Mateo slowly lowered her feet to the ground.

Her palms slid from his nape, across his wide shoulders, the friction creating pinpricks of awareness over her palms. She grabbed the strap of her small tote purse, slung messenger-bag-style across her torso, determined to thank him, then immediately be on her way.

"See, I'm fi—ow." Her left ankle gave out as she tried to step back, and she reached for Mateo, crumpling against him.

"Oof!" he grunted, grabbing on to her waist to catch her as she face-planted into his muscular chest.

Her hands fisted in his shirt for support at the same time his fingers tightened around her hips, drawing their bodies closer. With her forearms sandwiched between them, her nose squashed between his pecs, and his strong arms cocooning her safely, there was no denying that Mateo Garza kept himself in perfect shape.

Or that the man smelled and felt like an alarming mix of heaven and sin and trouble. Emphasis on the *sin* and the *trouble*. Especially for a woman with no interest in being swept off her feet. Figuratively or literally.

Both of which he had somehow managed to do tonight.

As he had with their chaste kiss all those years ago. And the first time they'd run into each other at a theatre event here in the city. Before she'd learned about his skills playing the field, much like her papi and her cheating ex.

"Coño, you okay?" Mateo asked.

Several other choice words ran through her head along with his *damn*. As for being okay? With his palms branding her hips, his long fingers splaying along the small of her back?

She wasn't sure.

Unfisting her hands, Vanessa smoothed out the wrinkles now crisscrossing his chest. Once. Twice. Madre de Dios, he was really ripped. A third . . .

Mateo cleared his throat, and she froze, hands splayed over his pecs. Embarrassed heat crawled up her face.

"Um, sorry, about that." She gulped, thankful for the muted lighting as she glanced at him from under her lashes. "I'm not usually one for the damsel-in-distress routine."

"Yeah, you've never struck me as the fainthearted maiden."

Good. She intended to keep it that way.

"Back in high school, you always gave off this confident, unruffled vibe," he added. A corner of his mouth lifted in an inviting half smile. "Remember that improv workshop we wound up in at Theatre Fest as juniors? You were kinda fearless. Then the next year, when we were paired up to sing . . . not that I . . . anyway, it kind of—" He shook his head, as if shaking away the memories. "Shit, never mind."

His throat moved with a swallow, leaving her to wonder if he held back something he wanted to say.

*It kind of* what?

The question teased the tip of her tongue. She bit down on it to stop herself from asking.

Their brief interactions over the years had stuck with her. Had it been the same for him? Another question she refused to voice.

Only once, at an industry after-party, had she and Mateo discussed their rival high school theatre connection.

Those community and school theatre days were long behind him, a man whose star now shone ever brighter. She rarely discussed her years as a performer. Before the sting of betrayal and its rippling consequences.

But, being around Mateo made her think about a different time. Back when she didn't question her choices. Or the people who were supposed to be closest to her.

She had turned a corner, was feeling confident with her new trajectory. Until that damn *Sin with Me* write-up. Until him.

Never mind was right. Obviously, they both had issues they didn't want to discuss.

Arching her back to create some distance between them, Vanessa stepped gingerly on her left toes, quickly hopping backward onto her right foot.

"I got it." She held up her palms in a back-off motion, stalling his outstretched hands. "Any chance I can ice my ankle for a bit while I drum up a ride to my place in Astoria? I'll be out of here as soon as I can."

Mateo's frown deepened as he dug his hands in the pockets of his chino shorts. Vanessa eyed the navy material with its trendy gray polka dots pattern, imagining it wasn't a look that many men could or would pull off. Of course, Mateo did.

Lips pressed together, he shifted his pensive gaze from her face to her foot, then back up again.

"Yeah, sure." The way he drew out the words told her he wasn't convinced by her I'm-all-right act. "We probably have a breakable ice pack in the first aid box. Have a seat, and I'll see what I can round up."

Ever the gentleman some journalists . . . not she . . . had written about, Mateo clasped her elbow to help her onto the stool. Instead of heading off to grab the kit, he surprised her by hunkering down at her feet. Gently he grasped her injured foot, cradling it in his large hands.

Desire and longing she did not want to feel tap-danced a duet up her calf.

His long fingers pressed softly around her ankle area. "Does this hurt?"

Vanessa shook her head, then realized that he was still focused on her foot. "Not too much."

Lie. She fully expected to spend most of the weekend limping around Ria's parents' place in Sag Harbor. Great excuse to lounge by the pool. "It's just a tweak. Give me a few minutes and I'll be fi—"

"Fine, I heard you the first time."

His frustrated tone surprised her.

"Hey, I'm the injured one here. I don't know what you're pissed about."

He scrubbed his forehead as if it pained him, then scowled up at her. Somehow the grimace only enhanced his tall, dark, and dangerous aura. It also reminded her of the womanizing heartbreaker he had portrayed in *Sin with Me*, the play she'd given a scathing review. Most notably of his performance.

"Excuse me for being pissed about our current situation." Mateo flung out an arm, indicating the empty theatre. "Tonight was *not* supposed to go like this. Shit! As soon as I saw you in the house, I had an inkling. No, more like a foreboding. Yeah, that's it, something told me—"

He broke off and rubbed a hand at the back of his neck as if it pained him. His shoulders rose and fell on an aggrieved sigh, then he pushed to his feet and strode away.

What the hell? Seeing her gave him an inkling of what?

Did he plan on finishing a thought eventually? Or was he purposely keeping her guessing?

Coño, what could he possibly blame her for?

That annoying pinprick of guilt she'd felt earlier in the evening stabbed at her conscience again. Greg Vickers *had* mentioned a rumor making the rounds in the months after her *Sin with Me* review had gone semi-viral. Something about the bad press it precipitated leading a conservative investor to pull out of *Clemente*.

Por favor.

If an investor got spooked by one measly bad review from an online magazine, they were in the wrong business. Sure, *The Fix* was the number one go-to for millennials and Gen Zers living in or visiting the city and surrounding areas, but still. One review was only one review.

No way could she have anticipated that a few bloggers would take her hypothesis and anonymous tip as fact. Then create a landslide of blogs and social media posts posing the question she hadn't so much implied as flat out stated. Had Mateo been playing the role of the dastardly, callous lothario in *Sin with Me* or had Broadway's darling simply been himself—a heartless mujeriego determined to have fun no matter whom he hurt in the process?

A simple question. Granted, one that had blown up, but it had also led *Sin with Me* ticket sales to soar.

Anyone in the business, even those like Vanessa who had stepped out of the performance ring earlier than anticipated, knew to expect negative feedback somewhere along the line. Few shows, few actors, pleased everyone. Hell, even *Hamilton*, as amazing as it was, had its detractors. Of course, those people were idiotas, if you asked her. But they existed.

If Mateo Garza held any ill will toward her because some lamebrain investor took the bad press her review had inadvertently precipitated to heart, bueno, there was nothing she could do about it. She wouldn't have gone there if the reports of his stepping out with one cast member after another hadn't been confirmed.

And yet . . .

Irritated by the sharp sliver of remorse slicing her belly, Vanessa snatched her tote bag off the floor beside the stool and wrenched open the zipper. She dug inside for her cell, anxious to order a car or call Ria to see about staying at her place in Chelsea.

This was basic Review Writing 101—the write-up was an individual's informed, yet subjective opinion. Naturally, that meant their personal perspective might come into play to some degree.

*Come into play, not blind them.*

Ria's quietly shared advice filtered through the argument in Vanessa's head. Ignoring it, she held up her phone.

Damn it. The face recognition couldn't register in the darkness. Irked by both her inability to squelch her doubts and the freaking power outage that had tanked her simple goal for the evening—confirm her glowing review of *Clemente* was warranted, not guilt driven—she thumbed in her security code with more force than necessary.

A groan pushed its way up her throat, her frustration mushrooming like the smelly exhaust from a diesel truck when her cell screen illuminated to show zero bars in the top corner.

No service.

Whether it was because of her location backstage in the old building or because everyone in the Manhattan area was no doubt desperately trying to reach someone on their phone, thus overloading the freaking cell towers, it didn't matter. The outcome was the same. She couldn't use the ride-share app or call for a cab. Texting Ria about staying at her place in Chelsea was a no-go. And without a ride, no way Vanessa could make it home. Walking over the bridge to Astoria with her bum ankle was out of the question.

"Thanks, Mike. I appreciate your waiting around for us." Mateo walked out from behind a large set piece, a flashlight emitting a long beam to brighten his path. In his other hand, he carried a white plastic box with a dark lid, a red cross marked on the top.

"I come bearing supplies," he announced, lifting the first aid box higher.

"Do we need to get out of here?" she asked. "I don't want to keep anyone from going home."

"It's okay. The others left, but Mike lives a few blocks over in Hell's Kitchen. He's good with sticking around until we get you taken care of."

"Thank you."

Mateo shrugged. Like it wasn't a big deal for the two of them to be sitting alone in a dimly lit theatre, with only a security guard somewhere she couldn't see, the entire city outside blanketed in darkness. The lack of cell service cutting them off from everyone else.

Onstage, maybe in a Rodgers & Hammerstein production, their situation would be prime for a romantic interlude. They'd break into a duet, lyrics rife with whimsy and innuendo. But in real life, there was nothing remotely romantic between them.

There couldn't be.

Not with her aversion to philandering jerks and Mateo's quips about loving all women and not being ready to settle down.

"Mike said there should be a bottle of Motrin in here." Mateo jiggled the kit and something rattled around inside it. "I grabbed you a fruit-and-nut bar, so you'd have something in your stomach. Gluten-free, right?"

Vanessa blinked, surprised at his thoughtfulness. That he somehow knew about her gluten intolerance.

"What?" he asked, confusion replacing the annoyed frown he'd worn before storming off. "You mentioned it at that Broadway Cares fundraiser."

Three years ago. Right before her review went viral.

Not that she would remind him of the timing.

Or be flattered that he remembered.

He drove a hand through his hair, mussing the sixties style in what she would have called a self-conscious gesture, had he been anyone but the confident leading man she knew him to be. Then he pulled the snack bar and a cold bottle of water from the left front pocket of his shorts, holding them both out to her.

"Um, thanks."

She took the proffered snack, tearing the fruit-and-nut bar's plastic wrapper and taking a hefty bite. Dinner had been hours ago. An apple with almond butter after picking up a last-minute substitute spot teaching a spin class at the gym and then racing home to get ready for the evening.

Mateo hunkered down at her feet again, setting the first aid kit on the floor beside him and propping the flashlight on its back end. The beam shot up to the rafters. Its glow spread out to softly illuminate them.

She waved him off, mumbling around a mouthful of the bar. "You don't have to—"

"You should have this elevated," he said, ignoring her attempt to dissuade him and gently grasping her injured foot.

Shifting to sit on his butt, he rested her calf on his bent knee to keep her foot propped up. Vanessa wedged her short skirt between her thighs, loath to give him a peep show. Even given the darkness.

He flicked the snap on the kit's lid with a thumb to open it, then removed a pill bottle and light blue pack. He shook two pills into his palm and held them out to her without a word.

While she chugged down the medicine with her water, she watched him out of the corner of her eye. His handsome face pensive, he squished the instant ice pack in one fist, then shook the little pouch to activate the cooling element inside.

"Looks like you're familiar with using that," she guessed.

"My first tour, I tweaked a knee two weeks in. Ice packs of all variety became my constant companions."

"Ow, that sucks." She swiped a droplet of water from the corner of her mouth. "*Guys and Dolls*, right?"

Hunched over her injured foot, Mateo paused. He slanted a glance at her, one dark brow arched in question.

"Oh, don't go getting any ideas. I'm not a registered member of the Mateo Garza fan club or anything." She grinned when he scoff-snorted.

He cupped her leg below her calf, and her pulse blipped. The heat from his palm spread like a wildfire, racing up her leg, heading straight to . . . she squeezed her thighs together.

"Any journalist on the arts-and-entertainment beat, if they're good at their job, knows the highlights of your career. Broadway's newest superstar, the brains and vision behind what many believe will be the breakout musical of the season. Of course, I—ooh!"

She gasped, flinching when he carefully pressed the ice pack to her left ankle. "¡Coño! That's freaking cold!"

"Uh, yeah, that's the idea," he deadpanned, but his dimple

winked at her, softening his bland tone. Also setting off a flutter of gray moths . . . she refused to think of them as colorful butterflies . . . in her belly.

His palm slid up and down her calf, caressing her skin. Wreaking havoc on her tightly wound libido. Battery-operated devices did not provide gentle ministrations like this. No matter how satisfying they were in other ways.

She needed to get a grip and come up with a way out of here.

"Hey, are you getting any service?" She jiggled her cell at him.

Mateo shifted onto his left hip. After making sure the ice pack would remain in place, he dug his phone out of his pocket and tapped at the screen.

Moments later, he shook his head. "Mike said it's still fairly crowded outside. People are having difficulty making calls. You're probably going to have a hard time getting a car service or cab to take you to Astoria."

He swiped the back of one hand across his forehead. Without the AC, the theatre was slowly becoming a hot box. They couldn't stay much longer, even if Mike weren't waiting around for them.

No doubt Mateo had someplace else he'd rather be than here playing nursemaid to her.

Frankly, she had already written this night off as a mistake. The power outage and twisted ankle were fate confirming what she already knew. The line of demarcation between personal and professional, the girl she had been and the woman she purported to be now, had become increasingly blurred when this man was involved.

It was time for her to disassociate the Mateo Garza of her past—a cute teen and worthy star of her schoolgirl theatrical fantasies—from the Mateo Garza of today—a pulse-thrumming, beguiling man who should only star in her reviews.

Sound advice.

She could heed it now by keeping things professional and getting the hell out of here.

"Look, I'm good hanging outside until a car frees up or I'm able to jump in one with a group of people heading my direction. That way you and Mike can leave."

She moved to slide her leg off Mateo's raised knee, stretching her left arm out to grab the ice pack.

Mateo's grip on her calf tightened. "Is there a friend's place close by where you can go?"

She hesitated, a mistake on her part because he pounced on it.

"Nuh-uh. No way am I deserting you." His voice was grim but determined.

His back straightened, shoulders stiff, like the gallant knight he had played in a regional production of *Spamalot* years ago, now refusing to leave the damsel in distress. No matter how annoying he found her.

"Look, my place is off Columbus Circle."

"Uh, no thanks," she quickly interrupted. "I am not going home with you."

He huffed out breath. "Now who's getting the wrong idea? I did not mean, 'Hey, babe, let's go to my place.' "

When he pitched his voice all low and sexy like that she could totally see why many women might fall for that line from him. Not her.

"Despite what you may think or write about me, I do have some morals." There was no missing the accusation in his words. Or the flash of anger and . . . something she couldn't place . . . in his dark eyes, the muscles flexing along his jaw.

Shit. There it was. The grenade she had tossed in between them, about to blow.

Her gut tightened with shame.

Eventually she was going to have to sacrifice her pride and throw herself on top of it. Admit to him that her comments had been fueled in large part by her papi's antics with his latest mistress. Finding out that she had a half-sibling while on the N train into Manhattan to see Mateo's play, hearing that her mother had known about the love child but turned the other cheek, *again*. Letting her husband continue living at home with her. It had made Vanessa's blood boil. Sent her spiraling back to the first time she'd caught her papi with another woman.

Arriving at the theatre and having to sit through a play about a man living the same lies as her papi . . . watching Mateo's incredibly gifted performance after having also watched his video interviews and heard the rumors of his making the rounds with a string of actresses . . . Vanessa hadn't been able to separate fact from fiction.

Or assuage her keen disappointment that success had gone to his head, turning him into someone she would group with her papi and college boyfriend.

Mateo scrubbed a palm over his face, frustration dripping from him like sweat as if he were in a sauna. Which was what the theatre was quickly becoming.

"Look, my roommate Jeff and his longtime girlfriend Nicole were planning to stay in tonight, so they'll be home. If we're lucky, we'll get you in a car headed to Astoria before we even reach my place. If not, you can hang out with us. No big deal."

The frown curving his lips downward said the opposite. But what other option did she have?

Ay Dios mío, how could this be happening to her? She bit her lip, sending another *Oh my God* prayer to the heavens.

She sure hoped He was listening, because right now she needed divine intervention in the form of the power coming back on or an empty taxi materializing when they made their way outside.

"Okay then, I guess it's decided." Mateo removed the ice pack from her swollen ankle. "Let's go."

Releasing her leg, he gently set it on the ground, then cupped her elbows to help her stand. Once she was steady, he turned his back toward her and squatted.

Confused, Vanessa leaned to the side to peer at him. "Um, excuse me. What are you doing?"

Still squatting, Mateo gazed over his shoulder at her. "Giving you a piggyback ride. You can't walk on that ankle."

"What? No way." She waved her hands as if she could wipe away this bizarre situation.

"My place is about a mile up Eighth Ave. You can't hobble that far. Come on." He reached across his chest with his right arm to pat himself on the back of his left shoulder. "Hop on."

Vanessa swallowed nervously. She stared down at the hem of her minidress. The idea of wrapping her legs around his waist, pressing herself against him as she clung to his broad back, had parts of her body perking up with interest. This was not a wise idea. For multiple reasons.

"You two about ready?" Mike called out.

Mateo gave her a squinty-eyed, What-are-you-waiting-for? look.

Slinging her tote over her head, Vanessa took a deep breath and nodded.

Holy shit. Could this night get any worse?

She sure as hell hoped not.

# Chapter 4

Mateo drew to a stop near the curb at Fifty-Ninth Street, in front of a busy Columbus Circle.

Central Park loomed across the street to their right. Tall trees stood sentinel above the shadowy paths where bicycle lights flickered like fireflies flitting down the park's winding trails.

A bead of sweat slipped from his left sideburn to trickle down his face. Growing up in Tampa, he was used to oppressive summer heat and humidity. But in the city, surrounded by concrete and buildings, it morphed from oppressive to stifling. A sheen of sweat covered every inch of his skin. His damp T-shirt clung to his chest. But the day's heat still radiating from the city sidewalks couldn't compare to the heat radiating from Vanessa Ríos's tempting body pressed against his back.

Her shapely legs hooked around his waist, his palms cradling her thighs, holding her in place. One block into their trek, after being jolted by the frantic crowd, she had looped her arms around his shoulders and clasped her hands at his chest in a tight hug that left her pert breasts cushioned between his shoulder blades. The friction between their bodies heightened his awareness of every inch of them that touched. Blood pooled low in his body, making it clear that his racing pulse had little to do with the effort of carrying her twenty blocks up Eighth Avenue and more to do with his attraction to the woman currently plastered to his body like the jellyfish he'd been stung by at Clearwater Beach in high school.

Her pointy chin rested on his right shoulder, and Mateo caught a faint coconut scent emanating from her hair. If he turned his head just so, his lips could almost touch her smooth temple.

He knew because his lips had butterfly-kissed her smooth skin back when he had stopped on the corner of Eighth Avenue and Fifty-Second Street, waiting for a break in the traffic to cross. He'd craned his neck to check on her, not realizing how close their heads actually were.

The brush of his lips against her temple had been the lightest of touches. Infinitesimal, really. But enough to leave his skin hypersensitized. Craving more.

"It's so strange, isn't it?" she asked, her question nearly lost in the cacophony of honking horns and raised voices.

That was one word for it.

Never in his wildest dreams would he have imagined finding himself in this predicament with her.

"I was at the August Wilson with a friend last week," Vanessa continued. "Now look at it. And the Neil Simon."

Her chin shifted on his shoulder, and he realized she was staring down Fifty-Second, referring to the well-known theatres, now shuttered for the evening. The black-and-white Neil Simon Theatre marquee was no longer a beacon high on the building's facade. The shows at both locations had closed for the night. Maybe longer.

Like his.

Frustration roiled in his stomach. A fist-size knot tightened in his chest. All those years he'd spent dreaming about bringing his abuelo's Clemente stories to life on the stage. This was not the homage to them he had envisioned. It definitely wasn't the opening night Tommy, Vicki, and he had worked their asses off to achieve.

Fuck, what were the odds of something this freakish happening? How would it affect the financials, especially for investors like his familia and friends?

Por favor—he gave a mental sign of the cross out of habit—don't let tonight's outcome be a foreshadowing of the future. An early closing for the passion project they had all sacrificed so much for.

Vanessa wiggled her hips as if to get more comfortable, and his mental pity party screeched to an abrupt halt. Her hip action rippled up her torso, and she shifted slightly side to side, her breasts teasing his upper back. Lust shot through him like a jolt of the electricity the city needed. Reminding him that for all those "dating around" rumors, since *Sin with Me* had closed, he lived more like a monk. Dedicated to the theatre gods.

And yet, somehow, once again, this woman had managed to play a role in what was yet another hellish blow to his professional career. And this was before her *Clemente* review had even hit the internet.

"I don't know that I'd call this strange," he muttered, resentment cooling his body's ardent reaction to hers. "More like screwed up."

"I wouldn't—oh!" She broke off on a gasp as the traffic stopped and he surged off the curb.

Mateo tightened his hold on her lower thighs as he strode between a yellow cab whose driver demonstrated an affinity for the horn and a beat-up white delivery truck.

They needed to hurry up and get to his place, where Jeff and Nicole would be a welcome buffer between him and Vanessa.

Increasing his pace, Mateo sidestepped a group of teens hanging out on the sidewalk, in no apparent rush to go anywhere.

Their progress bogged down at the next intersection, where either a plainclothes cop or a random citizen using his cell's flashlight app directed traffic.

"You are so sweet," crooned an older lady standing beside Mateo and Vanessa. Head tilted to the side, she gazed adoringly at him. "Carrying your girlfriend like that is quite heroic."

Mateo smiled politely at the woman and the gray-haired man she linked elbows with, barely keeping his skepticism to himself.

Sweet? Him? Not when it came to Vanessa Ríos.

Pissed. Stymied. Hell, even turned on, though he mostly tried to ignore that response to her.

Still, as the traffic cop waved them forward, Mateo realized that to anyone else on the crowded street, he and Vanessa probably looked like an average couple. Young lovers comfortable in each other's embrace, making the trek home like the rest of the masses stuck hoofing it since the subway was shut down.

Only he and this enticing woman—who'd once been his adolescent crush, and in more recent years his nemesis—were far from an "average couple."

There was nothing in the least *average* about Vanessa Ríos. The mesmerizing girl he never got the courage to ask out in high school. Nor the confident, alluring woman who popped up in his thoughts at inopportune moments.

In actuality, he hadn't had the time or inclination to be part of a couple in ages. Something *Sin with Me*'s publicity team had used to their advantage. Much to his mami's chagrin. Not to mention his roommate's teasing.

No, his lover, the one filling his days and nights, bringing him joy and hair-pulling irritation . . . that had been *Clemente* for most of Mateo's twenties.

"I don't know that I'd necessarily call you sweet," Vanessa grumbled once they had left the older couple behind them.

Her breath tickled his right ear while her words brought a disgruntled tilt to his lips.

"Back at you," he returned.

She humphed in response and squeezed her arms around his shoulders. Her inner thighs tightened around his waist, rocking her pelvis into his lower back as if she was afraid she might slip off. Instinctively he reached behind him to give her ass a boost. His fingers accidentally slipped under the hem of her short skirt, skimming her bare butt cheek.

Her yelp of surprise blasted his eardrum at the same time she smacked his hand away and jerked her skirt down.

"Sorry," he growled, clasping her lower thigh above her knee again. A much safer place to touch, though her smooth skin had him imagining the type of thong she must be wearing under that short minidress. Cotton? Lace? Red?

Damn if his crotch didn't perk up as he pictured a red lacy thong against her tanned skin.

He squeezed his eyes shut and shook off the image. Coño, he was going to need a cold shower as soon as he dumped Vanessa on Jeff and Nicole. With any luck, the two women would hit it off and he could disappear to his room.

Thanks to the discord of frenetic city noise and the over-crowded sidewalks, he and Vanessa didn't have to speak much the rest of the way. Not that he could have engaged in conversation. The physical exertion of carrying her while maneuvering through the harried crowd had his legs complaining. His side ached from oxygen deprivation.

Sucking in a deep breath through his nose, Mateo focused on the line of vehicles snaking their way toward Central Park and Lincoln Square, where the apartment was. Red taillights and blinding headlights gleamed. Around them buildings sat still and quiet. Generators had kicked on in the larger ones, but the normal Big Apple brightness remained peculiarly dim.

Much like his mood.

True to Murphy's Law, he and Vanessa had no luck snagging a car with room for her. Not one heading to Astoria anyway.

Also true to his evening's theme, cell service remained crappy. That meant she hadn't been able to reach out to any of her friends, and he hadn't been able to give Jeff a heads-up that he was bringing company home.

"Almost there, right? You said West Sixty-Fifth?" Vanessa asked.

He grunted a yes, keeping an eye on another random citizen directing traffic at the next intersection. The guy held his hands out at his sides, palms up, signaling for the vehicles to stop. Then he motioned for Mateo and Vanessa, along with a group of college-aged kids more than likely headed toward Fordham Law, to cross Fifty-Ninth.

Six not nearly short enough blocks later, Mateo turned left onto his street.

"Home sweet home," he wheezed, stopping in front of his seven-story brick apartment building, its white pillars bracketing the glass front door a welcome sight.

"Do you need your keys?" Vanessa shifted, probably reaching for his bag, slung on her back. Once again, the movement had her breasts rubbing against him. Mateo bit back a groan. Who would have thought a piggyback ride could be so damn erotic.

Before he could answer, a figure in black slacks and a gray button-down strolled from the back of the foyer. A flashlight cast its beam across the white-and-black-tiled floor, illuminating Freddie's friendly face. The doorman bent to unlock the two dead bolts, then pushed the glass door open.

"You two okay?"

"Yeah. Thanks, Freddie." Mateo stuck out his foot to anchor the door. "She twisted her ankle outside the theatre. And finding an empty cab was an exercise in futility."

Vanessa straightened her left knee to show off her swollen ankle. Too late, Mateo realized he should have at least loosened the thin strap circling her leg above her dainty ankle or removed her stiletto sandal entirely. The pressure had to be adding to her pain.

"Ow, bet that hurts." Freddie winced. "And who said chivalry is dead, huh? Vente pa'dentro." He stepped back, motioning them inside. "This heat and humidity are killing me. And it's getting just as bad in here."

Mateo nudged the door open wider and quickly moved inside before it swung back and bumped Vanessa. The usually frigid foyer had warmed considerably with the power off. No wonder Freddie was already complaining.

A Nuyorican around the same age as Mateo's papi, Freddie had bonded with Mateo over shared tales of their travels to Puerto Rico visiting familia. Freddie's wife made killer alcapurrias, and even though Mateo tried to stay away from fried foods, he kept a stash of her meat-filled yautía and small green-banana fritters in his freezer. Once in a while a man needed a taste of the island his familia called home.

Freddie was also a die-hard Yankees fan, like Mateo's abuelo on his dad's side. The affable doorman regularly peppered Mateo with questions about *Clemente* and had nearly fractured one of Mateo's ribs with his excited bear hug the day Mateo gifted his friend with two tickets to preview the show.

"Oye, pena que se fue la luz on opening night!" Freddie lamented, his disappointment about the power going out almost a match for Mateo's. The older man mopped a sweaty brow with a hand towel, frowning as he stuffed the rag into his pants pocket.

"Yeah, it's definitely a shame," Mateo agreed, swiping at his own brow with the back of a hand.

"Who do we have here?" Freddie waved the flashlight at Mateo and Vanessa, the older man's inquisitive gaze homing in on her.

Grabbing Mateo's left shoulder with one hand, she extended her right toward Freddie. "Vanessa Ríos, encantada."

"Freddie Pérez, a tu servicio. And I'm sure the pleasure's all mine." The wily doorman winked, his amiable grin widening. "Boricua?"

"By way of Tampa, pero my abuelos and much of our familia still live on the island. Both sets of my abuelos are in Bayamón," she answered.

"Ahhh, you finally bring a girl home for me to meet and she's one of us, muy bien," Freddie teased Mateo.

Mateo shot him a wide-eyed glare followed by a tiny, but forceful shake of his head. Freddie answered with a hearty laugh that deepened when Vanessa joined him.

"Oh, I'm sure there have been plenty of others," she said, her husky chuckle taunting Mateo.

He knew what she thought of him, and why. It was a bed he had helped make, even if he hadn't been altogether comfortable lying in it.

"Are you kidding me?" Freddie said. "This guy's practically a pries—"

"It's not like that between us," Mateo interrupted the overly chatty doorman, who was privy to the dire state of Mateo's nondating life. "We're just . . ." Coño, how would he describe his and Vanessa's relationship? Not that they actually had one.

"Old acquaintances," Vanessa filled in. She gave his shoulder a couple of surprisingly hearty smacks. "I knew this guy when his fans were mostly of the high school variety. No panty throwers in that crowd like he deals with now."

Freddie barked out a laugh, the flashlight beam waving around the empty foyer in his mirth. Mateo's face heated at Vanessa's teasing reference to the embarrassing time a woman had actually tossed a pair of black panties at him during a fan event.

He huffed out a breath, tucking his chin and angling his head to scowl at his exasperating "acquaintance."

Vanessa grinned up at him. Her hazel eyes sparkled with

mischief, transporting him to Theatre Fest their junior year, when the two of them had wound up in that improv workshop together. She had cajoled some poor guy from her show choir to volunteer with her.

Mateo couldn't remember much about the prompt they'd been given. Or the other guy who joined her. But he clearly pictured Vanessa. Light brown hair fashioned in some intricate braid, figure-hugging jeans, and a blue T-shirt with the event's logo across the front. Even more memorable, Vanessa's quick wit, self-deprecating humor, and the ease with which she adapted to whatever her nervous, inexperienced acting partner blurted out. Her eyes alight with humor and delight, much as they were now.

Just as it had then, the expression on her beautiful face was like a fist reaching in to squeeze his heart, pumping it to life.

"Where's Mateo been hiding you all this time?" Freddie asked Vanessa. "I keep telling him, all work and no play, no es bueno. Know what I mean?"

Sensing that Freddie's matchmaking was about to go into overdrive like his mami's, Mateo quickly changed the subject. "No, what's really not good is this freaking blackout. Any idea what caused the power outage?"

Freddie shrugged, walking with them toward the back of the foyer, past the elevators to the stairwell door. "I had cell service for a hot second. Long enough to hear that my relief might not make it at midnight. Apparently the problem's at the power-company level and this hit all the boroughs. Reminds me of the blackout of '03."

"God no, I've heard that one lasted close to thirty hours!"

Vanessa's dismayed cry mimicked Mateo's alarm at Freddie's nodding grimace. Coño, that would mean canceling both of tomorrow's performances, not to mention the huge disruption to the city as a whole.

Surely cell service would stabilize soon. He needed to get in touch with Tommy. Find out what his director suggested and if he'd heard from the main producers. This could not be as dire as Mateo feared.

Plus, if the towers were up, Vanessa could connect with one of the girlfriends she had mentioned, grab a ride share to their place if not all the way to Astoria.

"Let's hope whatever went wrong is resolved soon," Mateo said, trying to reassure himself as much as the others. "We better head up, put some ice on her ankle. Thanks for the info, Freddie."

"You gonna be okay getting up to the fifth floor?"

"Yeah, I'm good." No way would Mateo ask the older man to hoof it up five flights to help him with Vanessa. Not with this heat and Freddie's well-fed belly, proof of his aversion to exercise.

"Oh, hey, in case you decide to go up to the roof for some fresh air," Freddie said as he held the stairwell door open for Mateo and Vanessa to pass through, "be sure to prop the door open with the wooden block I left up there. They got someone coming tomorrow to check out the lock. Mr. Brantley in 4I got stuck on the roof earlier today when the lock jammed on him."

"Thanks for the tip," Mateo told his friend, who waved and let the door swing softly shut behind them.

Standing at the bottom of the stairwell, Mateo gazed up at the shadowy area above them, lit by the emergency lights on each level.

"Did he say fifth floor?" Vanessa asked, skepticism coloring her words.

"Uh-huh."

"Let me down." She smacked his shoulder again. "I can hop up the steps."

Mateo squeezed her lower thighs at the same time he jerked his torso forward, pitching her flush against his back. She yelped in surprise, then reached up to swipe her hair out of her face. Out of the corner of his eye he caught her annoyed glare.

"Are you doubting my manliness?"

She exhaled an annoyed *pffft*. "Ay Dios mío, deliver me from machismo. Enough already. Come on, let me try."

Another shoulder smack paired with her sensual hips-and-legs wiggle had him complying with her request. Her body slid down the back of his like a lover's caress.

Mateo swiped the sweat from his face with his shirtsleeve, then turned in time to catch Vanessa adjusting her dress. A yank on the hem that barely hit her midthigh, a lift of the elastic above her left breast where the dress became sleeveless.

"You just walked a freaking mile carrying me through the crowded streets. I think I can get myself up five measly flights of stairs." She slid his backpack off her shoulders, then held it out.

The determined jut of her chin told him it was pointless to argue. Her swollen ankle told him she had to be in pain. The smart course of action was to let her be and find out which would win out—her hardheadedness or the injury.

"Fine." He slung his backpack on, then waved her ahead of him. "After you."

Ten minutes later, they had made it as far as the first floor, with him making a concerted effort not to look at her curvy ass playing peekaboo with her dress hem.

Sweat glistened on Vanessa's upper lip and brow. Shimmered on her chest above the dark floral material of her dress.

At the half landing she had unzipped her small tote and dug around for a hair tie. She deftly finger-combed her tresses into a messy bun, the knot on top of her head wobbling precariously with each hop to the next step. By the time they stopped so she could catch her breath, a few loose tendrils curled along her neck, one sticking to the perspiration, giving her a hot-and-bothered look that had him all hot and bothered in a completely different way.

"This is harder than I thought," she admitted, her chest rising and falling on a deep exhalation of breath. "And I'm in good shape."

He laughed at her honest, surprised expression. "Damn, humble much?"

She grinned, dabbing the back of her right hand over her chin, upper lip, and forehead. "It's not bragging if it's the truth."

"I'll keep that in mind."

"Ho-kay, ready?" She breathed the word on an exhalation as if psyching herself up as she hopped, in her impractical stiletto sandal, up to the next step. She wobbled and pressed her left toes down to steady herself only to suck in a sharp breath and quickly transfer her weight back to her right.

Her knee buckled and she caught herself on the metal handrail before she fell.

Enough. Her sore ankle had to be throbbing. The longer they waited to put ice on it again, the worse it would be. At this rate, if she wasn't careful, she'd wind up hurting her other foot.

"Hold up," he ordered.

Vanessa's question-filled glance back at him was more than likely due to his sharp tone.

"Give me your purse."

"Why?"

Mateo held his arm out, palm up, then bent his fingers back and forth in a come-on gesture. Vanessa squinted at him, obviously wondering what he was up to. Good. If she wasn't expecting it, she couldn't object.

Slowly she lifted her black tote strap, ducking her head under it, then handing it off to him. Mateo slung the strap across his chest, the short length leaving it taut across his torso.

Vanessa eyed him warily. Wise of her to stay on guard, though her lack of faith in him did rankle a bit. And that was only about to get worse.

"I'm going to apologize now, but this is for your own good," Mateo announced. Then, while her delightfully expressive face was scrunched with confusion, he quickly bent down and flung her fireman-style over his shoulder.

"What the fu—!"

"Eh-eh, what would your mami say about that language?" he chastised, moving up the stairs two at a time.

Vanessa punched his ass with one hand while her other splayed over her butt to hold her dress material in place. No doubt she was worried about giving him a peek at what he had accidentally fondled earlier.

"Put me down, you big oaf!"

"I will, as soon as we get to my apartment. Ow!" Her punch to his lower back caught him off guard more than it actually hurt.

She quieted, her open palm gently pressing over the spot where her punch had landed. "Did that really hurt you?"

He didn't respond, concentrating instead on making it up the steps. His quads and calves were on fire. His lungs struggled for breath. His admiration for real firefighters and the difficulty of their jobs hit stratospheric levels.

"I'm just . . . trying to get you . . ." He stopped on the fourth-floor landing, his words punctuated by pants. ". . . on the couch . . ."

"Hey, what kind of girl do you think I am?" She smacked his lower back again, more softly this time.

"With an ice pack," he clarified.

"Uh-huh. That'd better be all you're thinking about giving me."

He snorted and couldn't help chuckling at her snark. Thankfully she stopped fussing, and he moved up the last flight more easily. Well, out of breath and his leg muscles screaming as if he'd just finished the military-style boot camp class at his gym.

"You on the couch, me in a cold shower," he finished once he'd reached his floor and neared his and Jeff's apartment.

He stopped in front of their door and knocked since his keys were in his bag.

"Please put me down now." Vanessa's forearms pressed into his lower back, raising her torso as she craned her neck to stare at him.

Mateo glanced at her. Her curtain of light brown hair hung in disarray around her captivating face, the hair tie she had dug out of her bag earlier lost somewhere on their trek up the stairs.

"I do not want to meet your roommate and his girlfriend with my ass hanging out," she admitted. "Please."

Good point. But it wasn't only her sound reasoning that convinced him. No way could he resist the worried plea in her hazel eyes.

Bending down, Mateo waited until she put her weight on her good foot, then he cupped one of her elbows to offer support as he rose to stand. Vanessa wove the fingers of one hand through her hair, combing it out of her face.

Without thinking, Mateo crooked a finger to release a few strands that clung to her lip gloss. The back of his forefinger skimmed her smooth skin, and he found himself wanting to touch more of it. More of her.

Vanessa drew back a little, a wary frown creating a tiny divot between her brows. "Um, thanks."

Mateo cleared his throat and shoved his hand deep in his pocket away from temptation. Shit, forget waiting for Jeff or Nicole to open up. He needed that cold shower. Now.

Suddenly anxious about bringing Vanessa—the one woman capable of convincing him to end his monk-like existence and unhealthy obsession with Clemente's success—to his place, Mateo ripped open the Velcro on the backpack's side pocket with more force than necessary to pull out his keys.

"Lean on my arm like a crutch and you can hobble to the living room couch. It's not far." Crooking his right elbow, he stiffened his arm and held it out to Vanessa. "Jeff and Nicole must be in his room watching something on his laptop. That's probably why they didn't answer."

Beside him, Vanessa sucked in and then blew out an audible breath. She tucked her hair behind her ears, fingers pausing to twist her tiny gold heart stud earrings. The fidgeting continued as she adjusted the elastic holding up the top of her dress, smoothed the tie cinching her slender waist, and ended with a final tug to her dress hem.

If he didn't know better, he'd say the woman whose opinion carried immense weight with countless readers thanks to her straight-talking, call-it-like-I-see-it perspective actually seemed nervous. About meeting his friends? About being inside his apartment?

About being with him?

He scoffed at the last one. Talk about projecting his own apprehension. Jeff and Nicole were the only ones who knew about Mateo's screwed-up nemesis-muse feelings for Vanessa. He could only hope they'd keep any wisecracks to themselves while she was here.

Hope but not hold his breath.

Reservations mounting, Mateo unlocked the dead bolt and ushered Vanessa inside the open common area.

"Hey, Jeff! Nicole!" he called out.

Nobody answered.

A harried check of Jeff's room later, Mateo mentally added a new word to his growing list of adjectives describing Vanessa Ríos: *pissed.*

Another word pretty much summed up his entire evening so far: *screwed.*

Jeff and Nicole hadn't answered his knock because, according to the note stuck to the front of the refrigerator, after he'd left for the theatre, her parents had invited them out to their place in the Hamptons.

Good news—Mateo didn't have to worry about Jeff and Nicole making any wisecracks about his long-denied interest in Vanessa.

Bad news—he and his tantalizing nemesis were holed up in his apartment. Alone.

# Chapter 5

The shower cut off in the apartment bathroom, and Vanessa's breath hitched.

Immediately she made herself release it, collapsing back on the sofa's cushioned armrest with a muttered "Get a grip, girl."

Easier said than done when she'd spent the past ten minutes imagining Mateo's incredible chest, broad shoulders, and expansive back bare, dripping with soap bubbles, water cascading over his rippling muscles. Calling herself all kinds of foolish and pendeja for doing so.

Yes, that was definitely her, an idiot in two different languages.

If she had learned anything from her mother's example, it was to not let herself fall for a charismatic guy with no interest in monogamy.

Doggedly, she swiped her mind clear of the pulse-pumping image of Mateo's naked body standing under the shower and concentrated on figuring out her next move.

Cell service remained spotty, which meant if she'd stayed behind at the Booth, she might still be there.

Given a choice between being stuck outside on her own in a frenzied Midtown caught up in the blackout or sprawled across Mateo's cushiony sofa with her left ankle propped up on two throw pillows and a bag of frozen peas draped over it—ha! That was a no-brainer.

Even if they had wound up alone.

So much for her plan to keep her distance at the opening-night after-party. They were having a private one of their own.

A wave of longing washed over her, filling her chest with a strange warmth.

Cursing her body's foolish reaction to the idea of being alone with him, Vanessa stretched forward to readjust the bag of peas. If only she could apply a cold compress to her heated thoughts about Mateo. Those kinds of impulses had no place here. Anywhere. Anytime. Not if he was involved.

But, coño . . . she had a hard time reconciling his reputation as an all-star at playing the field with the guy who'd carried her a full twenty blocks. His caveman routine on the stairs had thrown her, literally. But, hell, she'd probably still be hopping up those five flights if he hadn't pulled his He-Man act.

Plus, there was no use denying the view of his fine butt hadn't been all that bad.

A siren wailed over the muted sounds of city traffic drifting through the open windows. Comforting in its normalcy. The light breeze fluttering the gauzy drapes helped but didn't completely ease the stifling heat and humidity bearing down on the city. Had she been at her place, or Ria's or Alison's, she would already have stripped down to her panties and bra.

That was totally not happening here. In spite of—or, more like, *because of*—the erotic shower scenes playing through her mind for the past ten minutes.

Scooping her thick hair up with her hands, Vanessa pulled her last ponytail holder from her wrist and fashioned a quick, messy bun. While her fingers worked on her hair, her gaze trailed over the metal coffee table beside her. A flashlight and two burning candles were spread out across the surface. The flickering light danced over a pair of gray stone coasters and the latest copy of some finance magazine addressed to Jeff Campbell, the missing roommate.

The two men shared a great place in a prime location barely a block away from Central Park. Mateo had given her a quick verbal tour of the apartment thanks to her bum ankle. Apparently, the right side of their place housed Jeff's bedroom, the lone bathroom, a laundry closet, and the kitchen. On the left half, the entry and foyer opened to a large living room, where Vanessa currently lounged on a sofa positioned against the wall shared with Jeff's room. A matching armchair angled beside it in between the windows overlooking Sixty-Fifth Street.

On the far right end, behind a door off the living area, lay Mateo's smaller room. A private space she found herself intrigued by though she had no desire to visit.

*Liar.*

She shook off the errant thought and picked up her phone to check the time.

The soft click of the bathroom door opening followed by heavy footfalls on the wood flooring alerted her to Mateo's imminent return.

"How's it going out here?" His deep voice reached her before the glow of his candle did.

She glanced behind her to find him approaching, shirtless, a towel draped over his shoulders, doing absolutely nothing to cover his well-defined obliques and washboard abs. A pair of gray basketball shorts with a thick red stripe down each side seam rode low on his hips.

Madre de Dios. She gulped. Barefoot, his hair wet and tousled, Mateo Garza epitomized the cliché drop-dead sexy.

"Hey, you okay?"

His worried question put an abrupt stop to her ogling, and

she jerked around to face the far wall. The full moon shone through the window, casting a silvery trail along the wooden floor to the coffee table's edge, adding a dreamy feel to their surroundings.

"Y-yeah, I'm good. Checking the timer to see if I should remove the ice pack." She jiggled her phone as if proving her point, belatedly realizing she had turned it off to save the battery.

He strode through the living room toward his bedroom door. "Let me grab a shirt. Then I'll see what we can eat."

"Don't go to any trouble on my account."

"Putting on a shirt's no trouble."

"No, I meant—" She broke off when she caught his smirk in the flickering candlelight.

He disappeared into his room, returning shortly after, sans the towel, wearing a snug-fitting red T-shirt that tantalized the eye with the outline of his muscular pecs and six-pack abs. No doubt, this was an image she and her battery-operated BFF would be picturing in the near future.

"I've got leftover baked chicken breast and sautéed broccoli," he told her, sinking onto the armchair angled between the sofa and the wall facing the street. "And I might have enough quinoa and gandules for both of us. If you want something lighter, Nicole has some Greek yo—"

"Wait." She held up a hand. "Did you say 'quinoa and gandules'?"

"Pigeon peas?" There was no missing his implied *duh*. "You call yourself Puerto Rican and you don't know what gandules are?"

Vanessa sat up, affronted. The bag of peas slid off her ankle to lodge between the throw pillows and the back sofa cushion. "Of course I know what they are. I've just never . . . quinoa, huh?"

It actually sounded pretty tasty. Like something she might have experimented making herself.

She pictured her abuela's skeptical frown and often-voiced complaint when Vanessa asked for smaller portions or suggested baking instead of frying something. *Ay, nena, you and your healthy eating. Bleh!*

"Let me guess," Mateo said. "You're imagining your mom or abuela's reaction to healthier familia recipes, aren't you?"

"Maybe."

His husky chuckle sent delicious shivers across her shoulders like the brush of his fingertips up her spine.

Elbows propped on the sides of the armchair, Mateo balanced the lit candle on his right knee. The pale light danced across his face. It highlighted his knowing grin, kissed the dimple that practically dared her to ignore his appeal. The intimate ambience and his friendly teasing did a one-two punch on her resolve not to fall for his charm.

"My abuela's recipes are sacred, too." He placed a hand over his rock-hard abs, fingers spread. "But when your contract mandates maintaining a certain weight and you're craving a taste of home, you improvise."

"Aw, man, some days I miss my abuela's cooking so bad."

"I know, right?"

His guileless expression, their shared yearning for familia and comfort food, drew her to him almost more than his chiseled jaw and enchanting dimple. Though the competition for the top spot was fierce.

"Actually, one of the chorus dancers in *Clemente* put me onto this website by a Cuban athletic trainer-nutritionist from Key West," Mateo continued, oblivious to her mental fan fest in his honor. "Her site has a string of videos demonstrating how to whip up healthy Latinx options. I adapted her congrí recipe from red beans and rice to gandules and quinoa."

"Interesting. I'll have to get it from you. Maybe knowing there's a professional on my side will sway my abuela. You should have seen her reaction the first time I tried baking tostones." Vanessa pitched her voice a shade higher, adding her abuela's thick Spanish accent. " 'Ay, nena, por favor! They are called fried plantains for a good reason. El sabor.' "

Mateo tipped his head back on a laugh. Vanessa shook hers with chagrin, enjoying the chuckle rumbling from his chest, rumbly and husky.

"Because baked means no flavor, apparently," she complained.

"Believe me, I've heard the same." He stood, and the soft candlelight cast his shadow on the wall behind him, larger-than-life. Same as his reputation and the appeal she was having a hard time trying to ignore. "Give me a few minutes to heat things up. Thank God for gas stoves."

"Let me help." Vanessa carefully swung her legs off the sofa. She reached for a candle and pushed herself upright, putting all her weight on her right foot.

"I got it. Relax."

"As much as I may like being pampered occasionally, I'll go stir-crazy sitting here the whole night. I can stir a pot on the stove as well as anyone."

Mateo stopped a few feet away. Head tilted, he studied her, a question looming in his dark irises. "Are you always this hard-headed?"

"I like to think of it as determined."

"One-track-minded."

"Focused," she countered with a grin.

"And right now, you're focused on demonstrating your stellar pot-stirring skills, huh?" The edges of Mateo's mouth twitched.

"I'm also an expert wine-bottle opener."

"Duly noted." Crooking his elbow, he waited for her to grab hold of his forearm for support before taking a step. "I'm sure it's a skill you demonstrate with all your admirers."

"Ha!" His playful jab surprised a laugh out of her. "I think you're confusing your rep with mine. I'm the smart-mouthed one. You're the player."

His smile faded, and too late, she realized her gaffe.

Her joke had inadvertently reminded him of her review calling his character into question and, if Greg's insider info could be trusted, tangentially costing *Clemente* a prospective investor.

Their jovial mood dissipated. Still, Mateo held out an arm to help her limp-walk the short distance to the kitchen. Vanessa hung back in the open doorway, watching while Mateo grabbed two plastic containers and the ingredients for a salad from the fridge, placing them on the counter between the sink and the stove behind him. He bent to rummage through a cabinet next to the refrigerator, extracting a pot and a wooden cutting board, then stepped back to the counter where he began dicing the baked chicken breast.

"If you have another cutting board, I can slice the tomato and cucumber for the salad," she offered, pointing at the veggies.

Mateo glanced at her, his expression unreadable in the dim glow of their candles.

"Or, you cook, and I clean?" she suggested.

Call her crazy, but she missed his banter.

His natural ease and ability to connect with people had attracted her as a teen when their paths crossed. Comfortable on and off the stage, he had exuded charm. Of course, some of the guys in her school's show choir and theatre troupe used to grumble snidely that he was a show-off. Jealousy on their part.

Back then, she couldn't help but crush on a guy whose affable personality and heartthrob looks had so many gravitating toward him. Though she had tried to avoid falling into his orbit because fraternization between their rival theatre troupes would have been considered disloyal.

"Put you on kitchen duty? Are you kidding me?" Mateo complained. "My abuela and mami would wallop me with their chancletas if I had you washing dishes the first time you were over."

He mimed holding up a sandal, jiggling his wrist back and forth in the threat of a whack many misbehaving Latinx kids grew up fearing. Even into adulthood.

His wry grimace eased her worry that she had completely ruined their tentative friendship. Or whatever it was they had reached somewhere between his throwing her over his shoulder on the stairs and her verbal blunder.

"And mine would threaten the same if I didn't pull my weight," she answered.

"All one hundred pounds of it?"

His gaze traveled slowly from her head, down the length of her body to her bare feet, and back up again. Her gut tightened, her nipples pebbling as if he had physically caressed her.

Ignoring her visceral reaction to him, Vanessa limped over to the right-side counter and set her candle by the notepad and pen in front of a currently useless phone charger. Her gaze trailed over the note Mateo's roommate had left for him.

"How about you hop up there to get off your foot, and I'll act suitably impressed with your bottle-opening skills?" Mateo said, rinsing his hands under the nearby faucet, then drying them with a towel draped over a rod affixed to the low cabinet door in front of the sink.

Vanessa boosted herself onto the counter.

Mateo grabbed his candle, then strode out of the small kitchen. "Red or white?"

She recalled seeing a tall wine rack along the far wall in the foyer earlier and figured that was where he had disappeared to. "Any chance you have a good cab?"

"Jeff's a bit of a wine snob, so I'd guess anything he's got here would fall under the 'good' classification."

The sound of glasses clinking carried to her in the darkness. Mateo reappeared with a bottle of Joel Gott tucked under one arm and clutching two glasses, his candle, and an electric cork remover.

"It should still be fully charged. I await your skills with bated breath," he joked, holding out the gadget.

Vanessa shot him a wiseass glare as she took the glasses and bottle opener from him, setting the glasses on the counter by her hip.

"Gimme." She held a palm up and jiggled her fingers to indicate he should give up the cabernet.

Mateo held out the wine, but when Vanessa grabbed hold of it, he didn't release the bottle. She frowned at him in confusion and gave a gentle yank. He took a baby step closer. The elastic waistband of his basketball shorts grazed her kneecaps. Tantalizing tingles quickstepped up her thighs, double-timing it higher.

Sitting on the counter, she almost reached his height. If she opened her knees, would he fill the space they left for him? Was she foolish enough to do so?

"Truce?" he said, interrupting her inner debate.

"Excuse me?"

He leaned to his left, and his shoulder brushed her upper arm as he set his candle by hers. The clean smell of soap mixed with that of the melting vanilla candle, and an earthy, musky scent she was coming to associate with him teased her senses. His hand moved as if to touch her face and she held her breath. Waiting. Wanting . . . what, she wasn't exactly sure.

In the end, he curled his fingers into his palm, then set his fist on the counter next to her hip.

"We seem to rub each other wrong most of the time," he said.

"I wouldn't say—"

He shushed her with a gentle finger on her lips.

Her eyes widened in shocked surprise.

"I don't want to argue or debate. Honestly, I'd rather not think about your job or my job or the fact that what should have been one of the most important nights of my professional life was literally snuffed out. And I've yet to reach anyone to find out what the hell the ramifications might be."

The solemnity in Mateo's husky voice, the plea in his dark eyes, stalled any rebuttal she might have made at his move to quiet her. Surprisingly. Because being silenced, especially by a man, usually had the opposite effect on her. She had vowed years ago never to be like her mother, allowing a man to walk all over her at his whim.

"Can we pretend—role-play if it helps—that we're just two old high school, I don't know, almost friends reconnecting for the evening? No strings. No mind games. *No stress.*"

His gaze bored into hers, seeking what, she wasn't quite sure. But the intensity in his dark eyes, the way the muscles along his jaw flexed . . . they hinted at some importance, some indefinable need behind his request.

A strange desire to comfort him had her cupping his jaw with one hand.

His finger slipped from her lips, but a searing heat remained as if his touch had left a mark.

"Who are you calling old?" she teased softly.

Mateo's shoulders visibly relaxed.

"You remember that time those snooty kids from Miami beat us both at Theatre Fest?" she continued. "Freaking punks."

His lips curved. His dimple made its appearance, and she couldn't stop herself from tracing the little devil with her thumb.

"Thank you," he murmured, tilting his head the tiniest fraction into her palm.

If she slid her hand to his nape. Urged him closer. Would he kiss her? Did she want him to?

Afraid of the answer, Vanessa drew back.

Which Mateo Garza was the real one?

The hero who had swooped in to save her tonight, who cooked her dinner and offered her shelter? Or the serial costar dater who couldn't or wouldn't commit to one lover? Like her papi. And her college boyfriend.

Doubts circling like vultures, Vanessa pulled the wine bottle from Mateo's grasp. Better to keep things friendly between them. "You promised me a healthy Puerto Rican meal. Don't think I'm letting you back out. Chop-chop."

She set the wine aside and pretended to inspect the bottle opener.

"Bossy, aren't you?"

"And hungry." Her stomach grumbled as if on cue.

Mateo chuckled and moved back to the cutting board, where he scooped up the diced chicken breast with both hands, dumping it into the pot. Vanessa relaxed, temptation and potential morning-after regrets now several feet away.

Several minutes later she handed Mateo his wine.

"To a short-lived power outage," she said.

"To old acquaintances."

"Watch it. What did I say about that word?" she warned, narrowing her eyes at him.

"To intriguing ones, then." He clinked her glass, then took a sip.

Her heart fluttered like a baby bird trying out its wings, and she squirmed uncomfortably on the countertop. The rustle of paper drew her attention. Glancing down, she spotted his roommate's note.

Vanessa picked it up, intending to ask how the two men had met. A topic that would keep the conversation away from the two of them and their connection. But when she scanned the message, curiosity raised a different question.

*In a perfect world you're reading this in the early morning and you actually let yourself hang around the after-party and have some fun for once,* the note began.

Under Jeff's scrawling signature, in a clearly different handwriting that must belong to Nicole, the note concluded with an intriguing *P.S. We all know it's time for something real. I hope you followed my advice and were nice to her. She might surprise you in return. N*

"Who's the 'her' Nicole's giving you advice about?"

The knife Mateo held thunked against the wooden cutting board. His muttered curse followed.

"No one," he mumbled quickly.

Almost too quickly.

Interesting.

Setting aside the notepad, Vanessa took a sip of her cabernet, eyeing Mateo over the rim. His gaze slid away from hers to the note, then back to the cutting board and the tomato he'd been slicing.

Hmm, her there's-a-story-here radar blipped.

Was Mateo keeping a love interest secret?

A spurt of disappointment pricked her chest.

Vanessa ignored it, focusing on what could be a scoop for her column. *If* Mateo willingly shared the information before their blackout-induced friendly role-playing ended. *And* gave her permission to write about it, of course.

Would he?

Time would tell.

Ferreting out the truth might keep her mind occupied, off her inappropriate delusions about him shirtless, his six-pack abs within reach, his body heat mingling with hers to set them both on fire.

Coño, enough already with the fertile imagination.

She started to press her glass to her cheek to cool her flushed skin, but Mateo glanced up at her, so she opted for a hearty swig of wine instead.

Discovering little-known, fun facts about her subjects, deep diving into research, was part of what she loved about her job. She excelled at it and planned to hone those skills with the new human-interest column. The one time she hadn't done due diligence had been her review of *Sin with Me* and Mateo's role. Mostly because she'd been distracted all week by texts and calls from home. Trouble between her parents had been simmering for days, until it boiled over in a hot mess right before she had arrived at the theatre for Mateo's show.

No one wanted to find out via text message that her woman-izing father had a new baby with his latest side piece. A baby her mother had known about for months. Yet she hadn't kicked Vanessa's dad to the curb. Dios mío, the man still lived at home! Which was why Vanessa hadn't visited in nearly two years.

Also, the reason why she couldn't deny the possibility that her harsh review of Mateo hadn't been influenced by the fresh pain of her papi's betrayal. A truth that left an indelible ink stain on Vanessa's record. Even if no one else knew about it.

Good guy or Casanova. It didn't matter. As a professional, she owed Mateo an apology.

Personally, though, it did matter, and she'd be wise to steer clear of him.

As Mateo plated their quinoa and gandules with chicken breast next to the tossed salad he'd thrown together, a seductive chef cooking by candlelight, Vanessa realized that steering clear of his charming, nice-guy appeal was much easier said than done.

# Chapter 6

"Are you good?" Mateo backed away from the couch after handing Vanessa her tray of food.

She held it up and wiggled her hips, settling more comfortably on his sofa in a move that had him thinking about different couch activities they could engage in other than sharing a late-night meal.

"Smells scrumptious." Her lips curved in an enticing smile, her hazel-green eyes sparkling with a mischief. "I'm excited to sample your concoction. See if it would pass my abuela's inspection."

"Go for it." He motioned for her to start eating.

Vanessa shook her head, the messy bun balancing on top wobbling precariously. "I'll wait. Grab yours before it gets cold."

Mateo didn't have to be told twice. He hustled to the kitchen and had just set the open bottle on his tray when Vanessa called out, "Don't forget the wine."

"A woman after my own heart."

Her throaty chuckle pleased him, more than it probably should. Disconcerted by the realization, Mateo paused. He rubbed a hand over his chest, his head and his heart at odds with each other. When it came to Vanessa Ríos, his feelings were a mass of contradictions. Intrigued, annoyed, attracted, frustrated . . . none of which he had time to examine in the busyness of his life. Until now.

Until his city had gone dark, hitting pause on everything that had consumed him in recent years. Often to the detriment of relationships and his mental health. Greedily he wanted to take advantage of this bizarre blip in his daily routine of work, stress, more work, a little sleep, repeat in that same order.

Tonight's situation had a twilight-zone aura about it. Even knowing the ending of this little episode could leave him worse off than before the lights had gone out, Mateo wasn't about to cheat himself out of an intimate night for two with the only woman who had managed to infiltrate his single-minded focus on his passion project. A focus he needed to maintain because *Clemente* could make or break not only his career and bank account, but the expectations and financial status of his parents' business, as well as those of the loved ones in their comunidad in Tampa and Puerto Rico who had invested in *Clemente* to help him.

He couldn't afford distractions. And yet . . .

Leaving the thought unfinished—because he hadn't figured out the "yet" part and was pretty much relying on his improv skills—Mateo reached for Vanessa's wineglass to add to his tray. Jeff's note with Nicole's advice scribbled at the bottom lay on the counter beside Vanessa's drink.

*P.S. We all know it's time for something real. I hope you followed my advice and were nice to her. She might surprise you in return. N*

Vanessa's acquiescence to his détente had definitely surprised him.

He hadn't meant to suggest it. The words had slipped out in a moment of weakness.

While selecting the wine, he'd worried they had an endless

night of sparring ahead, that their time together would turn into one long interview for an article she might wind up writing. Which meant he'd have to be "on" the whole time. Making sure he didn't inadvertently offer up a sound-bite phrase that could be misconstrued or printed out of context.

If he had one night with Vanessa Ríos . . . finally . . . he didn't want anything to come between them, not the stress of their jobs or the choices he had made to bring *Clemente* this far.

"You okay in there?" she called out.

"On my way."

Moments later he dropped a throw pillow on the floor near the coffee table and sat down across from her.

He had drummed up a few extra candles from Jeff's room—thanking Nicole for her candle fetish. Now the living room and foyer resembled a cheesy romantic-movie set with candles of varying sizes casting wavy shadows and light across the hardwood floor and ivory-painted walls.

Vanessa scooped up a bite of quinoa and gandules, and Mateo watched as her mouth closed around her fork. Her eyes drifted closed. She chewed, swallowed, then her lips spread in a delectable grin.

"So, you're a whiz onstage and in the kitchen, huh?"

Pleasure bloomed in his chest. "I'm not opening up a food truck or anything, but my mami made sure I knew my way around a kitchen before I moved out. She was worried about me being a starving artist and, you know, wasting away."

"Let her know there's nothing to worry about." Vanessa waved her fork at him. "That hot bod of yours is definitely not wasting away."

She froze, her expressive eyes going wide as if her words had just registered in her brain.

Damn, if her inadvertent admission didn't have lust pooling, swift and low, in his body. "So, you think I'm—"

"It was just a figure of speech," she mumbled, pushing a few gandules around her plate and, he'd bet, purposely avoiding his gaze.

Interesting. Vanessa didn't strike him as the type to embarrass easily. And she rarely, if ever, held back her opinion in *The Fix*. That left him wondering . . . was it possible that she could be more interested in him than she let on?

He definitely wanted to find out.

"I take it you're a . . . how did you put it? A *hot bod* expert?" he teased.

She huffed out a breath and gave him a side-eyed glare before dropping her gaze to concentrate on playing with her food. "I call for a change of subject."

"Actually, I'm interested in hearing more about your area of expertise. Sure you don't wanna elaborate?"

He waited a few beats, milking the glorious moment of having her in the hot seat for a change. Eventually though, he caved. Not wanting to push his luck.

"Fiiiine." He drew out the word, faking a disgruntled mood. "But for the record, I will admit to having noticed, on multiple occasions, that you've got a hot bod yourself."

She stilled.

For a heartbeat Mateo wondered if he might have misinterpreted her banter and now had said too much.

Vanessa's top teeth bit into her lower lip in a move that had his gut tightening. His thoughts instantly segued to what she might taste like if he were nibbling on her lip instead.

"I will accept your admission in good faith," she finally said, setting down her fork to grab her glass off the coffee table. "However, I suggest we finish this bottle, probably sample another one, before we embark on a game of Truth or Dare. I like to play dirty."

Mateo coughed in surprise, and he reached for a napkin to cover his mouth.

Vanessa smirked over the rim of her wineglass as she took a hefty sip.

Coño, talk about a twilight-zone moment. A melding of the daring game he'd played as a teen with the very adult, sensual-as-sin woman presently driving him cross-eyed with desire. Her shapely legs draped along his sofa, her minidress skirt riding high enough to have his blood pounding through his veins. Headed in a direction that would embarrass him if she asked him to grab something from the kitchen right now.

There was a truth he'd like to ask: Did she really think as poorly of him as her review suggested?

Along with a dare. Or two. Or . . . hell, a lot more.

Keeping that truth to himself, Mateo wiped his mouth, amused and turned on by this playful side of the woman who regularly invaded his dreams. When he hadn't run himself so ragged working on *Clemente* that he didn't fall into the sleep of the dead when he finally put his head to pillow. Or sofa cushion. Or desktop as he was prone to do.

They ate in companionable silence for a few minutes. The city sounds outside the open living room and kitchen windows provided a comforting white noise he'd become accustomed to in the years since moving to Manhattan right out of college. The mix of sirens and horns and muffled traffic, even a helicopter hovering somewhere in the vicinity, soothed him like the ocean waves or the coquis singing in the trees during those summers spent in Puerto Rico in his youth.

"How about a little theatre-trivia contest?" Vanessa suggested.

"Contest?" He stabbed a piece of chicken with his fork, considering. Growing up a theatre nerd like him, and still working in the industry, no doubt she'd be a ringer for this topic on a trivia team. So would he. "As in, winner gets a prize?"

"Mmm-hmm," she hummed around a mouthful.

"*Any* prize?"

Vanessa threw her balled-up napkin at him. "Dios mío, does your mind always go to the gutter? You are—"

"Ahhhhh! We agreed on a friendly cease-fire, remember?" He held up a hand to ward off the disparaging description he anticipated.

He despised the "player" persona the publicity team at *Sin with Me* had pushed him to take on. Yes, it had served its purpose, heightening the buzz around the play and selling more tickets.

At first, he had balked. Then he realized the bonus they offered could go toward *Clemente*'s continued development. Plus, the contacts he'd made from *Sin with Me* had proven professionally beneficial in countless ways. It also didn't hurt that going along with their date-around plan gave him an out when one of his costars made it clear that she wouldn't mind turning their onstage pretend intimacy into reality.

But in the two years since *Sin with Me* had closed, he hadn't been able to shake the reputation.

"I was going to say, you are *so Wicked*," Vanessa finished. "Which opened on Broadway when?"

"Huh?"

Vanessa gazed expectantly back at him, showing no sign of the disdain he had come to expect from her since she had written about *Sin with Me*.

"Wow, already having to pass on the first question? This is gonna be easier than I thought." She grinned, then moved her food tray aside and stretched forward to adjust the bag of frozen veggies on her ankle.

The tension eased from Mateo's shoulders at her fun gamesmanship, and he sank deeper into the cushion on the floor. "October 2003."

"Ding, ding! Just under the buzzer."

"Based on the book by?" he countered.

Vanessa hooked her elbow on top of the back sofa cushion.

Cradling the side of her head in her palm, she rolled her eyes at him. "Por favor, don't go easy on me. Based on the book by Gregory Maguire. Is that a hint? You need me to throw you another softball?"

Damn if the smug tilt of the corners of her mouth didn't needle his competitive streak while also egging his libido to consider kissing the smirk off her lips. A move that would no doubt earn him a smack upside the head if he attempted it.

"What was Rodgers and Hammerstein's first collaboration?" she asked, as if quizzing a newbie in first-year theatre history instead of a veteran who lived and breathed and dreamed and made a living in the industry.

"Easy, *Oklahoma!* Okay, you want to play hardball?"

She flashed him an impish smile, eyes alight with glee.

For a hot second, Mateo nearly said screw trivia, bring on Truth or Dare. Let her see how dirty he could play.

Instead, he stayed safe by asking, "Who was the first Latino to win a Tony?"

Vanessa slapped her hands, then quickly rubbed them back and forth together. A cat-who-ate-the-canary grin plumped her cheeks. "Ooooh, papito, game on. José Ferrer in 1947 for Cyrano de Bergerac."

Gauntlet thrown. She did not mess around. Shame, because that's exactly what Mateo wanted to do.

In between bites of food and sips of wine or water, they lobbed questions back and forth. Some easy—which musical is based on the legend of Pygmalion: *My Fair Lady*—some more challenging—for which play did Rita Moreno win her one and only Tony: *The Ritz* in 1975. The year had been on the fringe of his recollection, but he couldn't place it until Vanessa had called time and given him the answer.

By the time their meal was done, they had finished off the bottle, and his chances of collecting the winner's prize were fading. Despite the challenge to his usual competitive streak,

Mateo wouldn't have given up the last half hour in Vanessa's company for anything.

A few minutes ago, she had dragged the hair tie from around her bun, slipping it onto her slender wrist and leaving her wavy tresses to tumble around her shoulders in delectable disarray. One errant curl played with the cleavage stretching the elastic band holding up her dress's dark floral material. Mateo's fingers itched to trace the edge along her bronze skin. Test the silky softness of that lucky curl between his thumb and forefinger. Slide his palm up the length of her elegant neck, slipping it behind to cup her nape as he lowered his head to sample her plump lips.

The elbow his chin leaned on slipped off the table's edge, jarring Mateo out of his lust-hazed stupor.

Thankfully Vanessa's eyes were closed, her hands buried in her hair as she fashioned it back into that messy bun that had him conjuring all kinds of just-rolled-out-of-bed thoughts.

"Any chance I can challenge you to a winner-take-all rapid-fire finale?" Mateo wiped his mouth with his napkin, mentally swiping at the drool that had him feeling like a horny teen.

"Maybe, though I'm sitting pretty right now." Propping her left elbow on the back of the sofa again, she tapped at her chin with a finger as if pondering an important question. "Already thinking about what prize I may want to claim."

Oh, she was definitely sitting pretty from his vantage point. Between the flickering candlelight and the moon's soft beams trailing over her, she seemed like an illusion induced by too much wine, stress, and longing.

As far as her prize was concerned, he certainly had some suggestions.

She leaned forward, stretching to set her TV tray on the table. He reached out for it, transferring her dishes on top of his, then rising to take everything to the kitchen.

"Thanks," she murmured.

The soft, appreciative smile curving her lips drew his attention to them. The tip of her tongue slipped out to run along her bottom lip seconds before she took a sip of wine.

Desire pulsed in his body.

"Refresh my memory again. How much am I beating you by?" she taunted jokingly.

"Humility is not your strong suit, is it?"

Her throaty chuckle turned into a full-on belly laugh when he narrowed his eyes and glared at her.

"How was I supposed to know you were a theatre-history savant?" he complained. "Usually that's my domain when Jeff, Nicole, and I meet up with friends for trivia night."

"You'll have to let me know the next time you go."

"Really?" He paused, his hand wrapped around the neck of the empty wine bottle.

Vanessa shrugged her bare shoulder. "Unless your team number is capped and already full. I'm usually down for team trivia with friends."

Friends.

Not necessarily what he wanted between them, but it was progress. Anything more would be foolish for him to consider. He didn't have time for a relationship. Not when so many depended on him and *Clemente*'s success.

"Should we open another one?" He jiggled the empty bottle.

Vanessa's gaze moved from the cabernet to his eyes. She bit her lower lip. A small but telling sign of uncertainty. He wouldn't push, unwilling to do anything that might lead to regrets later.

"How 'bout a water refill?" he suggested.

"Sure."

Her answer dripped with hesitancy, but Mateo left it at that and headed toward the darkened kitchen, where a lone candle flickered on the counter next to Jeff and Nicole's missive.

He set the tray down. Rested his hand on the lined notepad. *Have some fun for once.*

"I'm trying, buddy," Mateo mumbled. Though he had no idea what he hoped to gain from this strange interlude with Vanessa.

What he did know was that for the first time in . . . hell, he didn't know when . . . the stress and expectations surrounding *Clemente* hadn't been front-row, center-orchestra level in his mind.

No, that spot had been usurped by a certain brown-haired, hazel-eyed, enchanting woman whose quick wit, sharp mind, and alluring figure made it nearly impossible to focus on any-thing but her.

That could be dangerous for a guy so many others were counting on.

"Actually, I wouldn't turn down another glass of cab," Vanessa called out.

Temptation or a lifeline saving him from himself? Mateo wasn't sure which.

"Or a red blend, if you have one," she added.

Mateo snagged the bottle opener and strode to the wine rack.

Whether she was a temptation or a lifeline . . . it didn't matter.

At least for tonight. No way could he deny himself this time with his secret muse.

# Chapter 7

Mateo approached with a new bottle and the mischievous smile he flashed at the beginning of *Clemente* when he welcomed the audience to the show. The same smile that snagged Vanessa's heart like a fisherman's hook, reeling her in without much of a fight.

She didn't know what had possessed her to suggest more alcohol after he had dropped the suggestion. Switching to water was the smarter way to go.

Not that she always followed the smartest route suggested by the GPS of her life.

Case in point, while she had arrived at her intended destination, the Big Apple, she'd taken a completely different path from the one originally planned.

"You sure?" Mateo held the wine aloft.

"Truth?"

He grinned at her answer.

Coño, she could totally understand how his female costars were charmed by him. Working so closely with someone who effortlessly exuded this much magnetism? Fat chance of not falling under his spell.

But she could resist. She had to. At least until she knew for sure she could trust him.

Tonight, she'd seen signs pointing in that very direction.

"I hope there's always truth between us."

His serious tone gave her pause. Had her wondering if he was breaking his own rule by bringing in the past, the outside world he'd bidden her to hold at bay for the time being.

If so, there was a truth she owed him.

"But I've been known to rise to the challenge of a dare or two in my life," Mateo drawled. His dimple made its impish appearance, and Vanessa let the worry of apologies unspoken drift away.

While Mateo used the opener's attached blade to slice and remove the thick foil wrapped around the top of the bottle, Vanessa bent over her leg to remove the now room-temperature bag of vegetables. At this rate, she was going to owe Mateo and Jeff a week's worth of frozen food.

"How does it feel?" Mateo asked.

"Better. Though I can't be certain whether that's thanks to the pain meds you gave me earlier, the frozen veggie packs, or the wine."

"Probably a combination of all three. Here, let me take a look." He set down the opener and bottle, swapping them for the flashlight, then circled the metal coffee table as he stepped toward her.

Bending closer to her propped-up foot, Mateo shone the light over her ankle to examine her injury.

"You . . . you mind, if I . . ." He extended a hand toward her foot, stopping before he actually touched her.

Dios, how she wanted him to touch her. In a completely different way. For completely different reasons. Keeping those thoughts to herself, Vanessa bit her lip and tipped her head, indicating her assent.

Mateo slipped his hand under her foot to gently cup her heel. Damn if every cell in her body didn't perk up as if asking for his attention. He lifted her foot a little and bent lower, at what had to be an uncomfortable angle given his height.

"Feel free to sit down if you want," she suggested.

He turned his head to glance at her, his chiseled face a mix of light and dark shadows. His frown seemed to ask if she was sure, so she grabbed hold of the two throw pillows and pulled them out of the way. Mindful of her minidress, Vanessa dropped one pillow to the floor by her right foot and used the other to cover her lap.

Mateo slid under her extended left leg, taking care not to jostle it, his consideration for her injury another sign of his thoughtfulness.

Once situated, he set the flashlight on top of the sofa's back cushion, pointing toward the television and low entertainment center on the far wall. As he'd done backstage at the Booth, he held her foot in one hand while the fingers of the other gingerly pressed against her flesh. Vanessa winced and he immediately lessened the pressure. She sat forward, inspecting her ankle along with him.

"Swelling looks better. Don't you think?" he asked.

She murmured in agreement as she put her hand over his to gently move it out of the way. Their fingers laced. Held. Her gaze slowly lifted to meet his. Questioning. Wondering.

Did he feel this same connection between them? This need to satisfy an unknown, a desire to taste his kiss again. Without a room full of theatre kids, nor the pretense of playing a role. For real this time.

What had started out as innocent, teen adoration years ago had morphed into an intense adult desire. Pent-up and ignored. At first because he reminded her of a past before her father's betrayal. Then, because she had grouped the two men together.

Wrongly?

Guilt over that possibility had hounded her for a while. Tonight, it had caught up to her, compelling her to face truths she'd learned over the course of their forced intimacy.

Mateo gently set her foot on his lap. His free hand drifted from her heel, along the outside of her leg, stopping on the curve of her calf muscle. Heat ignited in the wake of his soft caress. The sensation traveled higher. Up her inner thigh, heading straight to the spot between her legs craving his attention.

Her breath lodged in her lungs. Her heart tripped, then gained speed, off to the races as if she was in the midst of a hard-core spin class.

His hand squeezed her calf, kneading the flesh. Desire undulated through her in sensual waves that lapped at her soul.

Her lids fluttered closed. A soft moan escaped her lips and Mateo's fingers tightened around hers. She opened her eyes to find his face taut with a longing that mimicked the hunger blazing through her insides. Threatening to turn her into a huge flame of passion and need bright enough to electrify the entire freaking state.

But he didn't make any move to come closer. Instead, he stayed on his end of the couch, one hand driving her crazy with his massage skills on her calf, the other clinging to hers, their fingers intertwined in an embrace she yearned to reenact with their bodies. Now.

His jaw tightened. His expression intense. Fervent. And yet, he kept his distance.

Confused, Vanessa searched his gaze. Suddenly worried that this might be part of his love 'em, then leave 'em wanting more game. Only they had yet to get to the love 'em part and her body was definitely craving more.

The answering desire darkening his eyes told her she wasn't the only one caught in this maelstrom of longing. As she stared back at him, moments from their evening together flashed by like scenes on a movie screen between them.

Mateo adamantly assuring her that he wasn't inviting her home to "have his way with her."

His gentlemanly, careful manner when he'd helped her to the couch, hovering until she was comfortable.

Freddie's comment downstairs about Mateo finally bringing a girl home. Like it was something new.

Jeff's note urging him to have some fun. As if Mateo rarely did.

His offer of water when she hesitated at his suggestion of more wine. Even giving her a chance to change her mind when he'd walked back to the living room with the unopened bottle she had requested.

The different moments converged, melding into a jumbled mass that awed like bright fireworks in a night sky, leaving only Mateo, silently watching her. Waiting.

Perhaps the water under his ladies' man facade ran much deeper than she had thought. Perhaps her perception had been skewed by her father's selfish machinations and her unfair projection of her papi's mistakes onto Mateo.

Worse, perhaps she had really misjudged him.

If he was the decent guy his friends and his actions tonight made him out to be, something told her he probably wouldn't make the first move. Not in light of her current position—a single woman, injured, here in good faith, not inebriated but not exactly sober. If she showed the smallest hint of reservation, Mateo would back off.

Good thing she had no problem letting her needs be known. And she was tired of denying herself. Especially when it came to him.

Squeezing her fingers tightly around his, Vanessa tugged Mateo toward her.

Excitement flared in his eyes seconds before his elbow knocked the flashlight off the sofa back. It landed facedown, lodged between the seat cushions.

The muted darkness heightened her senses.

The sound of muffled friction from his shorts sliding across the sofa's microfiber material as Mateo moved to the center cushion. The scent of his musky aftershave and crisp, clean soap when she sucked in a breath trembling with anticipation. The titillating sensation of his free hand slid from her calf, past her knee, drawing to a stop on her midthigh where his fingers played with her dress hem. Teasing her sensitive skin. Sending sparks of electricity flickering to all parts of her body.

Suddenly anxious, impatient for more, Vanessa untangled their fingers to drive hers into the close-cropped hair at his nape, urging him closer.

His lips found hers in a searing openmouthed kiss that had her gasping for breath. He grasped her waist, easily lifting her up so he could slide under her, settling her onto his lap while their mouths mated. Tongues caressing, savoring. Darting around and against each other in a heady dance. He tasted like fine wine and sin and deferred dreams finally realized.

Her hands traveled the expanse of his broad back, marveling at his taut muscles. He nibbled on her lower lip. Laved it with his tongue. A hoarse moan tore from her throat, and he broke their kiss to trail warm kisses along her jaw, over the pulse point in her neck. Ducking his head, he nuzzled her cleavage with his nose. Her nipples hardened, her breasts heavy with need for his attention.

As if he could read her thoughts, he suckled one of her breasts through her thin dress. Her nipple strained inside her lacy bra, aching for more. She arched backward, offering herself to him. He dragged his tongue along her skin above the elastic band holding up her dress, and she nearly reached up to pull the material down, desperate for there to be nothing between them. Craving only skin to skin.

"You taste so good," he groaned, seeking her mouth again. She opened willingly for him, hungry for his kiss.

One of his hands splayed across the center of her back, offering support. His other found its way to her thigh. Feathersoft caresses sent goose bumps trailing up and down her leg. He slipped his hand under her dress hem, his fingers spanning the breadth of her thigh. His thumb brushed a line of heat back and forth along her inner thigh, inching closer . . . closer . . . until the tip of his thumb lightly rubbed her center through her panties. Whisper soft. Then again. And again. Teasing. Seeking. Asking for permission.

She rocked her hips, encouraging his touch. Wanting more. Needing more. Needing *him.*

Her hands slid down his back in search of his T-shirt hem. Grabbing it, she dragged the cotton material up his long torso. They broke their kiss, panting. Mateo raised his arms high so she could pull his shirt all the way off, dropping it onto the pillow on the floor. Hands on his broad shoulders, she nudged him back against the sofa, her eyes greedily devouring him.

Now it was her turn to explore his steely muscles and smooth skin under the candle's wavering glow. With hands and mouth and tongue, she memorized every curve, every dip of his spectacular chest, the ridges of his rock-solid abs, his dark nipples that pebbled under her ardent attention. His erection tented the front of his basketball shorts and she fisted it. Instinctively she pumped slowly up, then down. Imitating the motion her body ached for.

"God, you're amazing," he groaned.

"I know," she teased, pleased at his bark of laughter.

He stilled her hand, surprising her. Pressing a kiss on his left pec, she glanced up at him through her lashes. His head was tilted to the side on the back cushion, lids heavy with desire, lips curved with chagrin.

"If we don't slow this down"—his voice was raspy with hunger—"I'm gonna wind up like a teen his first time up to bat, striking out on three fast pitches. I want to make this good for you, too."

"Promises, promises."

He shot her a rakish grin as he raised her hand to his lips. He kissed her palm, sucked her pointer finger into his warm mouth.

Carnal hunger coursed through, leaving her sex throbbing with need.

Mateo buried his face in her neck, grazed her sensitive skin with his teeth. Then he sampled his way to her ear, licking the lobe before softly blowing on her wet skin. Need long denied took hold of her.

Vanessa grasped his wrists, moving his hands to her breasts, letting him know what she wanted. He obliged, cupping her breasts to palm their weight. He dipped his head, his tongue sneaking under the dress's elastic band to lick her cleavage. Her nipples tightened even harder, straining for his attention.

His fingers crooked inside her dress's elastic band but stilled. Instead of pushing the material aside, he dropped a kiss in the center of her chest, then drew back to meet her gaze.

"We good?" His voice was a heady mix of gravel rough and whisper soft.

She blinked at him in surprise. Thinking she'd given him enough signs that, uh, yeah, she was more than good.

"We can pause. Stay clothes on," he clarified.

"In case you hadn't noticed, you're halfway past that stage already."

He chuckled. "Coño, you're cheeky, aren't you?"

"It's one of my finer traits."

"And there are many," he murmured, bending to kiss a delectable trail up her neck.

A deep foghorn blared in the room, startling them. They jerked apart, heads swiveling to find the source of what was now a loud vibration rattling somewhere in the room.

Mateo slid out from under her, and she pulled her left knee into her chest, out of his way. He fell to his knees on the hardwood floor, reaching for his cell phone, which was clattering like a live wire on the far edge of the metal coffee table.

"Apparently the cell tower is back in business," he said.

Vanessa grabbed her cell, remembering she had turned it off earlier to save power.

"Uh, in case we weren't aware, there's a power outage in the area." Mateo held his phone up for Vanessa to see the notification on the tiny screen. "Good to know the emergency alert system's working."

Shaking his head in disbelief, he leaned his elbows on the coffee table and looked down to read something on his cell.

Thanks to the real-world interruption, the fog of lust thinned around Vanessa. The magnitude of what they had almost done . . . taken a giant step they wouldn't be able to take back tomorrow . . . loomed between them.

She swiveled to sit properly on the couch. Knees pressed together. Hands gripping her cell and the link to reality it represented.

Doubts perched like pesky cartoon sidekicks on her shoulder, snickering in her ear.

Her thumb pressed the side button on her cell, and she waited impatiently for the screen to brighten, suddenly desperate to connect with Ria or Alison. They were the only two who would understand the flood of emotions whipping through her like a hurricane wind buffeting her carefully constructed walls. Erected to keep her father, then her ex . . . truthfully, any guy who showed the slightest indication of wanting a relationship, which would eventually lead to heartache . . . at bay.

But this wasn't some random hookup. Not that she engaged in those regularly, but a girl had needs that she couldn't always satisfy alone.

This was Mateo. The two of them shared a connection. Even if she had tried to bury it or snip it with her razor-sharp words. Purely out of a misguided need to protect herself.

Her gaze cut to him, hunkered next to the table. Broad shoulders hunched over his cell. Handsome face scrunched in thought while his blunt-tipped fingers tapped at the tiny screen.

He was part of her past. The Vanessa before her home life had blown up and her faith in those closest to her had been broken.

When they had first crossed paths in the city, she had entertained thoughts about connecting with him again. As adults now. Only, her keen disappointment in hearing that he'd grown up to become a serial womanizer like her father had crushed her youthful delusions.

That's why she hadn't heeded Greg's hint that she dig deeper into Mateo. Question more than one "anonymous source." Instead, she fired back. Not a warning shot. Oh, no, a full artillery blast.

She owed Mateo an apology for the personal attack in what should have been a professional review. For letting her messed-up home life color her professional one.

Only, how did you segue from being hot and bothered and ready to get naked with a guy on his couch to apologizing for implying to the entire theatre world that he had trouble keeping it in his pants. Especially when she was the one who'd been ready to whip it out for him moments ago.

Mortified, Vanessa tucked her chin and tapped her phone on her knee, anxious for it to load. This situation desperately called for Ria's calm perspective and a shot of Alison's girls-run-the-world attitude.

Eager to finally connect with her best friends and hoping their evenings weren't proving as unimaginable as hers, Vanessa peeked at her cell. Relief lightened her anxiety as she spotted a text from Alison that had come in earlier in the evening: *Operation: Magician Downfall is a go.*

Just as Vanessa started to reply, the words NO SERVICE popped up in the screen's upper left-hand corner. Her stomach dropped.

"What the fu—?" She swallowed the oath. "I don't have— do you—"

Mateo shook his head. His face crumpled with defeat. "It

dropped before I could send my text to Jeff. Or answer my mom's. The towers must still be overloaded."

Muttering a curse, Vanessa turned her phone off again, then let it clatter onto the metal table. She collapsed back against the cushions with an irritated sigh. Eyes closed, she tunneled her hands through her hair, squeezing her head between her palms.

So much for a BFF pep talk. She was on her own.

As if sounding a warning alarm for her personal life, that Emergency Alert System had done her a favor with its rude interruption.

Mateo Garza wasn't someone she could fool around with and ghost afterward to avoid potential messy feelings and relationship expectations. Not when they ran in the same professional circles.

Ria was right.

The reason Vanessa had been so angry, so hurt, by the thought of Mateo turning out like her papi was because despite her no-relationships mantra, he'd been the one guy she would have broken that rule for.

*Ay, nena, tremendo lío tienes.* Her abuela's often-heard phrase whenever Vanessa came to her with a problem brought a wistful smile to Vanessa's lips.

Sí, abuela, she had a tremendous mess on her hands.

Mateo cleared his throat.

Vanessa's eyes fluttered open to find him staring at her warily.

"I'm guessing. You and me. All of that." He gestured at the couch. "Not happening, huh?"

His good-humored tilt to one corner of his mouth let Vanessa know he wasn't pushing to start up where they'd left off. More like trying to break the awkward tension.

Hands clasped tightly in her lap, she slowly shook her head.

"Yeah, I didn't think so," he said softly.

Flattening his palms on the tabletop, he pushed himself to his feet, the muscles in his arms and bare chest flexing under his weight. He stood facing her, hands on his trim hips, drawing her attention to the curve of his obliques. Vanessa's mouth watered the way it did when her mami's flan came fresh out of the oven and she was eager for a taste.

"How about I refill our waters and we hold off on more wine and Truth or Dare. Maybe watch a movie that's already downloaded on my iPad instead?"

Damn if her heart didn't melt a little—something that never happened with a guy—at his wholesome suggestion. Sure, her lady parts got a little excited, too. How could they not when facing someone like Mateo, whose gorgeous physique was rivaled by his wide gentleman streak.

"Do I get to choose the movie?" She arched a brow in challenge.

"We could rock-paper-scissors for it."

She laughed. A full-on belly laugh that eased the guilt-fueled tension in her chest.

"Okaaaay," she muttered, bending over to snag his T-shirt off the floor. "But you gotta put this on."

She tossed the red tee at him and he caught it one-handed.

His dimple flashed along with his impish grin. "Too distracting for you, huh?"

"Go! Bring me some water. I have a movie to pick out."

His rumbly chuckle floated to her in the muted darkness.

First a friendly movie, while she searched for the words of apology. In between, no kissing. No fondling. No crossing outside of the friend zone.

Coño, that might not be too easy if they were sharing an iPad.

Maybe she should trust her skill with words and start with the apology.

# Chapter 8

"You cheated," Vanessa accused, her pouty tone matching her moued lips.

Mateo forced himself to slide his gaze away from her tempting lips to the iPad screen resting half on his lap, half on hers.

Obviously he hadn't thought through his let's-watch-a-movie idea before blurting it out earlier. Why else would he subject himself to the torturous experience of having her delectable body pressed up against his? Shoulders, hips, thighs—pressure points of heat searing his skin.

How the hell was he supposed to set her at ease, make it clear he was okay putting the brakes on their intimacy, when his entire body perked up at her slightest touch?

"I forgot I deleted the movies from my tablet. Without Wi-Fi we can't download one from the cloud. My bad." He shrugged, regretting the move when her bare arm rubbed against his.

"Uh-huh, likely story," she joked. "So our options are a Clemente documentary or a Clemente documentary. Gee, I wonder what I'll pick."

She tapped her pointer finger on her lips, head tilted as if she were deep in thought.

"Wiseass," he chided.

"Wise? Me? Definitely. But I'd call my ass fine, thank you very much."

"Man, I don't know how you get around this city without using the subway or a car service."

"What?" She scowled with confusion.

"With that big head of yours, it's obvious you can't fit inside either one," Mateo teased.

Her mouth opened on an affronted gasp and she smacked at his chest. "You're one to talk. Inviting a girl to watch a movie only to have the options ones that inevitably compel her to ask about you and your so-called passion project."

Heat crawled up his face and he was thankful they'd blown out a few candles in case they were needed later.

"Is it?" Shifting to face him, she crooked her left knee so it wound up resting on his thigh, her injured ankle on the sofa cushion.

"What do you mean?" he asked, finding it difficult to concentrate on their conversation when her dress rode up her golden thighs, reminding him of when his hand had followed that same delectable route.

"I have to break your rule."

The earnest note in her voice cooled his heated thoughts about her hem, his hand, her thigh . . .

"Meaning?" he asked warily.

She worried her lower lip and scooted a little closer, her knee riding up his thigh to brush his stomach.

He swallowed, forcing himself to ignore his body's heated reaction to hers.

"But, point of order," she said, "you started it with your unsuccessful movie-watching invite."

"I'm not following."

She took the iPad from him. After closing out of the app with the documentaries, she swiped to the last screen, where there were fewer icons. She held up the device as if presenting him with something, but he still had no idea what she meant.

"Your homescreen image. There's a copy of it in the Clemente display at the Booth, isn't there?" She pointed to the candid shot of an older Roberto Clemente wearing pants with a button-down shirt and tie, talking to several young ballplayers wearing their San Juan Senadores uniforms.

"Yeah. And?"

"And this guy looks eerily familiar." Vanessa tapped a finger on one of the ballplayers. One Mateo knew well. "Same hair and build. Same chiseled jaw. Same flash of dimple."

Now he understood her "point of order" comment. They'd had a deal. No shop talk. For one night he relished the idea of not stressing or worrying or feeling the weight of responsibility like Atlas balancing the world on his shoulders. And yet, he had opened the door with the documentary debacle, leading her to ask him about something he hadn't shared with anyone outside his closest circle.

With sudden clarity, he realized he wanted Vanessa to be a part of that group.

"It's you. Fifty-plus years ago." She combed her fingers through his hair. Her short nails gently scratched his scalp, and delicious pinpricks chased across his head, energizing and re-laxing him at the same time. "Something tells me this is a big part of the *passion* behind your project. Am I right?"

"It's my abuelo on my papi's side. I haven't really talked much about my personal connection. It's important that the focus stay on Clemente, the mentor, the activist, the man who positively affected the lives of so many. My abuelo is only one of them. But the Clemente stories Abuelo tells. There's so much orgullo when he talks about those days with Clemente managing his winter-ball team."

A similar pride filled Mateo's chest.

"So, your abuelo played ball?"

Mateo nodded. He stared at the iPad screen, remembering his abuelo talking about when the picture was taken.

"He'll tell you this was a regular game day. Clemente passing along words of wisdom like usual. Advice about the game. About life. About standing up for what was right. Demanding Latinos in the league be treated fairly. With respect."

"What an incredible experience, being mentored by someone like him." Awe colored Vanessa's whispered words.

"My abuelo would say yes, it was. He nearly quit the game when Clemente died. Played a few more years, then gave it up after injuring his shoulder one too many times. But as a kid, my summers with my abuelo were filled with countless Clemente stories. The two of us watching Yankees games on the TV together. Listening to them on his staticky radio. He used to drop me off at Clemente's Sports Complex for baseball camp. Then he'd listen to me yammer on about my day over dinner with him and my abuela."

Nostalgia for those simple days filled Mateo and he rubbed at the ache in his chest.

"I didn't know you played."

"Until sophomore year of high school. Then the coach made me choose: the team or the spring musical."

"Yeah, that happened with a couple guys in our theatre troupe." She cupped Mateo's nape, gently massaging the base of his neck, as if she knew that the tension headaches he battled always originated in that exact spot.

"I never thought it was fair to make the guys choose. That's a tough decision for anyone to make," she said.

"Naw." Mateo shook his head. "The decision itself wasn't hard. Not for me."

"Really?"

"Theatre, show choir. They've always been more than an extracurricular for me. Onstage, I can be anything. Become anyone. The thrill of taking someone's words and breathing life into them. There's nothing like it. I'm sure you get that."

She nodded as her fingers sifted through his hair again, soothing the antsiness talking about Clemente inevitably brought.

"Telling my abuelo I was quitting the game—" Mateo stared at the television screen on the wall in front of them, his thoughts far away. "*That* was hard. I didn't want him to be disappointed. And now . . ."

The fear he'd felt that day swept over him again, for different reasons, but equally as potent. He sucked in a deep breath, blowing it out through puffed cheeks.

"Now what?"

"I started writing *Clemente* in undergrad. At first as a way to save the stories my abuelo had shared. Then it became him reliving his memories of the legend who had impacted him, and others. Then I found myself randomly humming bars of music, catching lyrics tumbling in my head. Fiddling with ideas at my keyboard. Alek was a year ahead of Tommy and me. And we had already collaborated on a few ideas in school. It was only natural for them to jump on board."

"The Dynamic Trio."

Mateo tore his gaze away from the imaginary memory montage playing on the blank TV screen to meet Vanessa's smiling eyes.

"Alek despises that nickname. Says it lacks imagination."

"He's right. I could come up with something better."

He chuckled. Something he rarely did lately when talking about *Clemente*. "You think so, huh?"

She blew a *pffft* between her lips as if to say, *Of course*.

Coño, her self-confidence was a total turn-on. Without thinking, he reached out to tuck her hair behind her right ear. Loathe to let go, he clasped a thick lock, sliding his fingers down its silky length.

He leaned toward her, stopping with his face inches from

hers. His gaze moved to her mouth, then back up to her eyes. "I dare you."

Her hazel eyes flared with interest. Her cheeks grew plump with a Cheshire-cat grin. "Ay, papito, you should know better than to dare me. Even if we never opened that second bottle."

"Believe me, I've got far more interesting dares than that one. If you're not too scared to play."

"Scared? Me? Yeah right."

But he caught a flash of something—uncertainty, maybe?—before she blinked and it was gone.

"Riddle me this," she said. "As a lifetime theatre nut, I'm dying to know what it's like taking a seed of an idea from this nugget inside your handsome head"—her fingers massaged his nape again, her words massaging his ego, whether she intended to or not—"to opening night, hottest-ticket-in-town status?"

As if a circuit breaker had been flipped inside him, that telltale tension seized his body. His shoulders bunched. The ever-present ache at the base of his skull that had disappeared with her as a distraction delivered a warning throb.

Mateo eased away, leaning back on the sofa cushion behind him with a tired sigh. "Change of subject."

"Aw, man, really?"

The warmth of her hand on his shoulder soothed him a little. Enough to have him turning his head on the back cushion to look at her through slitted eyes. Disappointment at his bid to end their discussion drew her mouth into a frown.

The idea of letting her down in any way made him feel worse.

"Here's the condensed, off-the-record version." He patted her knee, leaving his hand to rest there, testing to see if she would move away.

She held up a hand, her thumb tucking her pinkie finger down in what he thought might be the Girl Scout salute his little sister had practiced. "Vegas rules. What goes on here, stays here."

"Somehow, I don't think that's the Girl Scout credo."

"It's ours."

A sense of peace spread through him. He liked the sound of that. *Ours.*

"Okay. If you really want to know, it's gut clenching, and not in a good way. Anxiety inducing, sleep depriving. Hair pulling."

She cringed. "Yikes. That fun, huh?"

"Don't get me wrong," he rushed on. "It's also exhilarating. But my familia and close friends have put their hard-earned money into the show. Even though many of them are still struggling to get their businesses on an even keel in the aftermath of Hurricane María, the earthquakes, and hard economic times. I haven't had a peaceful night's sleep in ages worrying about the show flopping and how that would affect them. How I would disappoint them."

"You wouldn't."

He knew different. "I eat, sleep, and breathe *Clemente* and whatever job I have at the moment to help pay the bills and keep my health care. That revolving door of dates I did during *Sin with Me*? It was publicity stunts invented by the producers. I went along because it benefited the show. That job helped finance *Clemente*. The closest I've come to dating in years is with my laptop or keyboard."

Vanessa slapped a hand to her forehead, eyes wide with shock at his admission.

"Crazy, right? I don't have time for anything else. Alek and Tommy help me stay sane in the busyness of getting *Clemente* where we are today. Jeff and Nicole are the people I'm closest to outside of my professional life."

"Dios mío, I'm an idiot." Palm still pressed to her forehead, Vanessa sagged back against the padded armrest behind her as she murmured, " 'Have some fun for once.' "

"Excuse me?"

" 'Have some fun for once.' Jeff's note?" She sat up and

draped her left arm over the back of the sofa, her fingertips finding his nape again.

"Ahhh, yes. He likes to nag. Complains I work too much."

"Like Freddie, your doorman."

They shared a smile and Mateo found himself oddly comforted instead of his usual stressed when this topic came up.

"And Nicole's addendum?" Vanessa asked. "Who was she talking about?"

Ooh, he wasn't quite ready to admit his long-held infatuation with Vanessa. Although after having spent tonight with her, not the poison-pen reviewer or even the cute teen of his past, but the quick-witted, competitive, captivating woman he found easy to talk to, even about topics he didn't normally share with others, he found his infatuation had deepened.

"Nicole likes to think my soul mate is out there, waiting for me. She's itching for the four of us to double-date. Plan couples trips together. In her words, I deserve to be as happy as she and Jeff are. Sappy, believe me, I know."

That was the truth. He'd only left out the part about Nicole's being certain Mateo's soul mate might be the woman seated beside him right now. The girl he'd never been able to forget.

"She sounds like someone who cares about you. That's nice." Vanessa cupped his cheek. Her hazel eyes glistened, and he couldn't be sure if it was a trick of the flickering candlelight or if a sheen of tears shone in the hazel-green orbs. "I hope I can meet her sometime. Let her know she's right—you do deserve that. And I—"

Vanessa broke off. Pulled her hand away from his cheek, robbing him of the comfort of her touch.

"And I owe you an apology. Please!" She held a palm as if sensing his *For what?* question. "I should have said this a while ago. Tonight made that even more clear."

Mateo rolled his lips together, signaling his intent to keep quiet. She'd let him have his say. He could do the same.

"Right before high school graduation, I caught my papi with his mistress. And found out it wasn't the first one. Or the last."

If Vanessa had gut punched him, he wouldn't have been nearly as surprised as he was by her admission. Wanting to offer her the same comfort she'd given him, he covered her tightly clasped hands with one of his.

"Worse, my mami's known about it. Actually 'turns the other cheek' because our Church says there should be no divorce and she loves him. Can't live without him, apparently. Discovering that ripped the foundation of my life out from under me."

She shook her head, pain creasing her beautiful features.

"My papi used to say my desire for the limelight and the audience's adulation was a lot like his desire for attention. I didn't realize until then the kind of attention he meant." Her lip curled with derision, anger sweeping in to chase away the pain clouding her eyes. "I stopped acting in college when he showed up with a new woman, bragging to her about how I was his mini-me. I got so mad, I just . . . quit."

Vanessa blinked up at Mateo with what looked like surprise. He saw the hurt of a young girl betrayed by her papi, and he ached for her. Wanted to wrap her in his arms and wipe away the painful memories.

"To be honest, when we first ran into each other, I wondered what had made you change majors," he said. "Theatre Fest our senior year, you were BFA-in-musical-theatre bound, but then we met here and you're a journalist. Are you saying you regret your decision?"

Her messy bun wobbled as she slowly shook her head again. A wavy lock slid loose from the hair tie, curling softly down the side of her face. "Usually, no. I'm damn good at my job."

"Your self-confidence humbles me," he teased, relieved to see a whisper of her cheeky smile teasing her lips.

"Another one of my finer traits."

"Of which there are many." Unable to ignore his need to

touch her, Mateo tucked the lock of hair behind her ear. Then gently caressed the curve of her jaw, before easing away to give her space, sensing that her story wasn't finished.

"That pretending to be someone else onstage that you crave. My father did it my entire life, pretended to be a loving husband and dad. When he's a total mujeriego."

"Like Eric, the womanizing asshole I played in *Sin with Me*."

Vanessa's throat worked with a swallow as she nodded. "Right before I left to review *Sin with Me*, I found out his latest side piece had given birth to my new half brother. That *happy* news, along with the stories circulating about you loving and leaving your female costars and your innuendo-filled interviews . . . which I now know were all for show . . . set me off. Your performance was flawless, but I let my personal feelings color my review, and that was unprofessional of me. I am so sorry."

The anguish in her heartfelt apology had Mateo shifting on the couch to fully face her. He cupped her shoulders, his thumbs brushing across her collarbones as he sought to reassure her that he understood.

"I feel horrible about the way it all snowballed with the bloggers and gossip columnists. Later, I heard that it might have caused you to lose an investor for *Clemente*. And I didn't intend—"

"Hey, it's okay."

She dropped her gaze to her lap as if unable to meet his.

Mateo crooked a finger under her chin, gently nudging it up until she looked at him. "That guy had been yanking my chain. And one of the producer's, too. Making promises we found out he couldn't keep. Bad timing that he bowed out right after your review hit and things spiraled. But *Sin*'s producers were thrilled with the social media tizzy. No press is bad press if you ask them."

"It's not them I'm worried about." Her softly voiced admission arrowed right to his heart. "I'm sorry for questioning your integrity."

The brutal honesty in her words, the plea for his forgiveness in her expressive eyes and deeply furrowed brow, made it clear her apology was sincere. The confident woman of moments ago was readily admitting her mistake. That took guts, humility, and a generous soul.

"Thank you," he whispered, not trusting his voice through the sudden knot in his throat.

"Although I am not sorry for kicking your butt at theatre trivia earlier tonight."

He couldn't help but grin at her caveat, thinking her cheeky attitude added to her charm.

Vanessa Ríos was everything he wanted. Hoped he deserved.

"Truth or Dare?" he asked her.

A tremulous smile wobbled on her lips as she searched his eyes. He willed her to see his acceptance of her apology in the teasing olive branch he offered.

Her chest rose and fell on a weighty sigh. Her head dropped back, exposing her slender neck as she groaned up at the ceiling. "Ay. Dios. Mío. I've had enough of the truth for one night."

"Good. 'Cuz I dare you to give me one kiss to soothe the ache of my hurt feelings," he challenged.

She laugh-snorted, which he took as a positive sign. An impish grin curved her lips when she gazed back at him, delight easing the worry from her eyes.

"Ay, papito, dare accepted."

His stomach clenched with anticipation as she cupped his cheeks with her palms and leaned closer to brush her lips softly over his. The tip of her tongue licked his lower lip and he opened his mouth, allowing her to deepen their kiss.

Mateo's eyes drifted shut. Desire consumed him as their

tongues tangled, stroked, savoring the intimacy. Needing more, he clasped her waist and dragged her closer. She whimpered and he jerked back, realizing her sore ankle was on the couch between them.

"Here, move down." She pushed his shoulders, indicating he should slide to the far end. Then she straightened her leg, tucking it against the back seat cushion and scooting her ass toward him until she lay across the full length of the couch.

He kneeled between her legs, tipping forward, a forearm braced on either side of her until his torso hovered inches above hers. "You sure about this?"

"One hundred percent." As if he might doubt her words, Vanessa clasped her hands behind his head and drew him down on top of her.

Her soft curves molded to the harder ridges and planes of his body. Like yin to yang, they fit perfectly together. Arching up, she suckled his earlobe in her warm mouth, traced the curve of her ear with her tongue. Mateo strained against her and she rocked her pelvis against his. He groaned with pleasure-pain as their bodies rubbed against each other, dry humping as if they were teens making out in his familia's living room.

Mateo claimed her mouth, hungry for her taste. For all of her. Their tongues twisted and stroked, while his hands molded her breasts in his palms. He reveled as her nipples tightened in response.

She moaned her pleasure, nipping his lower lip with her teeth, then laving it with her tongue. He trailed a hand up the smooth skin along her inner thigh, seeking the secret spot he knew would bring her more pleasure. His fingers traced the edge of her panties, and his cock pulsed with the need to be inside her. To make her feel as out of control as he was quickly becoming.

"Yes," she murmured, rocking her hips in encouragement. "Touch me."

He didn't need to be told twice. Gently pushing her panties

aside, he slid a finger between her folds. She was wet and ready and his cock throbbed in his shorts. He slid his finger in, then slowly withdrew it. Her low, throaty moan met his second thrust, and he added a second finger, filling her tightness. His thumb circled her clit and she bucked her hips, a harsh "Yes" falling from her kiss-swollen lips.

Her hands explored his back as her teeth grazed his neck, his jaw, his chin.

"You taste so fucking delicious," she murmured.

He answered by dipping lower to suckle her breasts through her bra and dress, craving the taste of her skin. His body thrummed with the need to feel her naked and soft under him.

"You're overdressed," he growled.

"That goes both ways, papito."

"I know how to fix—" The sound of his phone vibrating on the metal table interrupted him.

Vanessa paused her handsy exploration of his back with a muttered "Ay, what crappy timing."

His phone continued its dance along the far edge of the table, signaling a call. Mateo pushed up onto his knees. Vanessa scooted backward so she could sit up again.

"Damn phone," he complained, adjusting himself in his basketball shorts.

Vanessa snickered as she eyed the tent action no amount of adjusting on his part could hide. She reached for her phone and pressed the on-off button.

Jeff's name scrolled across Mateo's cell screen. "I'd better take this, then send a text to my mom."

"Sure. I'll make my calls from the bathroom after I freshen up so we can both have some privacy."

Mateo watched as she limped to the bathroom, claiming her ankle was already feeling better. His phone silenced, then immediately began vibrating with a second call from Jeff. As soon as the bathroom door closed behind Vanessa, Mateo slid his thumb across the screen.

"How the hell are things over there?" Jeff asked by way of greeting.

Striding around the corner to the kitchen, Mateo quickly filled his best friend in on the surprising turn of events, starting with *Clemente*'s opening-night disaster.

"Shit, that sucks, man!"

"Hold up. Let me put you on speakerphone so I can wash the dishes. My headphones are back in my room."

While Mateo cleaned, he continued updating his best friend. Jeff laughed at Vanessa's piggyback ride up Eighth Avenue and poked for more juicy details about their time in the apartment. Claiming, of course, that Nicole would want them.

"So, you're buttering her up, gunning for a good review this time?" Jeff teased, knowing full well that was the last thing Mateo would do. "Hoping a little Garza charm up close and personal will do the trick?"

"Yeah, that's it," Mateo joked back. "You know me, do whatever has to be done for *Clemente*. Always willing to take one for the team."

Mateo swiped at the counter, mopping up water and crumbs, shaking his head as if his buddy could see his *Yeah, right* smirk.

Jeff had urged him to reach out to Vanessa, use their high school history as an in, after her nasty review for *Sin with Me*. Mateo had insisted he had no interest in using their loose connection for his professional gain. When the time was right . . . if it was ever right . . . he'd approach her about drinks, or coffee, or whatever she felt comfortable with. No shop talk. No smoke and mirrors like he normally used with the media.

His interest in her had absolutely nothing to do with their professional lives. He wanted to keep the two separate.

Just like this evening.

And tonight . . . Tonight had far exceeded Mateo's expectations.

A sound out in the foyer area drew his attention. "Hey, Jeff, let me go. I need to text my parents, then check on Vanessa. She'll probably need another veggie pack for her ankle."

"Yes, go pamper her. Heed my advice. And Nicole's. She's anxious to meet Vanessa for a couples' night."

After cautioning his friends to slow their roll, Mateo hung up, then reached for the kitchen towel to dry his hands.

"Vanessa? You doing okay?" he called.

No answer.

He strolled out of the kitchen and spotted the open bathroom door in the shadowy hallway off to the left. That was strange. A few steps later he found the living room empty. Unease trickled down his spine as he hurried to the foyer. Vanessa's small tote was missing from the entry table where he had dropped his keys into the glass bowl. Keys that were now gone.

Had she headed up to the rooftop patio alone?

During trivia he had wondered aloud if the stars might be visible with the city lights darkened. But why would she go up without mentioning it to him?

Unless.

An evil thought took root in Mateo's mind, quickly sprouting and growing as fast as Audrey II, the nefarious blood-sucking plant in *Little Shop of Horrors*.

¡Coño! Had she overheard Jeff's idiotic remarks about buttering her up?

Mateo burst into the hallway outside his apartment. He raced toward the stairs at the end, pushing open the door and glancing down the five flights. Empty. A grunt above him had Mateo leaning over the rail again, straining his eyes as he peered up the two flights above him.

Sure enough, there was Vanessa, limp-hopping up the steps, relying on the rail for help.

He took the stairs by twos and threes, desperate to reach her. To explain Jeff's stupid way of needling him.

At the top landing, he spotted her, barefoot like him, standing in the open doorway leading to the rooftop patio.

"Vanessa! Wait!"

She turned back, her expression mutinous. And hurt.

"Leave me alone," she cried. "I'll hang out here until morning. Then I'll call a car to take me home."

"Let me explain."

"That's okay, there's no need."

With that, she hobbled outside, taking the key that would unlock the roof door with her.

Mateo raced up the stairs, shouldering the door open just before it closed. He followed her outside, searching for her under the moonlight.

He finally spotted her, curled up in one of the wicker ottomans grouped around the circular bricked gas fireplace. She rested her forehead on her bent knees, right foot planted on the seat cushion, her left one held slightly aloft, arms wrapped around her shins as if she were hugging herself. Protecting herself from pain.

Pain caused unintentionally by him and Jeff but caused just the same.

Shame soured Mateo's mouth. He approached her slowly, but the crunch of the indoor-outdoor carpet gave him away.

"I said leave me alone," she muttered.

"Please, let me explain."

Heart in his throat, he waited, never wanting anything else as badly as he wanted a chance to make things right with her.

# Chapter 9

Vanessa felt more than heard Mateo approaching, despite her request for him to go away. Her muscles tightened as if preparing for a blow. But he'd already delivered one.

He and Jeff, whom she didn't know but had come to like. Even looked forward to maybe going on one of those double dates that Nicole apparently teased Mateo about.

That wouldn't happen. Not now.

Not if what she'd overheard was the truth.

A lump lodged in her throat, all sharp and jagged edged. She tried to swallow it, telling herself she deserved the discomfort after her foolishness in opening up to him. Damn it, she *knew* better.

Forehead pressed against her knees, she tucked her face into the crook of her arm. Why couldn't this night hurry up and end?

Back in the apartment, she hadn't been able to reach Ria or Alison. Which left her nervous and worried. Especially given Alison's particular plans.

Earlier, Vanessa had been excited to share how great her night had gone. That she had followed their advice and mustered up the courage to apologize. To lower the shield they always warned might keep her safe from being hurt but also kept her from experiencing the joy of connecting with someone. So, she'd taken a leap of faith and had been rewarded with mind-numbing kisses and the very real prospect of hot sex with an even hotter, sweeter guy than she could have imagined.

Ha!

Silver lining . . . she hadn't gushed to the girls so she wouldn't have to take it back. Plus, she and Mateo had stopped short of sleeping together, thanks to those interruptions. That meant one less regret about her night.

"Vanessa, please let me explain," Mateo repeated, closer this time.

His deep voice dripped with remorse. Maybe a dash of what sounded like sincerity.

The fake grass carpeting crunched, alerting her that he drew near. She peeked under her arm to find Mateo hunkered down in front of the wicker ottoman where she sat.

"I'm guessing you overheard Jeff being a silly ass. Pushing my buttons like he's wont to do. And me responding tongue in cheek, like usual. We have this sort of Abbott and Costello bit we've perfected since college."

"I'm supposed to buy that?" she asked, head still buried in her arms, aware she sounded childish. "Go back to your apartment. I'll be fine here alone. You don't owe me an apology."

"I know."

She sat up, surprised. "Excuse me?"

"You deserve an explanation from me. Same as I'd appreciate an explanation for why you immediately thought the worst of me and ran off."

Mateo wrapped his big hand around her left lower calf and applied gentle pressure. She relaxed, letting him straighten her leg to rest on top of his raised knees. Elevating her injured ankle.

His sweet gesture negated the harsh words about his selfishness she had muttered on her painful trek up the stairs.

"Maybe it's better if we go to our separate corners for the

rest of the night. Me up here. You back in your apartment," she suggested.

Her soul felt battered from her earlier admissions. Another heart-to-heart with him, given that she may have—probably had—overreacted, might leave her a blubbering mess, and she did not like to ugly cry in front of others. Especially a guy she'd been lusting after, secretly, for over a decade.

"I couldn't do that even if I wanted to," Mateo said. "Which I don't."

"You're speaking in riddles. Why?"

The moonlight cast his handsome face in shadows, which made it difficult for her to read his expression, but he hitched a muscular shoulder in a half-hearted shrug. "I didn't remember Freddie's warning about using the wooden block until after the door closed."

She gasped, sitting up and twisting her torso around to find the rooftop door closed.

"We'll have to give him a call to come open it for us," Mateo said. "Is your phone working? I ran out and left mine on the kitchen counter."

"Um." She slumped down in the ottoman, loath to admit she'd left hers behind, too.

*Dios mío*, could this situation get any worse?

Before she finished the thought, Vanessa rapped her knuckles on the ottoman's wicker stand. It was almost like knocking on wood, wasn't it? At this rate, she didn't want to tempt fate or the blackout gods or any entity. Her ill-conceived—okay, spur-of-the-moment, whatever—plan to get away from him had grossly backfired.

"Hand me your phone and I'll give Freddie a call." Mateo held his palm up toward her.

"I can't," she mumbled, angling away from him and resting her chin on top of her knee. Annoyed with herself, almost as much as she was with him. And that was saying a lot.

"Why not?"

"Because mine's downstairs next to the bathroom sink," she mumbled.

"What?" His slack-jawed shock mirrored the dismay swirling in her stomach. "Why the hell would you do that?"

"Excuse me, Mr. I Left My Phone Behind Too!" She huffed out an exasperated breath, embarrassed yet still hurt by his earlier words. "Excuse me if, after hearing you and Jeff, I didn't think about my phone, or lack of shoes, or the fact that storming down the hallway and lugging my ass up two freaking flights of stairs would make my ankle hurt like hell! So, my phone, like yours, is back in your damn apartment doing me a fat lot of good. And now I'm stuck up here with . . . with you, you . . . dumb jerk."

She jabbed a fist at his biceps in frustration, words failing her in a way they rarely did.

He took her lame punch, but grasped her wrist, refusing to let her go when she tugged on her arm. Instead, he slid his hand down to intertwine their fingers.

"Damn, we really make a good pair, don't we?" The self-deprecating humor lacing his voice made her chest tighten. Unshed tears burned her eyes.

"Stop. This won't work." She turned her head away, staring at the darkened Central Park less than a block away. Its towering treetops shadowy humps under the moonlight. He'd been right. With the normal glow of city lights absent, a tapestry of stars glittered across the inky-black sky. It reminded her of nights at St. Pete Beach and trips to Sanibel Island with her familia. Late nights sprawled on a shared blanket draped over the sand. In the before times. Before her father's duplicity and the depths of her mami's codependency were revealed.

Vanessa promised herself years ago never to fall prey to the same unhealthy relationship as her parents. Having no relationship was better than being in a hurtful one.

"I'm sorry," Mateo said, lowering her foot to the fake grass and edging closer. "I have nothing but respect for you. But, given what you shared earlier, I can see how you might have misconstrued our joking."

She let her eyes drift closed, her heart wanting to believe him. Trust him. Experience and pain cautioning her.

"I would never use the tentative friendship you and I had, much less any adult relationship we've formed tonight. I'm not hardwired that way. You deserve better than that, Vanessa. I want to treat you, give you, better than that."

His words rained down on the fires of hurt and humiliation burning inside her. Even as she told herself to fan their flames, drive him away. Save herself from further pain down the road.

Only, he wasn't leaving. And she wasn't really sure she wanted him to.

He had scooted close enough to rise up on his knees, place his hands on either side of her hips, and meet her almost eye to eye. He gazed at her, the reflection of stars above glittering in his nearly black irises.

"You're the 'she' Nicole referred to in her note. The one I'm supposed to play nice with. Hoping, praying, you'll surprise me. And you have. God, you have." He dragged in a shaky breath. Combed a hand through his hair, leaving it mussed. "For a long time now, I've been a skeleton of the friend they've both known for years. Too wrapped up in *Clemente* and the responsibility I've taken on to think about anything or anyone else. Except you."

He cupped her cheek, and his thumb swiped a lone tear from her cheek. "So, I'd go to charity events, attend wrap parties with friends or on my own, while finagling a way to get myself seated at your table. But I'm tired of fake dates and feeling alone. Of not having a special someone to celebrate, commiserate, and curse fate with when crap like a blackout happens. If the lights go out again, there isn't anyone else I want to carry piggyback down Eighth Ave. or firefighter toss over my shoulder, treating me to a glimpse of her shapely butt. No one else

I'd willingly lose theatre trivia to if my consolation prize is more time with you. I—"

Vanessa shushed him with a close-mouthed kiss.

"I'm sorry, too," she admitted. "I overreacted. It's something my therapist and I often discuss. But I'd like to work on it, get better at trusting. With you. If you don't mind another passion project?"

He stared at her intently, and she held her breath. Praying her baggage wasn't too much of a load when he already carried so much on his shoulders.

Her heart soared when he grinned and his dimple winked at her. Then he scooped her up in his arms to spin her around. She laughed and grabbed on to his shoulders, throwing her head back to watch the stars circling above them.

"I take it that's a yes?" she asked, moments later when he sat her back on the ottoman and knelt in the space between her knees.

"Most definitely."

He bent to brush her lips with his, and she wrapped her arms around his waist. Their tongues mated, slow and sensual. As if they knew they had time now. No rushing to fit it all into one reality-suspended night.

Mateo cupped her jaw, his gentle touch making her feel precious and safe. She rubbed her hands along his broad back and reveled at his steely strength.

Their kiss deepened, then softened. She sucked on his lower lip. He nibbled along her jaw, then covered her mouth with his once more before they eventually pulled apart. Both gasping for breath but all smiles for each other.

"I'm sorry we hurt you," Mateo said, leaning his forehead against hers.

"I shouldn't have run. Old wounds still not healed. But being with you makes me want to heal them. Trust again."

She finger-combed his hair, her heart warming at the sincerity shining in his eyes.

"You want to trust. I'll do my best to earn it," he promised, pressing a kiss to her forehead.

"You need someone to remind you to stop and enjoy the fruits of your labor. I'd like to try and be that someone for you. I don't mind beating you at trivia and making out on your sofa, walking into a charity luncheon together instead of accidentally on purpose winding up at the same table. Deal?"

He nuzzled her nose with his. Ducked down to press a chaste kiss to her lips.

"Deal," he whispered.

Later, curled up on the patio sofa, wrapped in each other's arms, they watched the sunrise over Central Park. Kissed long and slow while dawn spread its pale yellow light over their city. Traffic bustled, horns blared, streetlights finally flickered on. The power outage was over.

Vanessa and Mateo stayed in their secret hideout a little longer, murmuring plans and promises, and, yes, she beat him at one last round of trivia.

Her prize . . . a toe-curling, lady-parts-tingling kiss from her leading man. And a piggyback ride down to his apartment when Freddie's relief made his check of the premises and wound up setting them free.

Back down in the apartment, while Mateo turned on the Keurig for their morning coffee, Vanessa found a "checking in" text from Ria.

Alison hadn't answered yet, so Vanessa quickly tapped out her response to her best friends: *You are not going to believe the AH-mazing night I had. Are we still on for Sag Harbor? Must share details . . . ALL GOOD!*

Mateo stepped around the corner from the kitchen into the hallway, two steaming cups of coffee in his hands, a broad smile softening his chiseled good looks. His dimple winked at her, and Vanessa found herself happily falling a little more for the guy who might just be her perfect leading man.

# Acknowledgments

Like all my books, the novella *Lights Out* came to fruition in part thanks to many others who helped or guided me at some point during the process. Muchísimas gracias to the following people for their love, support, and assistance:

Monica, Barbara, Jamie, Amy, Sabrina . . . the insight and advice you shared via your beta reading & feedback are truly, *truly* appreciated!

Tammie W. with the Shubert Organization who answered my "strange question" emails in the midst of a pandemic and provided insider info about the theatre since lockdown wouldn't allow me to visit again in person; I hope to safely catch another show at the Booth one day soon!

Jeff and Alexa, your brainstorming help led to a key scene near the end and your shared excitement for this novella fed mine! Looking forward to toasting this one together!

My editors, Esi and Norma—our Zoom chat provided beneficial insight about acting/actors, life in the city, and more, aiding me with infusing some believeability into both Mateo's and Vanessa's characters, while our chat also refilled my emotional well!

My agent, Rebecca, you're an amazing pep talk giver in the midst of my writing life madness! I sincerely appreciate having you on my team!

Maureen Lee Lenker, our phone chat allowed me to fill in Vanessa's resume at *The Fix* and get a better feel for her potential writing career. Here's to more beach days for us both!

Mia, Sabrina, and Alexis—our 4ChicasChat bond is fierce; I'm so blessed that we have each other in our corner!

The LatinxRom author comunidad, somos pocos pero creciendo (we're small but growing); mil gracias por su apoyo y amistad (a thousand thanks for your support and kinship)!

Mi familia, I hope reading this novella fills you with the same warmth and love that writing about memories of Gueli, the game we worship thanks to her, the Broadway shows we've attended together, and the city we all adore brought me. ¡Los quiero mucho!

# Mind Games

## SARAH SKILTON

*For my amazing sister, Rachel*

# Chapter 1

"Are you smiling or frowning?" Honey asked.

The nine-year-old's classmates had vanished ten minutes ago, enveloped by loud, cooing sounds of praise from parents and grandparents regarding the day's artwork. To keep Honey's mind off her being the last student to be picked up from Smocks & Brushes summer camp, Alison had volunteered as a portrait model.

The smell of warm, wet clay permeated the room. Outside, the city dripped with heat. Thankfully, periodic blasts of cold air from the newly installed air conditioner cut through the bog, courtesy of a fundraiser last Christmas.

Honey waited patiently for an answer, her charcoal pencil poised above her sketch pad.

"That's a good question. What do you see in my expression?" Alison asked.

Honey's nose scrunched up in concentration. Alison stifled a laugh; she couldn't remember the last time she'd been subjected to such scrutiny.

"There's no wrong answer," Alison assured her. "And no mistakes in art, right?"

Honey nodded. "I don't mean to be rude, but . . . you look angry, but also like you're happy about it."

Alison's hearty cackle startled them both. Honey was one hundred percent correct. Alison had felt "angry but happy about it" all day. (All week. All month.) She'd woken with vengeance in her heart, deliriously giddy over the knowledge that tonight golden-haired, happy-go-lucky Nicholas Finn would discover how it felt to have years of hard work used against him as fodder for mockery.

Her anticipation over this long-delayed righting of wrongs had grown with each passing minute, ticking ever closer to her impending victory this evening at the Ace Hotel, where Nick would be performing an intimate magic show.

Ideally, Alison hoped to join him onstage as a volunteer assistant. If he didn't select her, however, she could inflict damage via heckling. Not obnoxious heckling, no—her revenge would be subtle. A well-timed remark, delivered in a guileless voice: "Ohhhh, it was magnets, wasn't it?" or "He pocketed the card! Who else saw?"

Death by a thousand cuts.

Exposing his tricks wouldn't only affect Nick, of course. The dozen or so people in the audience would suffer collateral damage, and she felt conflicted about that, but they could always get their money back. They could always return another time to see a magician who *hadn't* forced Alison to transfer colleges senior year on a wave of embarrassment that, five years later, still sent shudders through her whenever she thought about it.

When the only man you've ever loved slips a shiv through your heart while you lie in his bed for the first time, naked and vulnerable—you don't easily forget it.

She'd studied hard for this assignment.

Six weeks ago, when she'd learned about Nick's performance, she'd realized revenge was within reach. Was she willing to put all her old study habits to use?

Yes. Yes, she was.

She glanced at Honey's drawing, which depicted a woman on the verge of triumph. At least, that's how Alison chose to interpret the image.

"Why are you dressed up?" Honey asked, sketching two neat slashes in opposite directions to indicate Alison's shoulders. Honey then bisected those lines to show the straps of Alison's little black dress, which Alison had changed into moments ago.

The dress was backless save for a delicate $X$ crisscrossing her bare skin. A princess-seamed bodice and plunging neckline, snug enough to keep her contained sans bra, completed the upper half of the design. The fitted waist flared into a skirt whose hem hit midthigh, making her legs look endless. She'd felt like a naughty ice-skater the first time she tried it on.

The cardigan she wore concealed the more risqué elements of the dress, but Honey's eyes were saucers as she looked Alison up and down.

"Are you going on a date?"

"No, oh, no," Alison corrected her student. Why did her heart race at the word *date*? "Just a . . ." *Well-planned attack.* "An evening of surprises. A boy I once knew is doing a magic show. So, hopefully it'll be fun."

*For me, anyway. For him it will be decidedly less so.* Out came that devilish grin again, curling the edges of her lips.

"Want to see?" Alison tugged a wrinkled printout from her purse and placed it on the table. The edges of the paper were torn from where she'd taped it to her desk at home for motivation.

Below a glossy image of Nick's smirkingly flawless face, a paragraph of hyperbole advertised, *In the heart of Manhattan, overlooking Central Park, the Ace Hotel on W. 80th presents master magician Nicholas Finn, in his New York City debut. Prestidigitation! Legerdemain! Feats of Mental Acuity that will leave you astonished and delighted! 90 minutes, $75 per person (drinks included)!*

Alison hadn't dated anyone in months. Her previous little black dresses covered a lot more of her slim frame and had only been worn during fundraisers for Smocks & Brushes. When it wasn't a summer camp, it operated as a nonprofit, low-cost after-school program: art lessons, tutoring, and homework help, with extended care offered until 6:00 p.m.

Her weekends were spent chasing down donors and prepping for the week ahead; hanging out with Ria and Vanessa when they were free; and, since May, obsessively viewing magic instruction DVDs as research. A yard sale in June had provided a bounty of magic material, and—in her mind—direct confirmation that the universe was on her side.

Her lack of "going-out" dresses wasn't the only reason for her limited social life. Dating had never come naturally to her, and the prospect of physical *or* emotional intimacy made her stomach hurt.

She had Nick to thank for that, as well.

As Honey continued sketching, Alison's gaze landed on the artist quote she'd pinned to the corkboard that week:

IN THE LONG RUN, THE SHARPEST WEAPON OF ALL IS A KIND AND GENTLE SPIRIT.—FRANZ MARC

She rolled her eyes. That was a fine message for children, but in the real world it meant jack crap.

She averted her gaze from the quote and batted away any lingering misgivings as though they were badminton birdies, which would hopefully be the sport on tap in Sag Harbor tomorrow, when this was all behind her.

Honey smiled. "Will there be a rabbit?"

"I don't think he works with animals."

*The Ace Hotel would never allow that, would they? Shit.* She'd made the assumption at the beginning of Operation: Magician Downfall that no animals would be involved. What if Nick showed up with a menagerie? She'd be useless against that. . . .

Alison swallowed hard. "But if he does, I'll be sure to tell you about it on Monday."

The dove refused to cooperate.

Nick's mentor, The Amazing Arthur, had a way of soothing the birds by holding them in one hand and applying pressure to the backs of their necks with the fingers of his other hand. When Nick tried that maneuver, the bird shit in his palm and dive-bombed away.

Scrubbing his hands clean and frowning at his reflection in the bathroom mirror, Nick took stock of the bird situation. *Arthur doesn't expect you to re-create his show,* he reminded himself for what felt like the millionth time. *He gave you permission to use his illusions, but only as a base from which to build your own lineup.*

At eighty-eight, Arthur remained razor-sharp intellectually, but when he broke his wrist and twisted his ankle during a fall, the siren song of retirement proved too seductive to ignore. Hotel management was ready to shutter the show and move on, until Arthur convinced them to hold auditions for a replacement and update the event for a younger crowd.

"Auditions?" Nick had fumed. "No fucking way." He was supposed to inherit Amazing Arthur's show, end of story.

At least, that had been the plan.

"You'll be the obvious front-runner," Amazing Arthur boomed happily. His eyes twinkled; he thought this turn of events was marvelous. "You'll benefit from the comparisons to lesser performers, and management will feel as though they've conducted due diligence. You can't *tell* people you're the best, you have to show them. So, let's show them!"

In other words, the dove had to go, Nick decided. Anything less than perfection would kill his chances.

Pacing the length of the room, an hour before showtime, Nick rearranged his set list to highlight his strengths and jettison his weaknesses. A ninety-minute parlor show with one intermission meant he couldn't front-load the first act with his best material; he had to spread things out, work the audience higher and higher toward an unforgettable climax that would leave them panting for more.

So to speak.

Nick thrived on the adrenaline that came from last-minute decision-making. He'd been the same way in college, pulling all-nighters on the eve of exams and waiting till the morning of to complete his term papers. His friends at the time—if they were even his friends, which in retrospect seemed unlikely—had nicknamed him Slick Nick because of his ability to sweet-talk his way out of any consequences to his actions. Whether it was a paper turned in late, too many absences, drunk and disorderly in the quad, or—

Well, there was that *one* consequence he hadn't been able to sweet-talk himself out of. The one that haunted him to this day, five years on.

He shook his head to dispel the memory. Flicked his collar down and studied himself in the gilt-framed mirror resting against the wall. His thick blond hair, prone to cowlicks now that he kept it short, was smoothed down and combed into a part, sideburns neatly trimmed. At six feet and lean, he cut a sharp figure in his crisp white button-down, blazer, and dark blue jeans over jackboots.

It drove his roommate crazy that Nick eschewed formal wear onstage. ("How do you not own a tuxedo? How will people even know you're a magician?")

Laypeople who assumed magicians required costumes had misinterpreted the past. The only reason magicians in previous eras carried silk handkerchiefs and squeezed themselves into tuxedos, cummerbunds, spats, bow ties, and top hats was because at the time that's what gentlemen wore for an evening at the theatre. *All* gentlemen.

Magicians hadn't been dressing up when they donned those outfits. They'd been blending in. It was the same reason David Blaine wore a T-shirt and jeans: that's what spectators of modern street magic wore.

Following those examples, Nick's collared shirt, blazer, and denim perfectly matched his audience's cocktail attire, and he used pens, cards, coins, and dollar bills for his illusions. They were commonplace, everyday items, the way top hats used to be.

A special outfit was pointless. His skill with magic spoke for itself.

The hotel suite serving as his performance space comfortably seated twelve people, one of whom would be analyzing the audience's reactions and either handing him a contract afterward or tearing one up. His competitors had flogged their wares last month. Now it was Nick's turn, and the final night of auditions. (Arthur had engineered it that way because the older man believed going last gave Nick an advantage.)

Ten minutes to showtime. Cards? Check. Coins? Check. Flash paper? Check and check. He preferred close-up magic, which was exactly what it sounded like: illusions performed inches from spectators' eyes, with objects that could be examined before and after. For the grand finale he'd throw in a little mentalism.

He cracked his knuckles, flexed his fingers, and gently rotated his neck. He positioned his custom-made table so it tilted toward the audience; placed his velvet close-up pad on top and rolled a lint remover across it; squared each deck of cards; neatly stacked his quarters; and rearranged his pitcher of water. Good. Everything was exactly where he wanted it.

Decked out as a casual performance space with chairs and a wardrobe closet, the suite contained secrets befitting its occupant: a small bar that sprang to life complete with mixologist at intermission (he or she entered via a trapdoor), and a hidden passage embedded in the bookshelves that opened into an adjoining bedroom. Nick was welcome to use the bedroom between sets and to sleep there at the end of the night if he chose. It was into that sanctuary he retreated when the sound of guests in the hall reached his ears.

A hole in the wall allowed him to observe everyone who entered the performance suite. Arthur had taught him to assess his audience beforehand whenever possible. If you see a drunk person, don't let them near the props. If you see someone using a walker or a wheelchair, go to them where they are for help with a trick, don't force them to maneuver through the aisle toward you.

A young white woman with chestnut hair that tumbled past her shoulders glided into the room. She wore a flirty, form-fitting black dress. The material gripped her slender waist as though painted on, then flared outward like a bell. A bell, he couldn't help but notice, that rocked from side to side. His gaze locked on to her twitching hips, then slid down her lovely bare legs, to discover her feet were encased in . . . tennis shoes, laces flap-snapping to the beat as she strutted through the room.

Why the hell did he find that sexy?

She turned to make pleasantries with another audience member, and his breath caught at the sight: her entire back was exposed, elegant and smooth and tender, save for tiny twin straps that crossed in a barely there *X* from each shoulder down to her hips.

She'd come here alone.

Glancing left and right, she positioned herself in the first row, dead center, and removed her tennis shoes, stuffed them in a bag, and replaced them with a pair of black kitten heels.

Ah, right. New York women knew all the survival tricks of a city made for walking. "Stash your heels until you arrive at the office / party" was probably their first lesson.

The room filled up and chatter ricocheted off the walls, but he couldn't tear his eyes from the woman with chestnut hair. Even the delicate ridge of her collarbone entranced him.

Her eyes appeared to meet his and he nearly staggered back, caught, until he realized she had no idea he was there; she was merely perusing the bookshelves. Because that's what she would do, of course, because she was . . .

His body figured it out before he did.

A bead of sweat gathered along his hairline, his throat ached, and his heart tripped forward as though he'd been pushed down a flight of stairs, his face smacking into each step as he fell.

He tilted his bottle of water to his dry, chapped lips and gulped heavily, his Adam's apple bobbing, until drops spilled onto his shirt. He wiped helplessly at them, never tearing his eyes from the woman.

She might be glammed up, and she might have ditched her glasses, but it was her.

Alison Cahill.

The consequence who got away.

# Chapter 2

Her affair with Nick started at the campus library.

(It couldn't have started anywhere else; she never *went* anywhere else.)

Friday night, fall of senior year, and Alison was studying.

It didn't feel like senior year, though; not to her, because she was only twenty years old. She'd chosen Shippensburg University in Pennsylvania because of its accelerated BSBA program. Having arrived with four AP credits from high school, she'd entered as a sophomore, guaranteed to graduate in three years. Saving a year's tuition, plus the fact that she already lived on the East Coast, meant "the Ship" was a sweet deal.

According to her father.

Was she passionate about her major? Not particularly; but her getting a degree in business was not up for debate, so widgets it was. Supply and demand. Profit margins. (ROI. B2B. They sounded like robots from a *Star Wars* film. Hell, maybe they were; she hadn't gone to the movies in ages.) No aspect of the business mind-set came naturally to her, which was why it was vital she succeed, and success meant no social life. She spent every waking minute studying her ass off.

She'd seen Nick around, of course. He was *pretty*. He was a business major, too, so it was inevitable they'd wind up in lecture halls together. He'd sat next to her once, sophomore year (which felt like freshman year to her), all ripped jeans, bleached-blond hair, and lightweight hoodie. He'd flashed her a smile so molten it made her insides clench.

She'd avoided him ever since.

As far as she could tell, he never took notes in class. The beginning of senior year, however, something changed. The entire month of September he'd barely looked up from his laptop, fingers flying across the keys. Had someone laid down the law at home? Tied his grade point average to tuition payments, the way her father had?

Friday night, 9:55 p.m., early October. The library would close in five minutes. Outside, all was dark except for the fuzzy glow from the campus streetlights, and inside, all was quiet except for the shuffling murmur of students gathering their items to leave. Alison wished she could stay another hour, inside the warmth and light and comfort of the library.

Suppressing a yawn, she ducked into the bathroom. When she returned for her belongings, Nick was there, elbows on the table, sitting across from her chair. People shared tables all the time, but why would he bother to do so right before closing?

The air between them crackled as he ran a hand through his floppy golden hair and looked up at her. His sudden appearance provoked an out-of-body sensation she'd not experienced since the previous Christmas when her car was stolen from the airport parking lot. She usually drove home to Brooklyn, but that year she'd taken a puddle jumper.

*A fork in the road,* she'd thought, tears poking at her eyes as she wandered around in the cold for half an hour. *This is how the next phase of my life begins. Filling out paperwork at a police station, trying to find money for a used car because Dad will blame me for this and tell me to take responsibility and get a part-time job, which will only cut into my studies, and then where will*

*I be? Screwed, that's where.* . . . And then she remembered she'd taken the bus to the airport; hadn't trusted her driving abilities after the stress and sleepless nights of final exams.

Unlike the "stolen" car, the moment in the library did turn out to be a fork in the road. Just not for the reasons she'd believed at the time.

"I'm in serious need of coffee," Nick said. "How about you? My treat."

She lived off campus by herself, in the bottom unit of a duplex that her dad owned and managed. Her father's presence was everywhere in the building, but it wasn't as though he *lived* there. He wouldn't know if, just once, she threw caution to the wind and stayed out late for no reason other than she was sick of studying and wanted a break.

"Okay," she said, trying to figure out where to put her arms.

Nick smiled, the same sly smile she remembered from the day he'd sat next to her in the lecture hall. The smile that made her insides twist.

"Does State Street diner work?" he asked, tapping at his phone. "I'll text you the address."

On the drive over, she blasted the radio, carefree. Rain peppered the roof and windows of her car, her movements guided by cat's-eye lights in the misty streets. She liked that Nick hadn't offered to drive, putting her in a position where she might feel trapped in his car at the end of the night, beholden to his decision about when to leave, or how and whether to linger in her driveway afterward. This way, they arrived separately and could leave separately.

It made her feel safe with him.

According to the neon sign in the window, the diner was open 24-7 and served breakfast around the clock. By the time she walked inside and retracted her damp umbrella, Nick had commandeered a corner booth, where a mug of steaming-hot coffee waited for her.

His hair was scattered across his forehead, wet and darkened from the rain. He looked as though he'd just gotten out of the shower. The idea of Nick in nothing but a towel made Alison blush.

"I should have asked if you wanted something stronger," he remarked, scooching along the bench to make room for her.

"Oh, no, thanks."

"Don't drink?"

"Can't drink." She shrugged. "I'm only twenty."

He laughed. Then he stopped. "Oh, you—you were serious." He cleared his throat and leaned toward her. Alison's heart fluttered in her chest, and she unconsciously mirrored his actions, moving closer to him. He smelled strongly of coffee and faintly of Old Spice.

"I'm going to tell you a secret," Nick whispered behind his large hand. "If you asked an upperclassman, and you batted those deadly eyelashes of yours, he would probably buy you a glass of something."

She affected the same whispering tone. "I *am* an upperclassman."

He leaned back, his expression curious, and she felt the loss of his nearness.

"How is it you're only twenty, then? Did you skip a grade?"

"Like a jump rope."

"And how is it we've never hung out before? And how do you like the Ship? And where are you from? And what do you think of breakfast for dinner?"

She grinned shyly. "What should I answer first?"

They chatted, leaning inexorably closer to each other again, until the waitress placed a plate between them, piled high with triangles of sourdough bread slathered in glistening layers of strawberry jam and creamy butter.

Breakfast for dinner. Conjured on his command.

Nick thanked the waitress and brought a sticky-wet slice to his mouth. Around a grin, he said to Alison, "It's not so much a piece of toast as it is a delivery system for butter. If you like that sort of thing."

She did like that sort of thing. She liked the look of it, too, especially when Nick licked his fingers clean like a cat with a secret.

She was garishly happy inside that neon diner in the rain, next to glowing, golden Nick, drinking her black coffee and eating bread weighed down by decadent goo, her own body sinking into the red leather banquette with stuffing coming out. The pulsing in her belly didn't make her nervous. Rather, it calmed her, like a weight keeping her in place.

Talking with him was shockingly easy. Their words slid together like gears rolling over and under one another in a continuous motion, no hesitation, filling each other's empty spaces, and she thought to herself, *I know you*. As though they'd been friends for years. As though they'd be friends for years to come.

In the secret corners of her heart she dared to wish for something beyond friendship. But she'd take this, too. Anything to be near him.

They'd both been raised by single parents. He spoke of his mother with reverence. She spoke of her father with halting excuses.

Two hours of conversation later, they exited the diner into great sheets of rain and a flooded parking lot. Nick wore Doc Martens, but Alison's tennis shoes would never survive the giant puddle between here and her car.

"Piggyback it?" Nick offered, crouching down.

She hesitated, then repositioned her umbrella, climbed aboard and tightened her arms around him, laughing. When they reached her car, he bent forward, and she slid slowly down his back until her feet hit solid ground.

"Thanks so much for dinner. I mean breakfast. Or, I guess, snack." *Stop babbling*, she ordered herself.

"I had a lot of fun tonight. Bye, Alison." He saluted her and splashed toward his own car.

The weekend passed without further communication, so she chalked up Friday's event to an enjoyable one-off.

On Tuesday afternoon, he sent her a text: *Are you busy on Saturday?*

She was *never* busy on Saturdays. She liked that he didn't realize this about her, or that if he did, he pretended not to. In her mind it was charming, old-fashioned; he'd taken on the persona of a gentleman caller who sent his request early in the week to beat out the other suitors.

Her response: *I'm free.*

Her thought: *But only for you.*

No one else could have lured her away from her studies.

Baggy eyed but jocular, Nick arrived on Saturday morning at ten to pick her up. He'd vacuumed his car and packed every conceivable item they would need for a day of hiking at Pine Grove Furnace State Park: hoodies and rain slickers, an overflowing picnic basket, a scratchy burlap blanket, bottles of water, and a graphic novel he thought she might like.

By the time they arrived at the park, the sun had sliced through the clouds in wide beams of light, 60 percent in their favor. She quashed a twinge of disappointment that she'd have no reason to wear his hoodie.

They hiked for an hour. Torch-bright fall foliage dotted the dark green landscape, decorating the pine trees in bursts of crimson and rusty ocher.

They picnicked by Laurel Lake and she laughed when Nick poured wine into an actual thimble for her.

"I don't see any Pinkerton detectives," he said conspiratorially. "I think we're safe."

"Cheers." She clinked her thimble against his thermos. "Where'd you get the thimble? If you like to sew in your spare time, I have a dress that needs taking in."

His gaze roved down her body, igniting her skin. "I'll bet you do."

She thrust out her thimble—which had the Shippensburg Raiders logo on it—for more.

He dutifully poured from his thermos but didn't tilt back in time. A splatter of red hit the blanket. "Oops," he said.

She laughed. "A glass would be fine with lunch."

"Thank God." He handed her a paper cup from his thermal picnic bag and instead filled that with wine. It smelled of fermented blackberries but tasted considerably less sweet, hitting her insides in a decadent gush and warming her body against the crisp, cold air.

They feasted happily on sandwiches and pasta salad.

"My mom collects them," he said a while later. "Thimbles."

"Oh, yeah?"

"She doesn't travel much, but any place she goes, she picks one up. I built her a display case in shop class back in high school."

They talked about their hobbies. Hers was searching for early editions of *A Tree Grows in Brooklyn* in used bookstores. His was fantasy baseball, every Sunday night with his buddies.

Nick came from Scottish and Danish stock, which prompted visions in her mind of him on a golf course or a ski slope somewhere, pale and grinning, the cheeks and tips of his ears burned by a cold sun. His body looked strong and athletic—his hiking abilities confirmed it—but his face retained a bit of baby fat, and the combination stirred something within her. They were both young and they were having fun together with nowhere to be and no rush to get there, and when was the last time she'd allowed that of herself?

Nick pointed at her with his fork. "Tell me something you've never told anyone."

Maybe it was the wine, or the rush of connecting with someone new, but she didn't mince words: "I hate being a business major."

He looked surprised. "But you're so good at it."

"How do you know?"

"Professor Rand never stumps you, you hustle to and from class like you're possessed by the spirit of Andrew Carnegie, and you got . . . what, one hundred percent on the last three pop quizzes?"

"Ninety-eight."

"What would you rather study?"

"Art," she said instantly. "Art history, art restoration, anything with art." The words tumbled out, knocking into one another. How extraordinary to say them out loud! "Oh, oh, oh, and childhood development. Something combining the two would be ideal, but I'm not—"

He was staring at her.

It made her self-conscious. "What?"

"I love the way your eyes sparkled just now."

"Your turn," she countered, looking away.

He wiped his mouth with a napkin. "I hate being a business major, too."

She flicked her empty paper cup at him. "You can't use *mine*," she protested. "You have to tell me a different one."

"Fair enough." He bit his bottom lip and her eyes softened. "Your secret's safe with me. I'm putting it in the vault."

"I want to be a magician." They gazed at each other for a beat. "You're thinking, 'Okay, magic dork, make this date disappear,' aren't you?"

"No, not at all," she said quickly. "I'm surprised, but I think it's great. What's stopping you?" The word *date* reverberated in her head like a pinball, lighting up the walls of her mind.

"Besides the fact that none of my friends or family know, because if they did, they'd make fun of me? How about the fact that it's almost impossible to make a living from it? Anyway, there's this club in California, a private club for studying magic, so I've been saving up, trying to make enough money to fly out there over spring break."

By the time the picnic was over, they'd conceived and jotted down a five-year plan for Nick so he could make his magician dream a reality. She leaned against a tree and he rested his head in her lap.

"I wish I could be relaxed," she said, stroking his hair. "Like you."

His brow wrinkled. "You think I'm relaxed?"

A movement by the lake caught her attention.

"What is she doing?" Alison groaned.

"Who?"

Frowning, Alison stood on tipsy legs and wove toward the water, where an older woman sat on a bench flinging chunks of bread at a group of ravenous ducks.

"Stop! It's terrible for them!" she shouted to the bread lady.

Laughing, Nick wrapped his arms around her from behind, lifted her off the ground, and swung her back in the direction of their picnic before she could escalate the confrontation.

"It stops them from eating the foods they really need. It turns to algae in the lake. It ruins the ducklings' wings," she insisted.

"They love it. They can't get enough."

"That doesn't mean it's good for them."

"Dork." He nuzzled her neck.

"You're the dork," she countered, smiling. "But yours is worse because you're a secret dork. At least I own it."

His face lost something then. It drooped, as though she'd snipped the strings holding his smile up. She regretted her words, wanted to bring back jovial, languid, careless Nick.

So she kissed him.

He deepened the kiss and brushed his thumb lightly across her nipple, catching her gasp of pleasure in his mouth as though it were a prize.

They got lost in the corn maze at Maple Lane Pumpkin Patch that Halloween, calling out to each other in laughing shouts.

Long drives and snowball fights filled the weeks that followed, along with recurrent games of Tell Me Something You've Never Told Anyone.

"I lost someone important to me this year," he told her, eyes lowered, on one such occasion. "But I'm not ready to say anything else yet."

Most of the time, their confessions were silly. "I *hate* the word *guesstimate*," she said. "The word *estimate* already means you're guessing. *Guesstimate* is trying to be clever but it's just dumb!" In response, he kissed her all over her face until she squealed happily and squirmed in his arms.

For her twenty-first birthday, he presented her with a 1947 edition of *A Tree Grows in Brooklyn*. The card said, *For my own Francie Nolan. Love, that dude who follows you around.*

"Where did you get this?" she asked, eyes wide, heart expanding. If he'd gone antiquing, she wanted to join him next time. She was afraid to touch the book, afraid she'd mar it with her unworthy hands.

"I have my ways," he replied.

An inscription on the inside cover, in faded pencil, read, *To my darling daughter on her 12th birthday, 1980.*

An inverted birthday gift from a past generation: 12 and 21. She'd mentioned her hobby *once*, weeks ago, and he'd filed it away. She'd never felt so seen, so heard, or so desired as she did that semester with Nick.

She hugged the book to her chest, inhaled the smell of its musty pages.

They both remained on campus for Thanksgiving, king and queen of the empty quad, joined at the hip for breakfast, lunch, and dinner. Two weeks later, after the Saints and Sinners costume party in mid-December, they stumbled into Nick's dorm room.

Nick wore a pair of devil's ears over a suit and tie, while Alison had crafted an angel outfit of wings, halo, and a silky-white baby-doll dress.

Door locked behind them, alone at last, they stared at each other, breathing hard.

"Come here," he said. They tore fitfully at each other's clothes. She could swear steam rose from their skin in contrast to the arctic weather outside.

When she stood naked before him, he groaned appreciatively and dropped to his knees in front of her. She'd had sex precisely once in high school, and while it hadn't been bad, it hadn't been good, either.

"I've wanted to taste you for so long." He clutched her hips, nudged her gently backward onto his bed, and buried his face between her thighs. She gleamed and ached beneath his tongue, and a gaping slickness blossomed inside her.

When she came, it was nothing like her usual experience, nothing like the gently sloping rise and fall she occasionally gave herself. This orgasm wracked her body.

He didn't stop until tears of ecstasy formed in her eyes. She floated back into herself with a dreamy smile and an astonished giggle. Nick soothed her with kisses, up her belly, nibbling at her skin, along her collarbone, the curve of her neck and jaw, her cheeks, and finally her lips.

"You're amazing," she whispered, arms limp around his neck.

He grinned and kissed her more. Again, and again.

"Should I get a condom?" He stood in the moonlight, his cock jutting out between strong thighs. She stared in awe. She wanted to slide the warm, rubbery head of his dick over her lips, lap at him, give him what he'd given her. She didn't have any experience with that, but she knew Nick would teach her, that he'd be sweet and appreciative.

"Definitely."

"They're in the bathroom." He grinned again and pointed at her. "Don't go anywhere."

She laughed. As if she could walk right now, even if she wanted to! In his haste, Nick knocked into a desk chair, and it toppled over, sending a notebook to the floor.

Moments later, he emerged from the private bathroom, his expression frustrated, his dick at half-mast. "I need to run out. My roommate was *supposed to* replenish the supply—"

"Is he coming here?" She pulled the sheets to her chin.

"No, no. He already left for Christmas break. I'm just gonna . . . Shouldn't take long." He grabbed a pair of jeans and a T-shirt from his dresser, yanked them on, and leaned over for a lingering kiss.

He didn't bother with shoes or socks, just a ratty pair of flip-flops with which to canvass his dormmates. While he was gone, Alison smiled to herself and swayed over to the bathroom for a drink of water. On the way back, she righted the chair he'd knocked over, and her eyes fell on the overturned notebook. Inside were several loose sheets of paper, printed from a computer, showing a complicated grid with dates, abbreviations, numbers, and symbols.

"Fantasy Gunners," read the title at the top.

*His sports hobby—must be the betting ledger.* What was a gunner? An image of clay shooting came to her. She'd had no idea people kept track of—shooting ranges? She crouched to pick it up. A key code explained the abbreviations.

HU = Hand Up
CA = Correct Answer
IA = Incorrect Answer
TR = Test Result

Perplexed, she flipped to another page, which contained funny pictures and stats in rectangles framed by dotted lines, like baseball cards you could tear out and keep in your wallet.

Nick's team, Nick's Ninjas, consisted of two boys and a girl. Not a girl, though. Not really. A caricature of an upright swamp creature, complete with glasses and a wide, toothy grin.

One clawed hand delved between its legs. Its eyes were shut, like it was in pain. Or extreme pleasure.

"Alligator Masturbator," read the girl's title.

Alligator. Allie. Alison.

*It's me. This picture is of me.*

Memories from the past semester flickered through her brain: Nick's sudden enthusiasm for note-taking in class. The flurry of movement around her each time she answered a question posed by Professor Rand. Other students had been keeping track of her. *Nick* had been keeping track of her.

She couldn't breathe. Alligator Masturbator.

It must have been obvious to their entire graduating class that although she wasn't technically a virgin, she'd never been *ravished*, never been *tasted*. Not until tonight, with Nick. Was it also obvious to everyone that she'd never achieved orgasm with another person before, that she relied on her hand?

It must have been.

"Hey, baby." Nick's voice dripped warm honey as he stood in the doorway.

She must have looked stricken because the next instant he was beside her on the bed, stroking the back of her knuckles with his thumb. She jerked away.

His eyes sought hers out. "What's wrong?"

"What's a gunner?"

He dropped her hand. His Adam's apple twitched. "You went through my stuff."

"What's a gunner?"

He twisted a hand through his hair, pulling so hard his scalp showed. "It wasn't my idea. I'm sorry, okay? I'm . . ."

"What's a gunner? . . . Nick."

"Always gunning to be the best," he said tonelessly. "Gunning for valedictorian, gunning for teacher's pet, or extra credit, or the best score. Gunning to show how much smarter they are than the rest of us."

That last line was delivered with an edge, a bitterness he didn't bother to disguise, which forced her to confront the awful truth: She didn't know him. Not anymore.

"It's been a tough year," he said quietly. "I was going to quit school, more than once, but this gave me a reason to get out of bed in the morning, a reason to go to class—"

" 'It's been a tough year'?" she echoed, her voice full of tears. "You think I care?"

She picked up her discarded clothes from where they'd landed. A baby-doll dress and feathery wings. It was freezing outside, layers upon layers of ice. The only reason she'd made it to his dorm room from the parking lot without shivering to death was because he'd given her his suit jacket and kept his arm around her the whole way.

Nick rustled through his dresser for the second time that night. Found a sweater and a pair of jeans and held them out to her.

For weeks afterward, all through Christmas break in Brooklyn, the only thing she could think about were those ducks at the lake on the day of their picnic, how Nick had fed her compliment after compliment and she'd opened her mouth and swallowed each one down her greedy throat, stuffing herself with something she was never supposed to have.

Nick was the person she'd fled from, so why did it feel as though she'd left *herself* behind? Why did it feel as though she'd gone missing?

The first week of January, she transferred to Brooklyn College.

# Chapter 3

Nick had planned to tell her about Fantasy Gunners. Eventually. He was going to split the money with her and invite her to California with him on spring break. He was going to hold hands with her at the beach and sip frothy cocktails with her at the magic club.

He was going to buy a ring and get down on one knee.

In his dumb brain, he'd envisioned a sappy future in which they recollected the circumstances of their union to their kids. Her: "Daddy used to bet on how many times I would raise my hand in class." Him: "Your mom was electric, and Daddy admired her from afar."

He honestly thought she'd be amused by the whole thing. (Maybe not *Alligator Masturbator*—he'd voted for *Hermione Brain-ger*—but the concept.) Because if he knew one thing about Alison, it was that she didn't care what anyone thought of her. How he'd envied that about her! She *must* have heard classmates snickering, *must* have known people rolled their eyes at her, long before the game existed. Other people's responses never cowed her. She was always perfectly herself, while Nick hid behind a self-constructed illusion of nonchalance. What had she said that day by the lake? "You're a secret dork, which is worse. At least I own it."

His dad had kicked off when Nick was little (cirrhosis of the liver), and his mom had passed the summer before senior year of college, three months before he and Alison got together.

He'd driven himself back to Shippensburg University that August uncertain why he was returning. He'd fought the urge to turn the car around at every mile marker of the eighty-five-mile trip from Leesburg, Virginia, his mother's final resting place.

The gunner competition was a good distraction, at first. His drinking buddies never noticed how rarely he spoke, how rarely he joined in when the mockery of their classmates became their only mode of communication. He didn't tell a single college friend about his mother. He didn't want pointless sympathy from people who hadn't known her and couldn't share his pain, so he spoke about her in the present tense and let people assume she was alive.

It was just easier that way. Graduation was so close. All he had to do was slink past the finish line without anyone noticing his misery.

When he chanced upon Alison in the library, he decided to cross the Rubicon. Gunner rules stipulated no contact with the subjects, lest the offender be accused of manipulating the score. Having quit all recreational sports, breaking rules was the only adrenaline booster left to him. And she'd looked so cute in her patchwork jeans and ponytail, her pouty lips pursed in concentration, her colored pencils lined up and sharpened to flu-shot points.

Her staggering course load meant they only saw each other on weekends. Also, they rarely interacted in class, which kept their relationship on the down-low. For two and a half months he'd loved her fiercely. Despite the short amount of time they were together, she'd changed the trajectory of his life. She'd taught him that if he wanted something, he shouldn't let anyone else's opinions stop him from pursuing his goals.

It had shocked him, the tenderness he felt for her. He'd tried to guard their relationship, cup it gently in his hands like an injured bird.

Instead he'd crushed it between his palms.

"Ladies and gentlemen, you are in for a treat tonight, and I'm not saying that because he paid me to! The man you are about to see is a master of prestidigitation known for his ability to fool even the most experienced audiences."

*We'll see about that,* Alison thought.

"After honing his craft for a few years on the West Coast, he's back to the best coast. May I present to you, the one, the only, Nicholas Finn!"

The squat, balding host with a neatly trimmed beard and dark brown skin walked offstage. All eyes remained on the front of the room.

Several seconds ticked by.

"I guess I have no choice now, huh?" Nick rose from one of the audience seats, startling the people on either side of him. Alison swiveled to look. He'd been hiding in plain sight for who knew how long, in a blazer and jeans to facilitate his camouflaged entrance. Frustrated that he'd already gotten one over on her, she vowed to pay better attention.

In college, Nick had been gut-twistingly handsome, but he'd also been all lion cub: floppy blond hair, large paws, rounded cheeks. Athletic but not overly muscular, he'd retained a softness to his form, a pale underbelly. Now, his hair shorn high and tight, his cheekbones angular, his eyes hungry, his body streamlined, he'd transformed himself into a wolf.

Wait. That was supposed to be her. *She* was the hunter. *He* was the prey.

He strolled to the front of the room, never once looking at her. Maybe he hadn't seen her.

"I'm going to be honest and lay this out for you," Nick said, sinking into a rolling chair and gliding from side to side, as though testing out the chair's speed and smoothness.

Alison smirked. *You couldn't be honest if your life depended on it.*

"My performance tonight is an audition, to book a permanent slot here. Hi, Stu." Nick waved to the balding guy in back, the one who'd introduced him. "Yep, I told everyone. Came right out and said it. Stu here is the entertainment director at the hotel, and the master of my fate. But here's the thing—Stu's well attuned to audience behavior. While you're watching me, he'll be watching you. Creepy, right?"

Laughter rippled through the room.

"And he'll know if you're faking. One of the rare men who can tell."

The woman next to Alison snorted with amusement, but Nick still didn't look over, still didn't seem aware of her presence.

"So only clap if you mean it, if you're genuinely moved to do so. I'll be destitute if you don't, but don't worry about me, I'll be okay. . . ."

He lowered his lashes, then slowly looked up and grinned. His charisma was an impenetrable shield. Surprise, frustration, and guilt tangled inside her. She'd assumed this evening was just another night for him, not a make-or-break performance.

Whatever. He was a pro. If he couldn't handle an unruly audience member, that was on him. "Stu here" should see him work in hostile conditions.

Also, who was to say it was even true? Maybe this was his standard Pity Me opening to earn the audience's affection as an underdog before he'd done a single trick. It was certainly possible.

*Was it* likely, *though? Ugh. Manipulative bastard!*

Nick placed both arms straight out in front of him and rolled up his sleeves to reveal bare wrists. He plucked a coin from thin air, and the woman next to Alison gasped. He displayed the coin for all to see, held between his thumb and forefinger. In a wide motion, he tossed the coin high in the air . . . where it turned into a dove.

More gasps. Pointed fingers as the bird swooped dramatically and circled the room, causing viewers to duck and squeal, before landing on Nick's outstretched finger.

Raucous applause followed.

"Shall we begin?" he said with a smile.

# Chapter 4

He wanted to impress her.

Might as well admit it. The moment she'd walked in, his set list had rearranged itself. Aspects of the show he'd deemed too risky only minutes before demanded their moment in the spotlight. The coin-to-dove trick was reckless and could have backfired, so when it went off without a hitch, he viewed the victory as a sign to continue in that vein.

His livelihood was at stake, but all he could think about was making Alison smile as much as possible over the next ninety minutes.

So why was Alison the only audience member *not* smiling? Blank-faced reactions were often attributable to shock, and once the shock wore off, the person would applaud like everyone else.

When this did not happen, he told himself it was fine. No, it was better than fine, it was *good*; he could use her lack of response as a litmus test. *If she leaps to her feet by the end, I'll know I have the job.*

"I have to ask everyone to please turn off your phones, or

put them on silent, and put them away. No photography allowed. . . . Everyone's cell phones on silent?"

Alison's hand shot up, and the hairs on the back of his neck rose. A premonition crept up his spine. Or was it a memory from all those times in class?

He returned the bird to its cage and swiveled to face her, hoping to convey casual recognition without having to acknowledge their history to an audience that could interpret it as subterfuge.

"Yes, you in the front, you have—a question?"

"Will you be in opening in Denver?" she asked earnestly.

"Uh, Denver?"

"With your little deck of cards. It's a popular place to open, I hear."

*What the . . . ?*

Denver Opener was the name of the first card trick on his roster tonight. (Hence the name *Opener*.) A classic crowd-pleaser, the trick required little patter, as the elegant, simple visuals did all the work. An audience member chose a card from a red-backed deck, memorized it, showed it to the rest of the spectators without Nick seeing, and replaced it in Nick's deck, at which point Nick fanned the cards out, facedown, on his velvet close-up pad, and revealed that one and only one card now had a *blue* back. And guess whose card it was?

"The Mile High City *is* a popular destination," he said, thinking fast, "but no plans so far. Why, is that where you live? Hoping I'll go on tour so you can bring your gaggle of girl-friends?" His voice was amiable and calm, but his heart sputtered fitfully in his chest.

"No, I'm a New York local. My gaggle is here. Just curious."

Nick cleared his throat. "For my first trick . . ." He rapidly cycled through his options for an alternative to Denver Opener, hoping its exclusion didn't trigger a domino effect that he couldn't yet perceive.

He dropped his original deck below the table, picked up a

different one in a smooth motion, and approached an older gentleman in the second row.

"Would you mind helping me out? . . . Terrific. I'm going to riffle through this deck and I'm going to ask you to say 'Stop' at any time, just say 'Stop.' "

"Stop."

"Okay, this one on top, or this one on the bottom? . . . Great. Now take this Sharpie and sign your name. Perfect." Developed many years prior to the Denver Opener, the illusion known as The Hero was one of the first Nick had learned, and an excellent practice routine for magicians starting out. He could perform it blindfolded and upside down.

Maybe he should've.

Maybe that's what it would take to coax a smile from Alison.

After the gentleman scribbled his name across the two of clubs and returned it to the middle of the deck, Nick squared the deck and tilted it while he snapped the fingers of his other hand. Then he thrust the deck back to his helper and said, "Turn over the top card."

Lo and behold, the man's signed two of clubs had risen to the top, through all the other cards, as though invisible.

Laughter and scattered claps from eleven of twelve audience members; stone face from Alison.

"That card sure is *heroic*, isn't it?" she said in a bright voice. "What a *valiant effort* from you."

What. The. Fuck.

Panic flared inside him.

The trick he'd intended to use first was Denver Opener; the trick he'd replaced it with was called The Hero; and Valiance was the name of his next one. Or at least, it *had* been. *She knows my routine. How does she know my routine?*

Under the guise of quenching his thirst with a cup of water, he turned and took several steadying breaths.

If he couldn't outrun her, he could still keep the audience entertained.

Back straight, grin affixed, he faced his executioners.

"Now, it's possible I have an entire deck of two of clubs with this gentleman's signature that I keep on me at all times . . . ," Nick quipped, and reached in his back pocket, swiveling slightly and popping his hip out so spectators could see. With his thumb and forefinger, he retrieved a card and flipped it over: the two of clubs with the man's signature. Chuckles, and a few shouts of "Oh my God!" rewarded him. His helper guffawed.

"But that would be stalker-y. Sorry, man, it's a perfectly normal deck."

He spread the cards in a wide, swooping arc on his close-up pad, faceup, to prove the man's card was unique.

"Let's try again."

"Can it be folded before you place it in the deck?" Alison asked.

Nick's jaw clenched. "It can," he gritted out. "Should it be, though?"

"Yes," the people closest to Alison cheered.

If he acquiesced to her demand, he became her hostage. But if he *didn't* fold the card now, it would look like he *couldn't*.

"Such an interactive audience," he said loudly. "What a fun surprise."

He folded the signed two of clubs in half. Allowed it to fall open, creased and tented, like someone standing with their legs apart. Slowly and carefully, he placed the folded card in the middle of the deck, where it stood out as an anomaly among the flat surfaces above and below it. As before, he snapped his fingers, and the folded card popped up at the top, as though it had teleported there, earning his best reaction thus far.

Alison's gaze darted among the happy spectators. She seemed irritated.

*Well, good.*

"Let's think outside the deck for a second," Nick continued, adrenaline taking over. "What's the craziest place this card could wind up? Anyone?"

Anyone but Alison.

"Your butt!" yelled the woman next to Alison. Alison's jaw dropped. The woman's friends giggled, sputtered, and shoved her, which knocked her into Alison.

"Wow," Nick deadpanned. "Card to anus. That's a new one. Let's keep it clean, folks."

"The ceiling," offered another audience member, a middle-aged woman with pink-dyed hair.

"Now we're talking. Where else?" Nick said.

"Your shoe," called a voice.

"Okay . . . anywhere else?"

"The bookshelf."

More ideas flew, and Nick caught or deflected each one. With the exception of his *ass*, he'd heard them all before. Most people looked around the room and based their ideas off their surroundings. All the while, Alison waited with her hand raised, prim and patient as a cobra waiting to strike.

It occurred to Nick he might be in hell. He'd died before coming onstage, and he was now doomed to watch Alison raise her hand for all eternity. He supposed it was fitting penance for his past transgressions.

Somehow this was worse than being interrupted because he'd brought it on himself by asking for the audience's suggestions. He'd have no choice but to call on her soon, since everyone else had had a say.

"Yes?" he asked, pointing to Alison. Their eyes met.

Silence blanketed the room.

"What's the craziest place this card could wind up?" he prompted.

"Citrus," Alison said, not breaking his gaze.

His shoulders slumped. He wanted to howl.

No layperson ever guessed lemon! That's what made it magical! Age ten, the first time he'd seen that trick, Nick had thought of little else for weeks afterward. The magician at the magic shop had taken a perfectly normal lemon out of a bowl full of them and sliced through it with a knife, to reveal a rolled-up card embedded within. Not just any card, the one *signed by Nick moments earlier.* The magician had taken something mundane—a common fruit—and imbued it with enchantment, like something out of a fairy tale.

"You're so very eager and vocal," Nick told Alison, his voice strained. "If I let *you* pick a card, will you promise to sit back and enjoy the rest of the show *quietly?*"

*Condescending prick!*

Alison frantically reviewed her options. She couldn't promise to be quiet and then break her promise; the audience would turn on her. So far, they'd been tolerant, even encouraging of her disruptions, believing the show to be freewheeling and off-the-cuff. They didn't comprehend what she was doing, and she wanted it to stay that way. She wanted Nick to spiral as she gaslighted him, wanted to witness the exact moment he realized escape was futile.

"If I'm enjoying it, why would you want me to be quiet?" Alison volleyed back.

"That's what *she* said," a guy at the opposite end of her row quipped. He received an elbow to his ribs from the girl next to him.

"I mean, isn't your applause-o-meter reliant on us making noise?" she continued innocently. "Your job *is* at stake, right? Isn't that what you said?"

"Pick a card, any card," Nick said in a loud monotone, presenting her with a deck and riffling angrily through it. "Do not let me influence you in any way."

A vein in his neck flexed, and his eyes dimmed.

*I'm winning,* she realized, and a crackle of electricity raced through her veins. Just as quickly, the flame receded, leaving ashes in its wake. If she defeated him, the game would be over.

"Actually, you know what, let's jump ahead," Nick shouted. "Let's throw out the rule book. Let's go nuts."

"Let's mix metaphors," Alison chirped.

He ignored her, as well as the snickers she'd produced from the others. He flung his hands in the air and called out, "Should we go nuts?"

"Yes!" everyone cheered.

Nick bent toward Alison, so they were eye to eye.

"What's your name?" he asked, head tilted.

*Oh, God.* For a horrible moment she wondered if he didn't remember.

No amount of revenge would fill the cracks in her heart if he didn't remember her.

"A-Alison," she faltered, breaking eye contact. She wanted to be sick. At one point he'd been the most significant person in her life. She'd loved him recklessly, wholeheartedly; the few people she'd slept with in the intervening years had been place-holders, bridges to an event she couldn't yet perceive.

That event was tonight.

Until she had closure with Nick, she'd never be capable of giving herself to anyone new. And closure meant destroying him. Didn't it?

Hovering on the knife's edge of victory or defeat made her woozy.

"Tell me about yourself, Alison. Wait, what am I saying? I'll read your mind and tell *you* about yourself." He stood and offered his hand so she could rise as well.

She stared at his hand. It still dwarfed hers. Slowly, reluctantly, she placed her hand in his and allowed herself to be led to the front. Her entire body hummed from the contact, the painful familiarity of it, even after all this time.

Everyone else in the room dropped off the edge of the world. Only Nick and Alison remained, connected by their hands, hovering in their own bubble of space and time. He squeezed her hand once before releasing it. Was that his way of saying he did remember her, and that she had nothing to worry about, or was it a standard thing he did with volunteers prior to letting go of their hands? She lifted her eyes to his and shivered at what she saw there: absolute recognition.

They stood three feet apart.

He did that annoying thing where he placed two fingers on his temple, as if summoning information from the ether.

Seeing his fingers splayed against his skin like that made her blush. If he *could* read her mind, he'd know she was recalling in vivid detail the way he'd once used his slippery fingertips to circle her nipples until they rose and tightened into bullets.

To her dismay, the memory combined with the harsh air-conditioning of the room caused her nipples to poke at the material of her dress. She fought the urge to cross her arms.

"Oh, this is interesting," Nick said in a low, knowing voice that only added to the images saturating her brain. "You came here with ill intentions. . . . You don't like magicians at all, do you?" he said, snapping her back to reality.

"Just one magician," she answered testily.

"Let's see. . . . You have always been good at studying. Book-smart, but not street-smart. Your sense of morality is extremely rigid."

Her eyes blazed. "Is it? Or do I just know right from wrong?"

"Everyone around you must be perfect at all times or you have no use for them."

"Damn," called an audience member.

"No second chances with *you*, I'll bet." Nick delivered his closing statement like a shark, all teeth.

Thirteen text messages.

That's how many he'd sent over Christmas break.

*I'm so sorry. I'm sorry, Alison. Can we please talk? Please give me a second chance. I'll make it up to you. I just want to explain. I know I don't deserve it. Please can I call you? Will you let me call you just once? Merry Christmas, Alison. Happy New Year, Alison. I'm so sorry.*

And the final one: *I miss you.*

Standing in front of him now, her back straight and proud, she didn't hesitate to respond. "Your assessment of me is vague enough to seem plausible. Do I often love crowds, but also being alone? At times do I crave acceptance, while at other times I value my independent streak?"

The room broke apart with astonished laughter.

*"Damn,"* called the same audience member.

In her pursuit of knowledge with which to flay Nick, she'd become familiar with leading questions, and the Barnum effect (named after P. T. "There's a sucker born every minute" Barnum). Like the A+ student she was and always would be, she launched into a presentation. Shifted her stance to face the audience. "A cold reading is a technique in which people are given descriptions about themselves that could apply to anyone, delivered in such a way that the words feel intimate and accurate. Horoscopes, psychic readings, and certain types of personality tests work the same way."

Nick's eyes darted frantically.

*I've got him!*

Oddly, it did not give her the satisfaction she'd predicted.

After an awkward, lengthy silence, punctuated by a few coughs from the audience, he jumped tracks and sent everyone careening in a new direction.

"Where's your phone?" he asked Alison.

"In my bag."

"Get it, please."

She did as told before she could think. The psychological

pressure to play along was palpable; she felt the audience's eyes on her, trusting her to keep the show running. She couldn't flat out refuse.

"I bet I can unlock it. Would that be impressive, if I could guess your pass code?" Nick said when she returned.

A rope of doubt wrapped around her stomach and squeezed. She'd never thought to research iPhone tricks. What kind of magician relied on technology? Wouldn't the audience think an app was involved?

Ah. Hence his request to use *her* phone, so no one could accuse him of preprogrammed trickery.

"I suppose," she replied. "Wouldn't it also be illegal?"

Snorts from the audience. They gorged on it, her bizarre insouciance.

Nick simply stared at her, his hand open, his eyebrows raised in anticipation.

Slowly, she placed her phone in his hand.

Their fingers brushed, and the rope around her stomach tightened further.

"Is your pass code personal to you, or was it randomly selected?"

He trusted her not to lie. Interesting.

Was that why he'd brought up her morals (aside from deriding them)? He was correct at any rate; she wasn't there to cheat. She was there to detonate him from the inside.

"Randomly selected," she said truthfully.

Nick squinted at her phone before announcing, "Yeah. Okay. Got it."

He held out the phone for the audience to see, then pivoted the screen back to himself. Looked at it one more time and nodded.

Alison moved closer to watch over his shoulder as he tapped out five of the six numbers required by the lock screen.

His sleeve rode up, and she glimpsed a delicate tattoo along the side of his wrist. A woman's name: Charlotte Adair, written in intricate cursive that merged into numbers below it. Alison tried to decipher its meaning, curious who the girl was. His current girlfriend? A previous girlfriend, affixed to him forever? (Heh heh.) The name plucked at the strings of her memory, but she couldn't place it.

He noticed her looking and tugged his sleeve down in jerky, agitated movements. Why did he care that she'd seen his tattoo?

"Abracadabra." He tapped the final number onto her screen. Unlocked!

He showed the audience, who rewarded him with rapturous applause. It went on and on.

Perhaps being his volunteer had happened too early in the show, and she should have held out longer. But magicians never tell you what you're volunteering for when you agree to help them. She'd surrendered control. His arena, his rules.

She'd been on the verge of success mere minutes ago; she'd seen it in Nick's eyes and in his bent posture. Now he paraded about like a peacock.

Incensed, Alison lunged for her phone, but he held it just out of reach.

"May I have it back, please?" she said, unsmiling.

"Of course." He presented it gallantly. "Don't forget to change the code."

"Why bother, you'll just crack it again," she retorted.

The audience laughter provided cover for his next words: "I texted myself, so you have my number," he whispered, and it was as though a tunnel formed around them, blocking out the world, and at the end of the tunnel stood a door to the past. It glowed so brightly it made her eyes sting. She wanted to run toward that door and barrel through it, arms wrapped around herself for protection, lest the shards of broken light slash her.

If she could go back, would she?

*Isn't that what this evening is really about?*

236 / Sarah Skilton

Her heart thundered in her chest, and though she stood stock-still, rigid as a statue, she feared that only made her heart's betrayal more obvious.

After what seemed like an eternity to her, she forced herself to place one kitten-heeled foot in front of the other. She hadn't gotten far when she felt Nick's hand, loose and light on her shoulder. Her skin melted like candle wax where he touched her, which was about right; hadn't he molded her into the person she was today?

"Alison, right?" His hand retreated, taking all warmth with it. "Before you go back to your seat, I need you for one more trick. If you think you can handle it, of course . . ."

"Oh, I can handle it," she hissed, lying through her teeth. The safe haven of her seat called to her, and if he thought he could *taunt* her into staying onstage, he was mistaken. "I just think it's time someone else had a chance."

The woman in the seat next to hers—the one who'd noticed how clutchable Nick's ass was—waved an arm in the air. "If she doesn't want to, I will!"

"You know what, actually, it's fine," Alison announced, propelled by possessiveness. She put her phone away and turned back to Nick, chin raised. "Bring it."

"You can be my next volunteer," he assured the other woman. "But for this trick to work, I need to build on the psychic bond I'm establishing with Alison. Everyone, give it up for Alison! Again!"

# Chapter 5

It had taken an embarrassingly long time for Nick to realize the solution to the Alison problem.

He'd been so flustered by (a) her presence and (b) her casual dismantling of his act that he'd flailed for a quarter of his show. His act had become a game of hot potato, each trick flung away the instant he chose it.

That type of scattershot behavior was fine for tableside magic at a restaurant. People neck deep in conversation didn't want to be interrupted by a lengthy performance; they wanted his flash-iest trick up front and then move it along, Card Boy. For a stage show, however, this approach was fatal. People had paid to see a beginning, middle, and end, a series of illusions that built upon one another within a theme. They'd paid to see live art.

Right now, his illusions had nothing in common. He'd lost any sense of a through line. The only story being told was of an ex-boyfriend forced to confront his biggest shame, and the only person who knew how the story ended was Alison.

She held all the cards, as it were.

As long as she hid in the shadows of the audience, she would remain in charge. To beat her, he needed to force her into the light. Neutralize the threat she posed by keeping her onstage as long as possible. *If she's beside you, you can control her. (Right?)*

With 95 percent of audience members, the answer would be yes. He wasn't so sure it would work on her, but what choice did he have? Allow her to continue interrupting him from her seat every five seconds?

In karate class as a kid, he'd learned to pull his enemies closer. The concept of using an attacker's momentum against the attacker had baffled Nick at first, but he'd quickly discovered why it worked: By yanking the enemy toward you, you'd catch the person off guard and gain the upper hand.

How did that concept translate to a magic show?

Simple.

He would stall like hell, keep her chained to his side, and run out the clock until intermission.

"Now that I've held one of your treasured objects, your mind is accessible to me. Let's further strengthen that pathway and see what develops."

Nick's grandiose words raised her hackles, and it must have shown because he added, "Don't worry, I'm not going to hypnotize you."

Her fist clenched, her fingernails leaving crescent-shaped marks in her palm. "If you make me squawk like a chicken, I swear to God . . ."

He guided her so they faced each other. "Look into my eyes. That's right. You take the lead, Alison, and I'll be your mirror. If you move your hand in a circle, I'll do the same. If you dance the Melbourne Shuffle, I'll try to keep up."

Murmurs of curiosity rose from the audience, several of whom shifted forward in their seats.

Alison stared at Nick, raised both her arms, and spread her hands open. He did the same, their fingers inches apart. Their bodies never touched, but she felt a vibration in the air between them, a pushback, molecular pressure. It was obviously her imagination.

(Was the power of suggestion that strong? Was everyone susceptible to it, or just her? Did he do this with all his female volunteers?)

It reminded her of the Ouija board she'd discovered in her friend's basement as a child.

She and her friend had spent an entire summer trying to master it, two sets of hands vying for dominance on that plastic triangle with the hole cut out, the window to the other side. She'd known it was fake, even as a kid, but that didn't diminish her desire for it to be real.

Eyes glued to Nick's—those translucent green irises flecked with gold—Alison tilted her head to the right, slowly, and back. Then to the left, slowly, and back. She stepped to the side and Nick kept pace. She flipped her hair and raised her arms, stretching languorously, like a cat arching its back. Was this her imagination as well, or did his pupils dilate at the sight of her dress inching up and her curves pushing out?

She clasped her hands together, lacing her fingers tightly, then opened them and waggled her fingers. He mimicked her every move as it occurred. Despite herself, she smiled, and when Nick smiled back, brighter than the sun, she had to look away.

The room fell still. Peaceful. Quiet.

Her heart no longer boomed like a bass drum between her ears. Instead, it fluttered, petals on a breeze. She could've played this game all evening. She wished they would.

*Of course you do,* she reprimanded herself. *Mirroring produces empathy, and you fell for it, like the idiot you are whenever Nick's involved.*

"Nice work," Nick told her. "We're on the same wavelength." He addressed the audience. "But what will happen when we can no longer see each other? If I remove her sight, will our bond be strengthened, or will it snap and break? I believe it'll be strengthened. I believe whatever I do will be felt by her, across the room."

He pulled a blindfold from his briefcase and handed it to a spectator to examine.

"Does it keep out all the light? Make sure it doesn't contain any hidden windows or slots to see through."

While various audience members assessed the blindfold's trustworthiness, he murmured to Alison, "Is this okay with you?"

"Why wouldn't it be?" she replied tartly.

"It involves touching. Nowhere intimate, but I'm worried your response might . . . embarrass you."

He grinned at her and let his eyes fall pointedly to her chest, where her nipples poked against the fabric of her dress.

"It's. Cold. In. Here," she hissed.

"Is it?" he drawled. "I feel warm."

Before she could come up with a rejoinder, Nick drifted away and took back the blindfold from the last person to hold it.

He approached Alison cautiously, as though attempting to slip a collar on a spitting raccoon.

"Hey, Alison." His voice was soft now, no longer joking. "Is this really okay with you?"

Her breath caught and her pulse raced. He smelled like clean, fresh bedsheets from the dryer. She breathed him in, slowly, as though she could pull a long cord of his essence into her lungs and keep it there inside her.

The problem was, her broken heart took up so much space, there was no room for anything else. Shattered pieces had spread throughout her body like shrapnel, each one bearing a different memory: tucking her head under his chin when they hugged. The way he used to trace her collarbone with his fingertips and mouth. The warmth of his kisses. Endless, unhurried explorations that left her weak-kneed and trembling.

Enfolded in his arms, she'd felt invincible. Cherished.

Their eyes locked.

"Do your worst," she said with a confidence she didn't feel.

Gently, he placed the blindfold around her face, his fingers light and swift as he tucked the straps around her ears. Then Nick moved away, and goose bumps pulled at her skin, calling him back to her. Despite her edict to get on with it, the moment he'd left her by herself in the dark, she felt chilled and vulnerable, and the urge to fling off the blindfold shot through her.

When he spoke, he seemed incredibly far away. Maybe the acoustics of the room were to blame?

"Alison, I'm standing across from you, like I did before, only farther apart. You can hear me, right?"

She nodded, puppeteered from afar.

"Great. Let's try something. Raise your hand if you feel something graze your shoulder."

Three seconds after he said this, a soft, melting pressure settled on her right shoulder, pleasantly warm. She jolted in surprise. Gasps from the audience.

It was redundant, but she did as requested and raised her hand.

"Show me where you felt it," Nick instructed her.

She touched her left palm to her right shoulder, and the audience let out another collective gasp. The spot where her palm rested grew warm, buoyed by some invisible force, as though she had placed her hand on top of Nick's.

*It's where he touched me earlier, to keep me onstage,* she reminded herself. *It's a residual feeling. This isn't real. He's messing with my head.*

*The way he always does, the way he always will.*

The next touch was featherlight, on the back of her neck, on the topmost bump of her spine. Skin tingling, she moved her hand to demonstrate where she felt the touch, and the crowd went wild again.

Immediately following that came a caress along her forehead, whisper soft. She shivered, and to her horror, a sigh worked its way out of her.

It wasn't possible.

None of this was possible.

She wanted more.

She ached for it.

The problem wasn't that she hated him. The problem was she couldn't forget how much she'd loved him. How much she'd *wanted* him. How she used to hold her breath whenever he entered the room, couldn't relax until he took her hand in his, confirming that, yes, he was here for *her*; he wasn't a fantasy; this gorgeous, kind, sexy guy was hers.

Except he hadn't been hers. He hadn't been kind. Misleading her about both those things had been his greatest magic trick.

*Why did he bother, though?* a soft voice asked. *What was the payoff? What was the purpose of the con?*

Hearing Alison sigh, and seeing the hint of a smile on her lips, was enough to drown Nick in memories of their tryst. Over the years, his brain had concocted a million different endings, each branching off from the moment he'd searched his dorm room for condoms. If his fucking roommate hadn't used up the stash, if Nick hadn't had to wander around in a horny stupor knocking on doors, if she'd never found his fucking notebook, and instead they'd finished what they'd started . . . would they have stayed together? Could he have spun his duplicity—lies of omission, really—into a story that didn't hurt her? Or had it already been too late for them, that evening in the library, that evening they talked for hours in the diner in the rain? Had it always been too late?

"Burn him," Nick deadpanned, after the applause died down. "He's a witch."

Alison tore off the blindfold, and Nick moved toward her,

acting cocksure and mischievous so she wouldn't know he was examining the past from yet another goddamn angle.

He'd scored a direct hit in this twisted game of hers. It was the best he could hope for. It would have to be enough.

"You look like you've seen a ghost," he remarked. Then, in a low voice for her ears only, he added, "Did it feel good?"

A voice from the audience: "Okay, do you guys know each other?"

Nick's back tensed. Slowly, he turned to face his accuser, a man in the second row. The man frowned. "Because I'm getting a vibe like you—"

"No," Alison said.

"Yes," Nick replied simultaneously.

The irritated man looked confused, then indignant. "Is she a plant?"

"Does it look like she's helping me?" Nick snapped.

"Not really," the man conceded.

"Confession time. We go way back . . . ," Nick said, amused by Alison's shocked expression.

"Seriously?" someone else groused, followed by groans and mutterings that increased in volume. In the first row, a woman flung her hands up.

". . . to ten minutes ago," Nick finished loudly, beaming.

Audience laughter, gilded with relief.

It was every magician's nightmare, that a volunteer would be labeled an insider. Once that thought was given voice, it spilled like ink over every preceding illusion, even the ones that hadn't involved assistants.

Frantic to deny the charge, he'd gone for the joke, hoping people would move on if he downplayed the situation. All he had to do was flick the switch to his college persona. Easygoing Nick, no cares in the world, look at him dance. Even Alison, who was the smartest person he knew, had fallen for it back then. She'd deemed him "relaxed."

The truth was she'd *preferred* him that way, she'd *wanted* him to be that way, neither of which made it real.

Regardless of whether the audience bought his act, her mere presence at this point was risky.

For *him*.

Her silky voice (particularly when she used it to cut him down); the luxurious smell of her hair; her firm, smooth-looking legs; that fiendishly tempting *X* across her bare back—like a treasure hunt's culmination—distracted him to an absurd degree. He yearned to slide his hand under that *X*, around to her front, and cup the gentle slope of her breast.

Standing so close to her, placing the blindfold around her face, and stroking her hair for the briefest of moments, he'd felt lost in time. If he could've waved a magic wand and made everyone else in the room disappear, he would've.

He wanted her to know he'd followed her plan precisely. He'd flown out to California, worked in sales by day, and studied magic under a mentor at the magic club by night. And when, a few years later, his mentor's friend back East said he needed a new personal assistant, Nick jumped at the opportunity. He didn't have the right to contact Alison, but sharing the city with her had sparked hope in his chest regardless.

Nick forced himself to return to the present. *Can't think straight, Nicky my boy?* It was Amazing Arthur's voice, spurring him on. *Then don't think straight. When she zigs, you zag.*

*Get her inside the box.*

It was the only way to salvage what was left of this performance. The only way to secure his job.

Nick pointed at the skeptical man and turned on the charm. "I like the way you think, though. Let's put her to work. Let's make it official. Ladies and gentlemen, my brand-new assistant for the rest of the show! She's lovely, she's tart tongued, she's quite the cutup! Shall we see how much of a cutup she can be?"

Nick darted over to a large cabinet against the far wall. With a grunt, he pushed the entire contraption on wheels to the center of the stage, toward Alison but facing outward.

He swept around to the front and opened the door with a flourish.

"If you would," he said, indicating that Alison should get inside.

"Am I going to be sawed in half?" she asked, rooted to the spot. She squinted at the cabinet, and for all he knew, she'd already assessed how it worked.

"Into thirds, actually. With blades. Why, is it a personal goal of yours? To be sawed in half?" More quietly, just for her: "Are you okay with small spaces?"

"Yes," she huffed.

"See you at intermission," he said, and swiftly guided her inside.

"Intermission? Wait, how long is that?"

"If I had to 'guesstimate,' I'd say five minutes."

Her eyes blazed and he choked back a laugh. The panel in front of her face was made of clear plastic so they could see each other through it. He shut the door on her livid expression and slid the metallic lock into place.

With no other recourse, she stuck her tongue out at him, which he ignored.

"Help me out?" he asked the skeptic, and the two of them pushed the cabinet back across the room. Not far enough away, he realized. What if she pounded on the walls or yelled?

"Actually, let's go this way." They pushed her across the room again. Nick opened the bookshelf door to the adjoining suite, wheeled Alison inside, and closed the door behind him.

"Yes, there's a bookshelf secret door," he acknowledged carelessly. "Now forget you saw it."

Unburdened and light on his feet, Nick swept back to the front of the room and addressed the audience, slapping his hands together. "Finally. A little peace and quiet! Am I right?"

The faces staring back at him seemed uncertain how to react. He could practically read their thoughts: Was this still part of the show? What was happening?

"Aren't you going to cut her in half?" the skeptic asked, giving voice to the majority.

Nick waved off the other man. "Yeah, no, we aren't doing that trick. Or any others with Alison. I just needed her out of the way. Shall we continue?"

Violent laughter filled the room. Nick floated on the sound, the rise and fall of it, his chest expanding. All the tension in the room had evaporated. Alison would be chalked up as an aberration in an otherwise stellar magic show. Hopefully.

As he pulled a rope from his briefcase, he wished he could leap past those five minutes until intermission and confront her *now*. She'd obviously done her homework, had obviously planned this stunt for ages. Why?

Keeping his promise to the woman who'd sat beside Alison—the one who wanted a card to appear in his *butt*—he called her and another giggling girlfriend up to assist in the rope routine. Nick had performed for drunk audiences plenty of times, but he'd never before seen such a group of hams all in one show. At least he'd cut the head off the rebellion.

Despite his rowdy accomplices, the rope trick couldn't have gone better. He wished Alison were still in the room to see it. Despite everything that had happened between them, he craved her approval and wondered what she'd thought of the show so far. Had she been swept away at any point, or was she thoroughly jaded from learning the lingo and secrets?

It made him sad to think she'd denied herself the experience of not knowing.

*Focus, Nick.*

On the heels of this private command, the lights cut out.

# Chapter 6

Alison's neck was stiff, and she felt as though she'd been sucking in her stomach for hours. That was the main qualification for a female assistant in magic, apparently: the ability to suck in one's stomach and contort into small spaces. The (male) magician could wear a freaking cape, puff himself up to twice his natural size, and swoop around the room like an enormous bat, but the women (still! in this day and age!) need only be small and know how to keep their mouths shut.

Just you wait, you *fucker*.

The instant he unlocked her prison, she would come out swinging. She would stomp back into the performance room and blow the lid off this trick, expose every detail in an evil, step-by-step, metaphorical PowerPoint presentation to Nick's audience.

Cramped spaces had never bothered her before, but then again, she'd never been shoved inside an upright coffin before. Her breathing sped up, shallow and frantic, which fogged up the clear, hard plastic panel in front of her face. This reminded her that things could always be worse. Not being able to *see* while shoved in an upright coffin, for example.

She forced herself to slow her breaths, count in her head with each inhale and exhale to conserve air. Once the small window cleared again, she took stock of her surroundings. Followed the swirling pattern of the vintage wallpaper with her eyes, let her gaze drift through the room, over the outline of the minifridge and freezer, the tray of coffee and tea supplies—she envisioned herself braining Nick with the coffeepot—the lush king-size bed, and the gauzy curtains for daytime nestled within the thick velvet ones that kept out the sunlight. Was this his preparation and dressing room, or did he *live* at the hotel? Was he like Eloise at the Plaza?

The thought made her chuckle.

Blindfolded, vulnerable, with the scent of his body and the heat of his presence surrounding her, she had almost tricked herself into believing he wanted her, too; that her longing for him was reciprocated, that it burned through him as fiercely as it burned through her.

She couldn't hear well; it felt as though someone had taken a wet washcloth and placed it over her ears. Muffled voices rose and fell from the adjoining room. Were they talking about her? Nick said he'd see her at intermission in a few minutes, but what if she took matters into her own hands before that? Maybe she could headbutt the face panel or kick her foot through the bottom.

She'd skimmed over escape tricks in her research, deeming them unlikely in a close-up magic act, and this gap in her knowledge galled her. Perhaps she should be grateful he hadn't tied her wrists behind her back and plopped her in a tank of water.

What was the endgame to Nick's little kidnapping stunt?

She'd no sooner asked herself this when her previous fear of not being able to see came true.

Her surroundings were plunged into darkness, and screams erupted from the adjoining room.

\* \* \*

No matter what Nick said, no one believed that it wasn't part of the show, until Stu, the entertainment director, cut through the chaos.

"Everyone, calm down and listen to me." Stu's deep voice made it clear he'd suffer no dissent. "Get out your phones, put on your flashlights."

Nick happily ceded control to the other man; his only concern was Alison and getting to her as swiftly as possible.

The rustling and murmurs dropped off as, one by one, phones were raised like tiny lighters at a concert, illuminating each holder's location.

"It's hotelwide, and they don't know what caused it," Stu announced a moment later, having read a text message from a colleague. "So, we're going to get everyone down to the lobby, and if the power's not fixed within twenty minutes, I'll issue refunds and tickets for a later date."

"The elevators will be stuck," a panicked voice called out.

"We'll take the stairs," Stu replied firmly. "It's a long way, but we'll be fine if we stick together."

"Here, everyone can hold on to this rope at fixed intervals." Nick tripped over a chair, righted himself with a grimace, and placed the longest rope from his collection into Stu's hand.

It would have to do.

"Aren't you coming?" Stu asked.

"I need to get Alison. We'll be right behind you."

Stu nodded and organized the group's exit. "Keep one hand free for your phone light, and use the other for the rope."

The dozen audience members wobbled out the door like an old freight train. With everyone gone, the room fell dark, Nick's own iPhone flashlight a pathetic beam in a black cave. He made his way carefully toward the bookshelf and pushed against it.

A minute later, Alison toppled out of the contraption and

into his arms. For a second, she went limp in his embrace, her back rising and falling with each intake of air.

"It's okay," he said into her hair, which smelled like vanilla and rosewood. "It's—"

She launched herself off him, her small hands pummeling his chest. "You *left* me here!"

*Wait a second. . . .* He squinted at her and tilted his head. "Was it you?"

"Was what me?"

"Did you . . . cause the power outage?"

"You know how you're not really a sorcerer?" she raged. "NEITHER AM I."

"Okay, all right, okay."

She shoved him and moved on shaky legs toward the window, arms braced in front of her. The thick velvet shades were open and the city below was an ocean of black.

"It's not just the hotel," she said. "It's everywhere."

His phone buzzed. He ignored it.

"What's it say?"

He looked down and read the message from Stu. "That you're right. It's all of Manhattan."

"Do they know what caused it?"

"Not yet. Stu's sending everyone home."

"Oh, God, I bet there's people trapped on the subway. I hope my friends are okay."

"I don't know how long the power is going to be out," Nick said, "and I'm not going to drain my battery looking for answers yet. But you don't have to go anywhere. Stay until power's restored."

"What are you talking about?"

"There's no reason to brave the craziness out there when you've got a comfortable hotel suite all to yourself. I'll hang out in the other room. Hopefully it won't last long."

She didn't answer, so he took a chance at conversation. "You can't fault me for asking if you had something to do with it. You had me running scared the entire show."

She frowned. "I'm not a supervillain. My plan to ruin your show was strictly verbal."

"You should be proud then. You almost succeeded."

"Until you locked me in a box," she snapped.

"And you made an excellent box jumper," he said with a laugh, using the industry term for magician's assistant. "Should we take our show on the road?"

His pulse jumped when he realized she was . . . shaking? And not from merriment.

He reached a tentative hand out, but before he could touch her, she whirled around, inches from his face.

"You know what? Fuck you. Not everything is a joke. *I'm* not a joke. You've always treated me like one—"

"No, I haven't!"

"Spare me." She dripped venom and he swallowed tightly.

He knew he shouldn't refute her, but he couldn't help himself; he needed her to see the truth.

"I never thought you were a joke—"

"Don't. I mean it, Nick. . . ."

"Are you still hung up on that stupid game? It was a *game*, it wasn't personal, it didn't mean I didn't think the world of you!" he cried.

"I'd had sex *one time* before you, and I've had boyfriends since you, but that night in your dorm room *shattered* my ideas about what sex could be." Her voice cracked on the word *shattered*, and he silently begged her to continue. "Pleasure I've never known before or since. I opened myself to you completely, and seconds later I find out you've been making fun of me for months. So, I mean, it's *great* that it wasn't personal for you. It was personal for *me*. It was everything, and tonight was supposed to be payback, but you won. Again. Find me a way out of here and leave me be, just leave me be."

It sounded as though tears clogged her throat.

He couldn't speak. He couldn't move.

"And you know what?" she roared, pain turning back into anger. "There is nothing wrong with masturbation!"

Surprised, he coughed uncontrollably. "Of course, there isn't—"

"It tells you what you like, it feels great—"

"Of course, it does."

"So, thanks for making me feel like a freak on top of everything else."

"I never, ever thought you were a freak." He took a chance and cupped her face in his hands, waited until her puffy eyes turned toward his. "I wanted to be like you. Do you hear me? You were everything I wanted to be."

"You had a funny way of showing it," she muttered.

The words poured out of his mouth, pure instinct. "Let me make it up to you."

"How?" she scoffed.

"'Pleasure you hadn't known was possible,'" he quoted. "'Pleasure you haven't felt before or since.'"

His offer hung in the air, decadent and heavy.

A car horn honked outside, followed by shouts, but the only sound in the room he noticed was Alison's shallow, rapid breathing.

*This is insane. Isn't it?*

*I'd be insane to say yes.*

*So why am I not saying no?*

"I remember every moment of that night." Nick's voice was languid, and his words unraveled something inside her, a carnal longing she'd suppressed for five years.

He pulled her to his chest, so she faced outward, nestling her within his embrace. She couldn't see him, but she could feel the heat of his sweet breath as he bent his mouth to the shell of her ear. "I could re-create it for you. Every touch, every gasp, every stroke, the way you spread yourself wide for me, how smooth your thighs were, how delicious you tasted."

She was stunned; she thought she was the only one who'd been so affected by that night. Nick had had so much experience, she was sure of it, a guy as good-looking and good-natured as he would never lack for bed partners, but Alison—

She closed her eyes as he continued painting a lush picture for her, his voice rich with promise.

"I bet I could pull the same exact sounds from you that you made that night, the way you moaned, those fast little breaths, like you were trying to hold them in but you just *couldn't*. I know now, you were discovering what your body could do, if only someone would bring it all to the surface. I can give you that again, I can give you anything you want, as many times as you want, as many as you can stand, and I *want* to, let me do that for you. We're alone here in this great hotel, let's have *fun* with it. . . ."

Her breathing grew ragged, unhinged. She twisted in his arms, stood on her tiptoes, and brought her mouth close to his.

But instead of kissing him, she hovered there, their breaths mingling. "And when you're done," she said, "when I *decide* you're done—you get nothing. No relief, no gratification. You'll go to sleep in the other room, and as soon as the power comes back on, we go our separate ways."

He didn't hesitate. "Done."

Her pulse raced. She hadn't ruined his show, but she could still get something out of tonight. Satisfaction of a different sort. He was willing, and she was *owed*.

It had all been foreplay, he realized. From the moment he'd seen her tonight, no one and nothing else had mattered to him. He'd performed for an audience of one. The entire evening of power games and verbal hide-and-seek had been leading to this, and he couldn't pretend otherwise any longer.

He also couldn't pretend he hadn't been turned on by her mischief during the show.

If he hadn't shoved her offstage, he had no doubt she'd have continued to bat him around like a cat with a mouse.

The rare, casual relationships he'd had in the past few years had been like magazines at a doctor's office—fine to read in a pinch, but you'd never subscribe—and none of the women in question had shown much interest in his work.

That Alison had studied magic, memorized so many routines, and *prepared* for seeing him swelled more than his ego.

He loved her wild and cruel. He loved her daring. He loved her kindness, too, her intelligence and her ferocious drive.

How had she gone from a business major terrified to use her weekends for anything other than studying to a confident, brash woman who'd cast off her father's directive and followed her bliss? (He'd looked her up. He knew about Smocks. He knew all sorts of things.)

But she didn't want to talk, she didn't want his apologies, and she certainly hadn't offered any of her own. If this marked his only chance to show her how much he'd missed her, and if bringing her to screaming completion was the only way he was allowed to do it, well . . . giddyap.

The heat coming off her was extraordinary.

He slid his thumb along the center of her panties, which contained a perfect silky damp line. She moaned softly and rocked her hips while he rolled his thumb in circles, spreading her liquid heat up and around, orbiting her sweet spot like the sun, giving her some of what she needed but not *all*.

A gift and a denial.

Abruptly, he drew away.

"Take off your dress," he ordered, breathing hard, and sat back to give her room.

She lurched upward, fingers flying to unzip and shimmy free. He could only watch, enchanted, as she obeyed without hesitation.

"You are so beautiful," he groaned.

He swept her into his arms and carried her slowly across the room to the bed. Luckily, it wasn't far and nothing hindered their arrival.

He drew her wrists behind her head, pinning them in place. "Don't let go," he told her.

She felt the cool cotton of the pillow behind her and gripped it between her fingers.

He lowered his face and kissed the breast nearest him, licking and sucking her nipple to an aching, shiny-wet peak. She fairly hummed with pleasure and offered up a prayer that he wouldn't go *too* slowly.

He moved downward, across her belly. She raised her hips, and he made like he was going south, but then moved back up to her breasts again, lashing at her other nipple with his tongue. It was as though he'd wound a chord from her chest to the pulse between her legs, and touching one sent vibrations to the other, until she became one long, quivering body part for him to toy with.

"Nick . . . ," she whispered.

"Mmm?"

"How are you so—"

"Good? Talented? Intoxicating?"

"*Maddening.* Tell me," she said between gasps. "Is the blindfold trick your go-to seduction technique? Leaving girls sopping wet across the country?"

He tapped her lips with his finger, and she opened for him, darted her tongue across his fingertip. "Such a dirty mouth," he admonished her.

"Tell me."

"I wouldn't know. You're the only one I've tried it on."

"How did it work?" she begged.

"The same way this works. . . ." He eased her nipple back

into his mouth and sucked until she became a tumult of movement below. "Because I *know* you."

At long last, he dipped his head, spread her thighs, and latched on to her clit with his warm, wet mouth.

She hadn't thought it was possible for her insides to twist any tighter, but within seconds the knot inside her clenched one last time and released. She cried out as pleasure washed over her in competing, sloppy waves.

She arched toward him and touched his face, his neck, and his back, her fingers digging into his arms, everywhere she could reach.

They kissed and she tasted herself on his tongue. He moaned and she pulled at his bottom lip, stretching it and letting it bounce back. He chased her with his mouth, ready for more kisses.

She smirked. "Bye."

# Chapter 7

"Here's the thing," Nick said, standing by the bed in the dark as Alison tugged the sheets up to her neck.

"Our agreement stipulated you would not sleep here with me."

"Our agreement also stipulated that I wasn't allowed to get off," he replied bluntly. "If I'm in the other room, you won't be able to monitor my chastity."

"Do you really plan on"—she jerked her fist up and down beneath the sheet (How was it possible that he felt it on his dick?)—"in your *workplace*?"

"We've already defiled my workplace. And, yes, I do. There's nothing wrong with masturbation, as a wise woman once told me. So you'd better keep an eye on me if you want to stop me."

"Ugh, fine." She rolled onto her stomach and gathered pillows.

"Are you making a fort?"

"A barrier. You'll stay on your side, I'll stay on mine, and I better not feel the mattress shake."

"I'm not sleeping. I'm hungry. Do you think room service would tell us to fuck off?"

"Probably."

"I'd kill for a burger right now. *Someone* had me running around like a madman tonight."

She conceded his point with a shrug. "I think they have more important things to do at the moment. But that's a good point. I'm thirsty, too. Does the bathroom sink have water, do you think?"

"It runs on electric pumps, so we can't count on it for long. The minifridge probably has a thousand-dollar bottle of Fiji water just waiting for a power outage and a couple of desperate idiots, though."

"It's on your tab, right? Dibs."

"I'll bill you for half." He held out his hand to her. She ignored it, and her dismissal stung. He let his proffered hand fall to his side.

"Where is the minifridge?"

"Not sure. Search the room?"

She shrugged again. "Okay."

They located her dress on the floor and he helped her back into it, trying not to let his hands linger on the smooth skin of her back. His jeans pressed painfully against his erection.

"First one to find it distributes the spoils. *If* she's feeling generous." Alison turned and promptly banged into a desk. "Ow."

He laughed. "Shit. You okay?"

"That wasn't always there, was it?"

"Second chance to go in on it together," he said, sliding his hand through hers. "Strength in numbers."

"Scared I'll win?" she countered. But she didn't let go.

"Always."

"I'll allow it." She shifted him so he stood in front of her. To his delight, she placed her hands on his hips. "You'll be my human buffer."

"Oh, I see how it is. No problem if *Nick* gets banged up."

"You always were too pretty."

Silence cloaked them then, as though any positive reference to the past must never be acknowledged.

She held on to his waist as he moved about the room like a ship, dragging her with him.

"We're scavengers," he said after a while.

"Hunter-gatherers."

"I think I see it!" He lurched forward and she slammed into his back, her breasts flattening against him. "Wait, no, that's the safe. Sorry about that. Please don't sue me."

"Why would I sue you?"

"For injuring you with my godlike back muscles, I don't know. Aren't you out to get me? A lawsuit might be next on your list."

She poked him in the middle of his spine. "I've decided you're more useful as an ally at the moment."

"Is it in the showroom?" he muttered to himself.

"Remind me, how is it you don't know?" He could practically feel her eyebrows arch behind him.

"Because I've never had to think about it before. This is my boss's place. Let's see, when I come into the room from the service elevator, I usually turn . . . right."

His hand covered hers where it still rested on his hip. Slowly, he led her to the other side of the room, groping the air in front with his free hand and startling her with a pleased yelp.

They knelt by the minifridge and Alison swung it open. Cold air swept out, but no light greeted them.

"That's eerie," Alison said. "As a kid I was fascinated by the way the light was triggered in the fridge. I'd try in vain to 'catch it' turning on."

"Yes," Nick gloated, bringing his prize up to his face to read the label. "Mozzarella-tomato panini."

"Should we ration it?"

He grabbed other items and set them on the floor. "There's also mixed nuts, a tin of Pringles, and a salad."

"Half now, half later?"

"If we don't eat it, it'll go bad."

"The sandwich and salad, yeah, but the nuts and chips can wait."

"Deal. And five waters. Sweet." He uncapped one of the bottles and began to chug.

" 'One, two, three-four-five, that's enough to stay alive. Six, seven, eight-nine-ten, I don't want to count again,' " Alison sang.

He sputtered and lowered the bottle, which was now half-empty. Had she lost her mind? "What the hell was that?"

She grinned. "It's what we tell our kids, at the place I work."

"Smocks, right?"

Her mouth dropped open.

"You really think I never looked you up?" he asked softly. "That after you left my dorm room that night, I forgot about you?"

She didn't respond, and silence stretched between them again, a tightrope with no takers.

"There's only one water fountain, so if we don't set a boundary, it's chaos," she explained. "We taught the kids a chant so they could self-regulate when they're in line to use it."

"*That's* not creepy."

"Hey, it works."

"What do you think caused the blackout?" Nick asked, after devouring his portion of the panini.

"No clue, but if this is because of a downed power line in Akron, Ohio, I'm going to be pissed," she said, referring to the 2003 Northeast blackout. "Did that one get you? I was seven."

"Yeah, I was eight. Our ice cream melted so we ate it really fast. Best soup ever."

She made a sound that was half exhale, half chuckle and that had to count for something, he thought. "Wait, wasn't it because of a tree nobody bothered to trim?" he continued. "In Akron, I mean."

"Yeah, one crashed into an old power line, I think." She opened the can of nuts and held it out to him. He took a handful.

"I wonder if the hotel has backup generators," Alison said.

"I have no idea. Think we're in for twenty-nine hours of this, or twenty-nine days?"

"Twenty-nine days was the ice storm. And it wasn't twenty-nine days, it was twenty-one," she corrected him.

"Oh, that's all right then. I was about to panic, but if it's only *twenty-one days*..." He trailed off sarcastically, before shifting gears. "So, I've gotta ask. What exactly was your end-game tonight, with my show?"

"To distract you so much you'd throw in the towel, at which point I would dismantle your program piece by piece, like one of those torture movies where people have to saw off their own limbs while a puppet watches."

He choked on a startled laugh. "You really hate me that much?"

She sighed. "Let's eat."

He moved closer. "You get that this is my livelihood, right? You get that I won't have another chance to earn this job?"

She refused to meet his gaze. "Well, I *didn't* know that, not until I arrived. I figured it was just another show for you. What was that whole thing you said at the beginning? 'You guys are the restaurant critics and I'm the food, please love me'?"

"Not really what I said, but sure. Make fun of my attempts to survive."

When she didn't volley back, he moved even closer. Alison pivoted, her back to him, and gripped her middle, arms overlapped and squeezing herself.

"Locking me in the cabinet was a dirty trick," she muttered. "There was a moment when I was breathing so fast I fogged up the glass and I couldn't see, and I didn't know when you were coming back."

"I had to put a stop to your rampage. I didn't know what else to do."

Without conscious thought, driven by the simple desire to help her feel better, he placed one light hand on her shoulder. When she didn't flinch, bristle, or jolt him off, he kept it there and began to rub the back of her neck with his thumb in smooth, lazy circles.

Miraculously, she allowed it, leaning into his touch.

"We're not thinking about that right now." He kept his voice slow and calm and steady. "We're only thinking about each breath as it comes into our lungs and strengthens us and cleanses us and gives us everything we need, and then we're letting it flow back out again, taking our fears and worries and concerns with it. Right? Slow, deep breaths. That's the only thing we're thinking about, the only thing that matters."

She bit her lip, uncertain, then nodded, and swiveled to face him.

"Here, we'll do it together." They sat cross-legged, eyes locked in the darkness. He inhaled, letting his chest fill and expand, and watched as she did the same. By unspoken agreement, they held the air loosely within them for seven seconds and exhaled simultaneously.

Facing each other and mimicking each other's movements, they replicated the mirror trick from his show, but either she hadn't realized it, or she didn't mind. With each breath their hostility toward each other lessened. He envisioned a cave forming around them, protecting them as they created their own place of respite.

He wasn't sure how long they meditated that way; he only knew he never wanted it to end. Sitting there with Alison, upright, spines strong, their eyes adjusting to the lack of light, pupils dilated as they gazed at each other in peaceful silence, was a gift he was pretty sure he didn't deserve.

"Better?" he asked. She nodded and his chest constricted.

It was bittersweet, ending their connection, but he owed her space, didn't want to force his company on her any longer, now that she appeared calm.

"You'll get another chance," she blurted out, and if her words were meant more for herself, to assuage her guilt, that was okay, he decided. "The show was interrupted by a force majeure. First me, then the blackout."

"You were a force of . . . something."

"The hotel will reset the clock, you'll perform your audition again to a *much* lovelier, more subdued crowd—"

"You really did rile them up. It was like an insurrection out there—"

"I could write a letter to the entertainment director, explaining," she offered quietly.

He cleared his throat. "It's okay. Anyway, I seem to be bonerless, so it's time for me to head to the other room and leave you be."

"Oh."

"Call out if you need anything." He moved slowly toward the swiveling bookshelf door that led to his showroom, arms in front of his body as a protective measure. His ego forbade him to crash or fumble in front of her; he wanted his exit to be as smooth as possible.

"Wait."

A patter of footsteps in the darkness, then slim fingers gripped his arm.

He swiveled to face her. They were centimeters apart.

"Don't go," Alison said, and if there were a world in which he denied her, he would've burned it down.

# Chapter 8

When Nick's hand found hers and squeezed, joy rippled through her.

She felt like a fool, a delirious fool in the midst of a dream. In the past ten minutes they'd grown comfortable touching each other, and she welcomed it, *needed* it. When the pad of his thumb stroked along the ridge of her knuckles, she nearly sighed with longing.

Everything that had happened during his show, in the light, seemed irrelevant now, as though an unseen hand had placed those events on the other side of a wall. And with that severing came a delicious sense of possibility. Who could they be? What would they do?

In the darkness they were allowed to peel off their hard outer shells and explore the softness underneath.

"I'm happy you ended up in the type of job you wanted," he said.

"So did you." The words *I'm proud of you* nearly tumbled from her mouth. But it wasn't her place to say them.

"Well . . . we'll see, won't we?" he muttered.

They stood by the window now, limbs touching, and gazed out at the only source of light available: car lights in the street below. Intermittent and weak though they were, those red and white beams were better than nothing.

"The irony is I'm here because of you," he said. "Do you remember that picnic by Laurel Lake?"

"I remember you got me so drunk I went off on a poor old woman feeding bread to the ducks." A laugh squawked out of her and she shook her head, embarrassed.

"(A) I didn't get you drunk, as I believe a literal thimble was involved, and (b), actually, that last part is true, you flipped your shit on that poor old lady," he teased.

"What were you going to say?"

"I told you I wanted to be a magician, and not only did you take me seriously, you never once made fun of me for it. You insisted on coming up with a five-year plan, and since it was you, the plan was well thought out and plausible, and it terrified me."

She tilted her head, fascinated. "Why?"

"Because what excuse could I possibly have not to follow it? And I did, to the letter—out to California, join the magic club, find a mentor, use my business skills to my advantage. As much as we both wanted to burst free from our business majors, my education set me apart from the magicians who didn't have that background, just as you predicted. I still have the paper you wrote the plan on, faded and folded in my wallet. I kept it as proof that . . ." He got bashful all of a sudden. Nick, as far as she knew, was *never* bashful.

Her breath caught in her throat. "Proof of what?"

"Proof that someone I admired and trusted believed in me. I'm a magician because of you," he finished simply.

Her brain stuttered to a halt on the previous sentence. The dream Alison had been enjoying with him split open, and she fell through the earth.

"You 'admired and trusted' me?" she repeated slowly. "Those are the words you'd use?" Her voice shook, and damn it, damn him, damn *herself*, for still feeling gut wrenched, five years on. "You always place bets on people you 'admire and trust'? You always try to make money off other people's hard work?"

"Here we go," he muttered, as though their previous truce had been a ruse, as though she'd lured him back into the room under false pretenses so they could have it out.

She'd had no intention of rehashing the past, but his impossibly ridiculous interpretation of what they'd been to each other could not stand.

"Yes. Here we go," she replied crisply. "We're stuck here together, for who knows how long, so I think it's time I had answers, don't you? So. Tell me. How did it work? Fantasy Gunners."

"Since you ask, it was a points system," he said, hitting the *p*'s and *t*'s hard as he spoke. "Certain actions earned more points than others. Raising a hand; whether or not they were called on; whether or not their answer was correct. Triple points if they asked an absurd question, which happened a lot by the way; and bonus points if they hung around after class. The biggest was one hundred points for whoever ended up getting the TA job for spring semester."

She'd been angling for that job. *Gunning* for it, in their view. Not because she wanted the extra responsibility, but because she thought it would help her learn the material if she was tasked with explaining it to someone else, and because she thought it would be nice to have spending money.

For dates with Nick.

"Why masturbator?" she asked in a dull voice.

He made a sound of frustration. "I didn't come up with it—"

"I don't care!"

"That look you got when you were concentrating on an answer in class—it just made us—I mean, it made the guy who drew it—wonder if that's what you looked like when you were, um . . ."

"And is it?" she asked darkly. "Is it what I look like?"

"No," he said firmly.

She held up her hands to prevent him from moving any closer.

"No," he insisted. "You're gorgeous when you come." Softer, now: "The most beautiful woman I've ever seen."

Hadn't she thought the same thing about him? How beautiful he'd looked that cold December night in his dorm room, ready to ravish her?

It wasn't enough, though. She needed everything to come to light, and if it took darkness and raised voices and painful confessions, so be it. "All those times you asked, 'How'd you do on the quiz?' So curious about my grades and my percentages, it was all to gather data to make fun of me. I didn't even want to be a business major, and you *knew* that. It was the only way my dad would foot the bill. I'd been working my ass off because contrary to what you and your friends thought, it *didn't* come easily to me. None of it ever has. I wasn't lording it over the rest of you about how 'smart' I was. I barely slept. I never went out." Her voice lowered to a whisper. "Not until you."

"I know, and—just—listen to me for a second. Long before we started hanging out, I was rooting for you. I was cheering you on. That's why I picked you for my team."

"You didn't get our names out of a hat?"

"I traded for you because you were the best," he said in a rush, the words smacking into one another. "I paid two hundred and fifty dollars all in. It was winner take all, ten times that amount. And, Alison, I was going to tell you. I was going to split the money with you, use it to take us both to California. I was going to—" He cut off so abruptly and his voice was so high-pitched and crazed she felt dizzy.

"You were going to what?"

"I was going to propose," he yelled. "But, you know, I guess it's better I didn't, considering all the ways we hurt each other!"

She was gobsmacked. Confusion and anger warred within her. She couldn't process the first part—*proposal proposal proposal*—so she leaped to the second part. "How did *I* hurt *you*?"

"Are you kidding me? You left and you never came back! And you never apologized!"

"What did I need to apologize for?"

"For never letting me be a real person! One mistake and that was it! You never dug any deeper, never asked *why* my year had been tough, *why* I would play that kind of game with my classmates. I tried to tell you, I tried to explain. 'You think I care?' you said. How do you think it felt when you ignored my texts, when you disappeared, and January came around and you were just . . . gone?"

"You were always so happy," she stuttered. "So relaxed and carefree. I didn't think you'd—"

"I was completely depressed that fall. My mother had just died."

Her throat went dry and tears spilled from her eyes. She couldn't breathe; she wanted to gasp, wanted to gulp air until her dizziness subsided, but this wasn't about her, and she forced herself to calm down. "I didn't know."

He sniffed in the darkness. Swiped an arm across his face. "Yeah. Well."

"I . . . I don't know what to say." Her hands gripped each other, twisting and flexing. She longed to pull him toward her, to kiss his pain away.

"When I got there in September, I was numb, looking for a way to blow off steam. The contest kept me invested." He sniffed again and cleared his throat, a rough scraping sound that pulled more tears from Alison. "She would have been ashamed of the way I treated you. The book I gave you, that old copy of *A Tree Grows in Brooklyn*? It was hers. I drove back and forth to Virginia one night to get it for you."

Frozen in place, Alison let the tears slide down her cheeks, petrified that if she moved a muscle to wipe them away, Nick might curl up into himself and retreat. Sensing he had more to say, she waited.

"Was what I did so awful that you had to change schools?" He sounded far away, or like he was underwater. She wanted to press herself against his chest, wrap her arms around him and hold him.

"I didn't drop out because of that night," she replied quietly. "Well, partly, but not for the reasons you think. I dropped out because you were having fun, and I wasn't. I was so sick of doing what my father wanted, instead of what I wanted. I wanted to be like you, so badly, I wanted to lap you up, I couldn't get enough of you, which was why it hurt so much."

He made a sound between a laugh and a sob. "*I* wanted to be like *you* because you didn't care what anyone thought of you."

"I cared what other people thought," she said, perplexed. "Or at least, I cared what *you* thought."

"I was hobbled by other people's opinions. Terrified to show them who I was, or what I wanted. But you went through life doing and being exactly who you were."

She swallowed around the lump in her throat. "I think if I'd found out about the game under different circumstances, I could have laughed it off. But I felt so raw and exposed after the wonderful things you'd done to me in your bed, and combined with my nickname, it was too much. I was twenty, and I couldn't deal."

"I get that. Raw and exposed, like me, up there onstage tonight."

"Yes."

They regarded each other in silence, but it was a soothing, light silence, not a heavy, burdened one. Their fight had been a storm at sea, but now they'd washed ashore, drenched but alive.

"I'm here because of you, too," she said. "At my art job, I mean." The realization caused a pleasant zing throughout her body. Because it was so obviously true, yet she'd never known it until this moment. "I never would have stood up to my dad and rerouted my degree and gone for what I wanted, found my own happiness, if I hadn't dropped out."

It was her turn to offer him a hand, and she braced herself for his refusal, but Nick accepted, and they meandered awkwardly through the room. A single armchair swam into view, the only furniture besides the bed, so they sat on the floor to continue their conversation. Their hands drifted apart. She lamented the loss.

"Did you have enough acrylics this year? Enough paint supplies, I mean?"

"I know what acrylics are," she said with a smile. "How did you know we needed them?"

"Like I said, I looked you up. Came across the site."

"We don't post our wish list on the site. Only in the newsletter to donors. Did you . . . donate?"

He brushed her off. "Nothing much, like five bucks or something."

She was in charge of sorting through the donor list, curating the newsletter, and matching donors to kids (the sponsorships were a big hit—those who provided funds loved to see where their money went, the joy it brought, the artistic expression it bolstered), and no one who'd donated had given less than $20 in the past year. If he'd contributed, it would have been at least that amount.

Why was he downplaying his contribution?

*He's not,* Alison told herself. *He just forgot.*

*But I would've seen his name.*

"I think what you do there is incredible." He sounded awed, which would have swelled her heart, had she heard him.

Her brain churned, trying to reel in the answer to her questions. It dangled there on a hook beneath the water, waiting for her to wind it closer.

She and her colleagues relied on one particular donor above the rest, a woman who'd sent $1,500 at Christmas each of the last three years, a guardian angel who'd kept them in high-quality paintbrushes and canvases ever since Alison had begun working there. The donor was a mystery benefactress no one had met or heard of. She didn't show up to the annual holiday party, never attended showcase nights, and hadn't responded to Alison's requests to profile her for the newsletter or Alison's suggestion that they place a commemorative plaque on the wall.

Their nickname for her was Mrs. Claus because of the timing of her gifts. That's how they usually referred to her, which explained why Alison hadn't recognized her real name.

Charlotte. Charlotte Adair.

The name tattooed on Nick's wrist.

"You," she whispered. She couldn't reconcile this information with her assumptions about how he'd spent the past several years. The puzzle pieces remained scattered along the floor.

"What?"

"Who's Charlotte Adair?"

He pulled away, ducked his head. "I don't . . ."

Gently, she drew his sleeve up and traced the line of his inner forearm, the radial bone beneath the skin.

He cleared his throat, captured her questing fingertip, and returned her hand to her.

"Nick?"

"She's my mother," he admitted softly.

*Yes*, Alison thought. *Of course. Nick's maternal grandparents were Scottish. Adair.*

"She loved art, and she would've loved you, too." His voice rang out hot, ardent. "Because no matter what you think, and no matter how you remember things, I loved you. I did."

She didn't decide to kiss him so much as give in to the relentless current that had been pulling her toward him all night.

The darkness of the room only heightened her awareness of his lips against hers, how pliable they were, how smooth and soft, and how expertly they responded to her movements.

In this dance, they were partners at last, not fighting for dominance as they had onstage.

"You're crying," he said when they broke for air. "I can't do this if you're crying. It's too much like the last time we saw each other."

"These are happy tears," she promised him.

"Are you sure?"

"I was crazy about you, Nick, and you broke my heart, but tonight you mended it. And I'll be damned if I'm going to waste another second denying myself what I want."

They stared at each other, chests rising and falling in perfect, breathless coordination, until she could no longer tell which breaths were hers and which were his.

Her fingers caressed his handsome face, then slid harshly into his hair. Simultaneously, his arms snaked around her lower back, hauling her against him.

Their mouths met, pushing and pulling and tasting. Nick kissed his way under her chin and down along the delicate column of her throat, lavishing her with attention.

"You're burning up," he murmured against her skin.

"The AC's off. . . ." It had been off for at least an hour by then and the heat of the room reflected it.

He cupped the back of her neck and kissed her again, quickly, firmly. "Get into bed."

"Where are you going?" she asked, on the verge of panic. *Don't leave me here alone. . . .*

"To cool you off."

She nodded, trusting him, although she wasn't sure yet what he meant. Tears dry, she weaved toward the direction of the bed until her knees hit the mattress.

Next thing she knew, Nick was beside her, a tray of dripping, shrinking ice cubes in one hand, and a cube of ice in the other.

"One for me, one for you." He offered her a cube. She ate it from his fingers.

"Too bad there wasn't ice cream in the freezer," she said, referring to his childhood experience with a blackout.

"I know. I could've licked a scoop off your belly." His low voice pooled in her gut. "Did you know, I've been wanting to tear this dress off you all night?"

"Is that right?"

"Did you wear it just for me? Because that $X$ across your naked back distracted me during the show more than anything else you said or did."

He set the ice tray on top of the bedside table and gave her his full attention. She swore the room glowed from his presence. He'd brought the sun into her life regardless of the darkness surrounding them.

His hand coasted lightly across her back, sliding under the $X$ and tracing its shape, until she moaned softly and helped him divest her of the dress.

It made her feel wanton and sexy to be naked again while he remained fully clothed in his "work" attire. She ached to sit in his lap and press her bare skin against every texture, from his tight jeans to the white button-down shirt that clung to his skin. Even his sweat smelled delicious to her, and when she trailed her hands down his chest, his stomach muscles flexed against her fingertips.

He stripped off his shirt and jeans, and she changed her mind. Nick in nothing but boxer shorts was even better.

She arched her neck in surprise when he traced a piece of ice . . .

. . . along her temple . . .

. . . down her cheek . . .

. . . over her chin . . .

. . . against the hollow of her neck, lingering at her pulse point . . .

. . . along the ridge of her collarbone . . .

. . . and down between her breasts.

The ice melted and spread across her skin, going, going, gone, a race against the clock before the morsel in his hand disappeared completely.

The water dripping along her hot skin felt like paint smeared along a fresh blank canvas.

She was a work of art.

She was brand-new.

His tongue followed the same path, caressing her and catching the drips, in delicate, precise movements.

She sprang up, pulled his tented boxer shorts down his legs and whispered, "Show me what you like."

She would never have been so bold in the light. The darkness had stripped her of all self-consciousness. She felt free to say and do anything now.

Nick slid her first and second fingers in his hot-and-cold mouth, then guided her hand down to trace her fingertips along the sensitive head of his cock, the taut line of skin on the underside.

He gasped, as if she were tormenting him, and he never wanted it to stop.

She continued her exploration, circled her thumb there until she felt a bead of arousal emerge. Going on instinct, she spread the slippery dew along his shaft. He moved his hips, closed his eyes, and moaned. How was it possible that she wanted him more than ever right now, despite climaxing earlier?

*Because,* a voice in her head reminded her, *you never got to feel him inside you last time, and you still haven't.*

"Condoms are in the bedside drawer," he whispered, reading her thoughts. "Rumor has it, anyway. I've yet to find out."

She laughed. "Let's find out, then."

Reluctantly releasing him, she draped herself across the bed—his hand palmed her ass, making her squirm in delight—and opened the drawer. "Jackpot!"

He rolled the condom into place, and her eyes never strayed from his perfect hands. He sat up on the bed, his back to the headboard. She climbed on him and angled downward, so she could set the pace and depth.

They stared in each other's eyes as she sank down, inch by inch.

"Oh, Alison," he groaned.

She loved the way he filled her, loved the way her own slick walls pulsed tightly around him as she rose and fell, rose and fell.

When she indicated she was tired, he rolled them so she was on her back. Hands gripping her hips, he slid more deeply inside her. She wrapped her legs around his waist and pulled him in farther, and farther still. Buried her face in his neck and whispered, "You smell so good."

Happy moans filled the air as they finally finished what they'd started in his dorm.

She'd waited five years for him, even when she didn't know that's what she was doing. And now she could finally breathe again.

# Chapter 9

Nick missed the dry desert climate of Los Angeles, where the sun's disappearance meant a cool evening. No such luck in Manhattan, where humidity reigned 24-7 in the summer.

Of course, he'd take the humidity of the Congo if it meant Alison in his arms. She'd fallen asleep, her head on his chest, her chestnut hair cascading down in soft waves. He inhaled the rosewood-and-vanilla scent of her shampoo, the smell of her skin, her sweat mingled with his. They were two purring cats wrapped around each other.

When she stirred, gazing up at him, he formed a list of questions, eager to hear more about her life. He'd happily waited for answers earlier, while they communicated in other ways, but now he craved information.

"Tell me what you do at Smocks," he said, tapping out a light drumbeat on her damp, warm back.

"Okay, I will," she said happily. Snuggling closer, she described the visiting artists, and the ways in which selecting them had expanded her social circle; the emphasis on exploration, the main lesson being that there are no mistakes in art; and how you'd never guess which kids would love which style of creativity, and which ones would start out hating something and later declare it to be their favorite one. So many public schools had been forced to shutter their art and music programs that, in her view, it was more vital than ever to provide an outlet for kids who wouldn't otherwise have creative outlets in their lives.

His pride over her words, her sense of purpose, and her altruism made him hug her tighter. He never wanted to let go.

When she finished talking, she tilted her head and bit her lip. "Your turn. Last five years. Go."

"After you left me, I felt like Houdini tying knots even he can't get out of, and there he is in the trunk, and he feels the water seeping in, and he's saying to himself, 'I've done myself in. I tied those ropes.' " Nick shook his head to clear it of the melodrama. "That sounds dire, but it was how I felt at the time. I knew it was my fault that you left, and my pain was all wrapped up in missing my mom."

"I'm so sorry—"

He stroked her chin in absolution. "I got counseling eventually, talked through some shit, and used your five-year plan like a lifeline."

"I wish I'd listened, that night. I wish I hadn't shut you down. I'm not saying I wouldn't have left, but I wish I'd been kinder."

He stroked her forehead, delved his hand into her hair. "Me, too. Not that *you'd* been kinder, but that *I* had."

"And I wish you'd told me about your mom. All those months we dated, and I had no idea. Nick, that must have been so difficult for you."

Her eyes sought his and he swallowed tightly. A rush of memories filled his head, all those moments he could have said something but didn't, both with her and his drinking buddies. What had he been so afraid of? Why hadn't he said the words, gotten them out so they couldn't eat him up inside?

In hindsight, the answer was blindingly clear: Creating an illusion had always come naturally to him. Why not live inside one as long as he could?

"I hid it from everyone," he confessed. "I thought if I didn't talk about her, and people assumed she was still alive, then she sort of would be. It's not like I went home that often during the school year, so pretending seemed easier than burdening anyone with it. I guess I figured if the collective unconscious kept her alive, it would hurt less.

"She died of lung cancer, but the thing was, she never even smoked, so it felt like she was paying for someone else's sin. Or that God had made a mistake."

"I wish I could have met her. You mentioned she loved art?"

"She was the Picture Lady at school. When I was in fourth grade, she'd show up in the classroom once a month with a large, mounted copy of a famous painting." He paused, lost in the image of his mom with her bright, gentle smile. "We'd discuss the image with her, how it made us feel, the way certain colors evoked certain feelings, how the brushstrokes and choice of paint added to the story being told. Most teachers talked *at* the kids, but my mom showed us the art and sat back. She wanted to hear the kids' observations, wanted to hear what *they* thought about it."

"We have a saying at work, it's a Tim Burton quote: 'Anybody with artistic ambitions is always trying to reconnect with the way they saw things as a child.' What was she like before she got sick?"

Such a small question, yet it encompassed an entire person, an entire life. "Where do I start?"

"Pick a season."

So he did. Winter, in a bid to cool them off with the images. He talked of snow forts and ice-skating; the way his mom used to put his towels in the oven to warm him up when the hot-water heater broke; the special Sunday breakfasts she made him of little faces composed of doughnuts and fruit; the walks in the forest behind their house.

In turn, Alison told him about growing up with a strict dad, and how standing up to him was the toughest thing she'd ever done, but how rewarding it felt once he finally understood and respected her.

Nick told her that sometimes he envied the people who came to his shows. Magic tricks never feel like magic for the magician. They only felt like magic for the audience. Sometimes it made him sad that he'd given that up, the possibility of not knowing how something was done.

The sun rose, and still they talked.

She glowed, luminous and vibrant, in the sunlight streaming through the window, her eyes soft and loving.

"Did it fix things? Doing to me what I'd done to you?" he asked.

She shook her head vehemently. "No. And it took me a while to figure out why." She sat up, looking around.

"Want my shirt?"

She accepted instantly, sliding her arms through the long sleeves. It was a stark contrast to that awful night in his dorm when she'd cried, naked in his bed, and initially refused his clothing.

He wrapped her in a tight hug.

"Thank you," he murmured into her ear.

"What for?"

*A second chance.* "For being the wonderful person you are. Anyway, you were saying . . ."

She gifted him a peck on the lips. "Right. Do you know who Franz Marc is?"

"Should I?"

"He's a German artist we were teaching the kids about this week. He said, 'In the long run, the sharpest weapon of all is a kind and gentle spirit.' I conveniently ignored that fact while plotting your downfall."

"You dropped out because of me," he insisted quietly. "That's not nothing."

"I dropped out because of *me*. You were having fun, and I wasn't. Once I recognized how miserable I'd been, I had to escape. And sometimes escape means going home to start over."

"You were supposed to graduate in three years, though, and you *would* have—"

"Rushing through life never actually helped anyone, I don't think."

He knew he shouldn't push, but he couldn't stop tearing apart her arguments. He needed to make sure no residual resentment was left for either of them. Otherwise, his hope for a future with her would be dashed before it could start.

"How many years did it end up taking, once you changed majors?"

"Just two more. I applied most of my business credits to nonprofit management pretty easily. The part that took longer was minoring in art history, with a concentration in childhood development. But, Nick . . . even if I'd had to scrap everything and redo it all, it was the best choice I ever made."

"So in a way," he teased, "you have me to thank."

She tapped him on the nose. "Don't give yourself *all* the credit."

"Ten percent of it?"

She pretended to give it thought. "Maybe even twenty."

"I really wanted you to join me in California. I thought it would—I know it sounds dumb—but I thought it would fix everything if I used the money on both of us. Like that would make it all okay. I should've quit the contest once we got together."

"Or at the very least, told me about it so we could've rigged it." She grinned.

He tried to smile back but it didn't work.

"Hey"—her fingertips drifted over his cheek—"you were young, too."

"I was. Though not nearly as carefree as everyone seemed to think."

"And I cared a lot more about other people's opinions of me than I let on." She kissed him, again and again. "Guess what, though. Our misconceptions about each other fueled our greatest accomplishments."

"Imagine how powerful we'd be if we *really* got to know each other." He was half joking, but when Alison's expression changed from warm to serious, he tensed up.

"I know you're a good man." Her voice was quiet and resolute, and Nick felt a pleasant buzzing at her words.

He turned her to face the window and rested his chin on the back of her head. "It's morning. We're not stuck here anymore."

His heart pounded in his throat. Would she take off, now that she could?

"Close the blinds."

Laughing, he did so. When he returned to the bed, she was no longer wearing his shirt.

Nick propped himself up on his elbow and stroked his fingers through Alison's damp hair. In turn, she traced a pattern on his smooth chest. The AC was back on and the city had returned to life, but they remained sweat dampened from their recent exertions.

They napped together, dreamed together.

Nick's phone buzzed and chimed from its location on the floor, inside his jeans pocket.

The sound was more insistent than the rays of light outside, and less easy to ignore.

He groaned and flopped an arm over his face. "I should probably get that, but can I stay here instead?"

"Whoever it is might be in trouble."

"Yeah, you could be right."

She admired his naked backside as he wandered over to retrieve his phone. While he answered the call, she scanned her memories for the location of her own phone. It must be in the other room, inside her purse. She'd been so caught up in her reunion with Nick, she hadn't thought about her phone even once all night, which had to be a first.

A flurry of missed calls and texts lit up her screen when she retrieved her phone and brought it back to the bed with her. She couldn't wait to hear about Vanessa and Ria's adventures, and to tell them about hers. They would be *flabbergasted*. The messages they'd already sent her had her shaking her head in surprise.

Alison mentally composed some cheeky updates of her own:

*The mystery donor from Christmas has a new nickname: St. Nick.*

Or maybe . . . *Guess what, I learned a magic trick! How to make Nick's wand disappear and reappear.*

She snorted at her silliness, but before she could send any texts for real, Nick's voice cut through the happy fog she was in.

"It's Stu," he whispered urgently. "The entertainment director."

She hastened to gather her items. "Want me to give you some privacy?"

If he lost out on this job because of her, she vowed to do everything in her power to find him a new gig, a better one. Whatever it took, no matter how long, she'd dedicate herself to—

Abruptly, he was back in the bed with her, under the sheets, with the phone placed between them.

Also, Nick was grinning. Why was Nick grinning?

"Could you say that one more time? And you're on speaker now, by the way," he said into the phone.

Stu's voice came through, slightly muffled but loud and audible.

"Most people start with Denver Opener. You didn't go near it! Everything seemed spontaneous and fresh. Your lineup was surprising, and after a month of the same old tricks, card to lemon, card to wallet, trust me, I noticed. Oh, and you can tell me: Was that female heckler part of the show, or not? I kept changing my mind about that."

Nick glanced at Alison, his eyes mischievous. "No, she—"

"Good, good, I'm glad to hear it. You handled her expertly, by the way; so many performers freeze up when confronted with audience members who've had too much to drink."

Alison clapped a hand over her mouth so she wouldn't squeak out a protest. She took umbrage at the assumption that she'd been soused. Or she would have, if Nick hadn't wrapped an arm around her shoulders and squeezed, beaming.

"Your rapport with her was what clinched it. Nothing fazed you, and sometimes that matters even more than the illusions. As you know, magic is so much more than trying to fool people; it's about creating tension and drama, defying expectations. You had the courage to interact with that demented woman! Instead of fighting her, or pretending she wasn't there, you went with it, and that shows confidence and flexibility. You didn't run from her, you brought her onstage with you. I *would* like you to finish your set for me, though. I can tell you've got the chops, but let's schedule time for a one-on-one performance. And after that, assuming it goes well, can you start in two weeks?"

Nick made a silent fist pump. "I can, yes," he said calmly. "Absolutely."

Nick and Stu said their goodbyes, and Alison waited a few seconds before reacting, to be on the safe side.

"Demented!" she howled, tears of mirth pulling at her eyes.

Nick kissed her cheek. "Want to help me write my act?"

"I thought you'd never ask."

"Ten percent of ticket sales can go to Smocks, if you like. Sound good?"

"Throw in three tickets to the first performance so I can bring my friends Ria and Vanessa, and you've got a deal."

Twenty-four hours earlier, she'd been so hell-bent on revenge that her student couldn't decipher her expression. Apparently, the word they'd been searching for was *demented*, aka "angry but happy about it."

She much preferred today's emotions.

"You around later?" Nick asked.

"When?" She pulled up her phone's calendar.

"I don't know, the rest of your life?"

She hadn't stopped smiling since.

Please read on for an excerpt from *Anchored Hearts* by
Priscilla Oliveras, available now!

Sitting on the worn floral-print sofa in his familia's living room, Alejandro Miranda cursed the bad luck that had dragged him back to Key West. The island home he'd left behind over a decade ago, by choice and by force.

His mami sat on one side of him, his abuela on the other, their dark eyes pools of concern. Across from him, his sister-in-law, Cece, and two-year-old niece, Lulu, perched on the matching love seat pushed against the opposite wall, their gazes trained on him expectantly. His brother, Ernesto, leaned against the armrest, hovering at his wife's side, his brow furrowed with uncertainty.

Trapped by their intent stares, Alejandro jabbed his fingers through his hair in frustration. His mind randomly wandered to that old copy of Thomas Wolfe's *You Can't Go Home* he'd found at a secondhand bookstore in London several years ago. According to Wolfe, you could never return to your old life, your old ways, even your old hometown, and find things the same.

Ha! The guy obviously hadn't tried going back to a Cuban familia where the ties that bind might fray but rarely snapped.

Sure, some things had changed. Cece and Ernesto had been about to start high school, barely making heart eyes at each other, when Alejandro had flown the restrictive coop his papi ruled. Curly-haired, pudgy-cheeked Lulu hadn't even been a thought in her parents' prepubescent minds.

But the old portrait of his papi, mami, Ernesto, and him, snapped at the Sears studio twenty-plus years ago, still hung on the pale blue wall above the love seat. The clunky frame was a throwback you wouldn't find in any gallery that displayed Alejandro's prized photographs today.

Worse, the expectations on his mami's, abuela's, and Ernesto's faces weighed as heavily on his shoulders now as it had back then.

In the past, their expressions had creased with a piercing combination of desperation and hope. Pleading for him to stop pushing back against their expectations. Wanting him to follow in his papi's footsteps, working alongside their familia patriarch at their restaurant with the intent of Alejandro taking the reins down the road. A life sentence that would have shackled his dream of traveling and photographing the world.

Today, the hope stamping his mom's and abuela's lined faces, the resignation twisting Ernesto's lips, and the inquisitive gleams in his sister-in-law's and niece's dark brown eyes told him they wanted much more from him than Alejandro was prepared to give.

It was the reason why he'd stayed away for so long. One of several.

"Your papi is sorry he couldn't be here to welcome you home," his mom said. She slid to the edge of the sofa, leaning forward to plump the leaf-green throw pillows cushioning his extended left leg braced on top of the rattan coffee table.

"Por favor," he muttered. "Let's not pretend. If I hadn't been stupid enough to fall off that rock ledge in El Yunque and wind up in this damn—"

"¡Oye! Language!" Ernesto interrupted. He jerked a thumb at his daughter, busy murmuring something to the baby doll cradled in her tiny arms.

*¡Carajo!*

The second *damn* nearly slipped out before Alejandro stopped it. He wasn't used to having a kid around. Unless they were the subject of his picture, and then his camera helped him maintain his distance.

He dipped his head in apology at his brother and Cece.

"If I hadn't wound up in this position," Alejandro continued, "I'd be on my way to Belize for my next shoot. Not . . ."

He broke off before he said something in agitation that might wind up hurting their feelings.

Not here, surrounded by the people he had let down. Girding himself for when his father came home from the restaurant bearing their familia name. Miranda's was father's pride and joy. The legacy Alejandro had spit on by walking away.

"Dios tenía otros planes," his abuela said softly.

Yeah, God had other plans all right. He squelched a bark of sarcastic laughter. Crappy ones.

Alejandro kept the thought to himself, knowing better than to utter the complaint his mom and abuela would condemn as blasphemy.

"I can't say I agree with them, Abuela," he muttered instead.

Alejandro sagged back against the worn sofa cushions. His leg ached, signaling the time neared for him to swallow another over-the-counter pain pill. He had staunchly said no to the opioid and acetaminophen with codeine Dr. Pérez had tried prescribing postsurgery in Puerto Rico. No way would he risk developing any sort of dependency or addiction.

A friend of his had injured his back on a shoot once, then wound up dive-bombing his career popping pain pills uncontrollably.

While Alejandro had always maintained an arm's distance

from the recreational drugs often bandied about among models, photographers, and others in the various professional and personal circles he inhabited, there'd been a time after his divorce when he'd come way too close to relying on the bottle to dull his thoughts. Years later, that flirtation with dependency still haunted him.

Now he only drank during special occasions and made it clear to his friends that any type of drug use remained off-limits around him.

"How are you feeling, hijo?" His mami finger-combed his thick hair a few times, a gentle caress that reminded him of times past. When he'd lain on this same couch or the double bed in his room, and she'd soothed him when he was sick.

"Your face is pale," she complained. "And you feel a little warm. Are you hurting?"

He gave a tiny headshake, lying but unwilling to cause her more distress. His jaw clenched tightly against the pain radiating from two of the pin sites high on his shin, a couple inches below his knee. The other pin sites moving down his leg seemed fine. But the ones higher up had started aching his second day on the ship. Rather than struggle with maneuvering his wheelchair to the ship's doctor through the long, narrow hallways teeming with tourists, he'd washed his leg as best he could in his suite's bathroom. Then he'd taken to bed, where he'd stayed for most of the trip to Miami.

"Kiss it better, 'Buela," his little niece suggested.

Despite the fatigue and disillusion crushing him, Alejandro curved his lips to smile at Lulu. Her pudgy cheeks plumped even more with her wide grin.

"I'm not sure that's going to work, chiquita, but thank you for suggesting it." He winked, pleased when a cute giggle burst from her mouth. She hugged her bald baby doll to her chest, twisting from side to side.

Cece caressed her daughter's hair, her expression gentle with maternal love when she looked over at him. "It's good to see you, Ale. Even if it is like this."

She jutted her chin at the Ilizarov external fixator with its four rings and multiple K-wires and olive wires piercing through his shin, holding his tibia in place. Lulu had already been warned to keep her distance from the cyborg-looking contraption after racing over to greet him and nearly bumping against the rings.

*¡Carajo!* He winced just thinking about the agony that would have caused him.

"Gracias," Alejandro replied to Cece.

He wanted to tell her it was good to be here. But that would be a lie. Everyone knew it.

He didn't belong here. Among them. They all lived and breathed for the restaurant—both the income it provided and the comunidad of regulars who were like familia. He . . . he'd always itched to be outside, seeing their small island from behind the lens of his camera. Capturing the beauty, wonder, and details so many missed in the busyness of life.

Making his own way in the world, not following someone else's.

His eyes drifted shut as he sucked in a disgruntled breath.

This visit was only for a short time. Until he was healed enough to have the external fixator rings and pins removed. If they had to remain in place longer, hopefully he'd get to a point where he could rely on crutches rather than the wheelchair. That would enable him to handle the stairs at his town house, and he'd be fine on his own. As he had been for years now.

Getting out of the wheelchair meant he'd be one step closer to getting back to work. Back to the job that gave his life purpose. And helped silence the occasional cry of loneliness that howled in the dark of night when his defenses were low.

"I still think we should have driven straight to the emergency room when we arrived here," his mami said, concern lacing her words.

"That would have been a waste of time and money." He swiveled his head on the back sofa cushion to meet her worried gaze. "Let me rest a few minutes, then I'll remove the dressings and clean the sites. I'm sure everything's okay. I'm just tired."

"Bueno, I would feel better if you saw a professional." His mami ran her fingers through his hair once again. The loving gesture both soothed and pained him.

"I don't need to see a professional. That's not necessary."

"Hmmm, so it is not necessary for a mother to do all she can when caring for her child?" she demanded with a sniff.

Arms crossed as he leaned against the far wall, Ernesto returned Alejandro's exasperated grimace. The same one they had shared as kids when their mom was on a roll, determined to sway them to her will. When she was like this, you had better pack your bags. Elena Miranda had a first-class ticket for you on a guilt trip you couldn't avoid.

"A mother should not worry and want what's best for her children?" Alejandro's mami droned on.

"I didn't say—"

"Te sientes caliente," she interrupted, pressing the back of her wrist against his forehead, checking his temperature as she'd done when he was little.

Shit, he felt a hell of a lot more than hot. He felt as if he'd been dragged like shark chum on a fishing line churning in the cruise ship's wake the past four days. His body worn-out. His mind weary from the mental strain of ignoring the pain radiating up his leg.

"Bueno, since you refused to go see the doctor. I asked someone to come see you."

If he didn't feel like death warmed over, he might have laughed at her overprotective, ill-conceived idea. "Mami, few doctors make house calls anymore. Not the ones my insurance company will cover anyway."

"Which is why I didn't call a doctor. I called familia."

Fatigue weighing down his body, Alejandro slowly shook

his head, not following. They didn't have any physicians in their family. "What do you mean?"

Her brows furrowed, his mami exchanged a worried glance with his abuela, then sent a familiar *Don't say anything* parental warning at his brother, who in turn threw an apologetic frown Alejandro's way.

Unease slithered down his spine.

"We only need someone with enough medical experience to properly clean your wounds and tell me if I should make you go to the hospital," his mami said. "When the physical therapist comes later this week, I can ask any new questions I have."

"Someone with . . . wait . . ." Alejandro shot a *What the hell, how could you let her?* glare at his traitorous brother.

Ernesto ducked his head, a sure sign he knew what their mami was up to but refused to, or more likely was wise enough not to, get in her bulldozing way.

"Mami," Alejandro's voice sharpened. "Who did you call?"

Her eyes narrowed at his gruff tone. A warning for him to curb his disrespect.

The stubbornness tightening his mami's lips and the calming hand his abuela laid on his left forearm answered Alejandro's question.

*¡Coño!*

Dread descended in a dark storm cloud. Thunder rumbled as complaints clashed in his head in the seconds before a knock ripped through the heavy silence.

The wide-eyed expressions on his familia's faces were almost comical. If this crazy situation hadn't been happening to him, he might have laughed.

Maybe.

The hinges creaked in protest as the front door slowly opened. The rich, lilting voice that haunted his dreams, no matter how hard he tried to banish it, called out a hesitant "Hola" as Anamaría Navarro stepped into the living room.

"Anamawía!" Lulu squealed.

Dark curls bouncing, his niece hopped off the love seat. Her pink sandals slapped the gray-and-white tile as she ran with open arms toward the woman who'd unequivocally closed her heart to him.

The woman he hadn't spoken to since their last Skype video chat over a decade ago. The night she shattered his youthful, naive dreams.

Lulu's skinny arms wrapped around Anamaría's thighs in a tight squeeze. Joy lit his ex's hazel eyes, sucker punching him with vivid memories of her greeting him with a similar glee.

She bent to rub a hand on his niece's back, her long dark ponytail swooping over her shoulder. "Hola, Lulu, this is a nice surprise."

Lulu craned her neck to look up at Anamaría, adoration dawning over Lulu's cute face. Damn if Alejandro couldn't help but understand exactly how the kid felt. No matter how often he called himself a fool for yearning for someone who obviously hadn't felt the same.

"Tío Ale tiene an owie," Lulu announced. Like the Frankenstein contraption encircling his leg wasn't clue enough.

"Yes, he does have an owie," Anamaría answered. "A pretty big one. But your abuela and abuelita are going to take good care of him. Just like they do with you."

"Will you come pway wif me soon?"

"I hope so. I need me some Lulu time." Anamaría hunkered down and tugged one of Lulu's curls, eliciting a sweet giggle from the child.

The closeness between the two—the niece he'd only seen the one time Ernesto, Cece, and Lulu had visited him in Atlanta, and the woman who'd basically said he wasn't enough—felt like a poisonous lance in his side. He might not fit in here, but Anamaría obviously still did. Without him.

Holding her bald baby doll tightly against her chest, Lulu skipped back to her parents. "Anamawía gonna babysit me!"

"Not today. But we'll see when." Ernesto gave his daughter's butt a nudge to help her clamber onto the love seat.

"Text me, Cece, and I'll let you know when I'm free. I'm sure you two could use a date night before your bundle of joy arrives."

Cece circled a hand over her huge, beach-ball-size belly that stretched the material of her soft blue short-sleeved top. A tired smile tugged up the corners of Alejandro's sister-in-law's wide mouth as she murmured her thanks.

Sending Lulu a wink, Anamaría rose from her haunches.

His shock waning, Alejandro allowed himself to take in her hyperfit figure, on gorgeous display thanks to a pair of form-fitting black leggings and a tight pink tank, the words AM FITNESS in a scrawling black font across the front. With her matching black-and-pink Nike sneakers and the long dark ponytail draping over her left shoulder to fall along the side of her breast, she looked primed for an athletic photo shoot.

Hell, she would have fit right in with the models for the *Women's Health* spread he'd shot in the Bahamas last year.

Without acknowledging him, she made the round of hello kisses and hugs with Ernesto and his family, even tickling Lulu's baby doll under the chin. The move elicited another precious giggle from his little niece.

Anamaría approached the couch. The scent of the tropical lotion she had always preferred tickled his nose when she stooped to brush a kiss on his abuela's wrinkled cheek. The two exchanged warm smiles as his abuela patted Anamaría's hand with a murmured, "Dios te bendiga, nena."

The age-old wish for God's blessing might be a trite phrase easily tossed out by many. But in this house, with the mini-altar in the far corner, its pillar candle lit during his abuela's daily prayer of the rosary, words of blessing held weight.

His mami had already stopped at their altar earlier to give thanks for her answered prayers now that he had returned.

Only after Anamaría had hugged his mami, waving off the offer of a drink, did she set her black backpack on the tile floor next to the coffee table and finally, *finally*, turn to him.

He fought to maintain a neutral expression. All the while he cataloged the features he had conjured in his dreams.

Her oval-shaped face with its high cheekbones, expressive hazel eyes, and roundly pointed chin remained as beautiful as ever. Even more so with age and maturity.

The tiny crow's-feet barely visible to the untrained eye added to her allure. Telltale signs of laughter and days squinting under the bright Key West sun. The serious slant of her full lips made him ache for the enticing grin she'd so readily flashed at him in years past. The tiny dark brown beauty mark an inch below the right corner of her mouth made him itch to press a kiss to it. Only, he was no longer free to do so.

That right had been taken away from him the moment she changed her mind and chose to stay here. Refusing to follow him to Spain like she had promised.

He hadn't expected her to leave right away, not after her papi's heart attack. But he *had* thought she'd eventually join him as they'd planned. Not break it off, claiming it had become obvious they wanted different things in life. As if wanting each other, him wanting her, her promising that she wanted him, wasn't enough.

As if *he* wasn't enough.

"So, I hear someone needs a little medical attention." Hands fisted on her trim hips, she got down to business, not wasting time with small talk. Or even a hello. "Lucky for you, making house calls is in my job description. And I'm in a generous mood."

Generous but not forgiving.

As if she were the one who'd been wronged here. Instead of the one who reneged on their shared dream. Then pushed him away without another thought.

Seeing as how she was about to poke around the leg that had started to throb like an alien had implanted itself under his skin and suddenly decided now was the perfect time to explode out, Alejandro kept his accusation to himself.

The sooner they got this over with and she left, the sooner he could go back to reminding himself that he was better off without any of the pressures and recriminations being back in Key West presented. Better off without her.

Anamaría bent to peer at his leg. Her cool hand touched his left knee above the top external fixator ring, a soft caress that sent heat searing through him. He tensed, his breath trapped in his lungs.

Her sharp, intuitive gaze swung his way.

Something dark and primitive passed between them.

Coño, he'd been right. If he was smart, he wouldn't even consider unpacking his bags. Especially the emotional ones he'd carried for so long their weight had become a natural part of his anatomy. Always there. Unexamined.

No good would come from doing that anyway.

Anamaría blinked and glanced away, breaking their connection. She leaned closer to peer at his leg.

"Okay, let's see what we're dealing with here," she said matter-of-factly, as if the spark between them hadn't singed her the same way it had him.

Shit, he knew what he was dealing with all right. His own personal hell.

Having what he craved at his fingertips. But life, in all its Murphy's Law glory, making it impossible for him to grab it.

Because, news flash, another unchanged fun fact that grated on him . . .

Anamaría appeared to be just fine without him.

Based on their warm greetings, she'd practically replaced him as a member of his familia.

There was nothing for him here in Key West. He'd known it all along.

Unzipping her backpack, Anamaría removed a first aid kit, then opened and set it on the coffee table. She tugged on a pair of light blue medical gloves with practiced ease. The snap of the rubbery material against her skin sounded loud in the quiet living room. All eyes were trained on her motions. Lulu's were wide with concern for him.

"You ready?" Anamaría asked him.

No. For a slew of reasons he refused to admit.

With a brisk nod, he braced himself for the discomfort her ministrations would bring—to his leg, as well as his traitorous heart.